THE FIRE
I CALLED

THE FIRE
I CALLED

M. DANE

CHAPTER 1

- CHALIA -

It was a perfect day in London, right until I found the pool of blood staining the pavement in front of his house. There were no such things as perfect days after that. There was no such thing as perfect.

The sun, liberated from the usual blanket of dreary clouds, had a mind to play that day. Its toasty rays decreed it a sin to attend school, and, not one to disappoint, I obeyed.

That's how they found me. I was sipping a warm beer as I crossed Queen's Park on my way to the rendezvous, when an eruption of sirens split the air. I jumped and spun to face the approaching coppers, and bile clawed up the back of my throat. They were about as welcome as an ass hair.

"Figures," I muttered, eying the blue and green checkered wagon. The driver's window wound down, revealing the bloated face of a woman with greased cooking-twine hair. I cursed. Her name was McCullough, and it'd been five glorious months since I last saw her mug. That time she threw me in the cells for looking at her in a suspicious manner. I was just trying to figure out how she breathed through that mess she called a mouth.

McCullough squeezed her head out of the car like an angry boil. "We know it was you, Chalia!" she shouted. "Come'n have a chat and not nothing else needs be done of it."

I scoffed. "You're about as sharp as a sack full of marbles if you think I'm falling for that," I fired back. "Go on and waddle back to your village. They must be terribly upset they've lost their idiot."

McCullough's face reddened. She pointed a fat finger at me as though she were picking an item from a menu. "I'll have your neck for that—"

"Come on then," I said, stale of the game of pig and mouse. I pelted my beer bottle at her. She ducked and hit her head on the door as the bottle crashed on the hood.

I laughed.

Then the sirens screamed.

Then I ran. Faster than a chav with a sausage hanging out his ass at the dog track.

I hurdled the park fence, my backpack bouncing on my shoulders, and sprinted across the road to skid around the corner onto Second Street.

Tires screeched behind me, the bumper groping for my ass. I leaped onto the curb, narrowly avoiding the police car as it fired past.

"Tramp!" I screamed. She'd never openly tried to kill me in public. I dodged the beggars who choked the footpath, and ran for all I was worth, desperate to reach the Warrens before they netted me.

Second Street ended in a T-intersection, where heavy traffic cinched a knot. Beyond it stood two red-brick apartment buildings leaning on each other. Underneath their bumping shoulders was an entrance to the Warrens, a maze of alleyways, and a haven for the city's riffraff.

The police car, just ahead of me, slammed on their brakes and I drew level with them. The passenger, a walrus of a man named Langley, reached out the window with a taser gun aimed at my noggin.

I gasped and shielded my face with my arms. "There're children about, ya dolt!"

The gun cracked, and I tensed, waiting for the lightning. It didn't come. The prongs sailed harmlessly behind me and buried into an electronic store. Not waiting for Langley to figure out how to unholster his pistol, I leaped over Mario's fruit stand and rocketed into the traffic.

A car flashed before me, its side-view mirror grazing my hand. I skittered across the next three lanes before jumping onto the footpath. I didn't slow until I reached the shadow of the Warrens.

McCullough sped into the first lane and quickly became wedged in the press. Cars piled up to the left of her, and the street filled with the fury of honking horns. She slammed her chunky hands onto the dash and shouted something lost to the roar.

I sucked in a few deep breaths, wiped the sweat from my eyes, then waved to McCullough, hoping to calm the poor scrubber before she had a heart attack.

McCullough's face turned beet red. She punched the glass windshield like a kid having a tantrum.

Maybe my intent got lost in the mail. I waved a two-finger salute at her, certain she would mellow out. Instead, her expression darkened to that of someone who'd just cultivated hemorrhoids.

Well, I couldn't win them all. I brushed aside my fringe, tied my boot laces, readjusted my backpack, and then hurried deeper into the Warrens.

A few turns in, and the world muted. By the time I reached the heart, the only sounds were my own footsteps and the rustle of rats as they scampered over the last century's garbage.

Even though I'd lived in Barden my whole life, I still got a twist of lungs when I walked the Warrens. If Barden was the stain on London's map, the Warrens was the cigarette hole punched through it. It was that sickly kid at school who no one wanted nothing to do with. The one with food smeared around his face and snot on his lip, who made you fear touching him. It was a dangerous place, but in its chaos was a structure I understood. It did not treat me differently because I was only fifteen and a lass, and that made all the difference.

I zigzagged through the maze at a trot and reached the rendez-vous at two forty-nine; nineteen minutes late.

It was deserted.

I cursed and kicked the wall. How could Kingsley be later than me? It was a special day, a day for everyone suppressed by the fascist rule of adults, a day for us to show we aren't afraid to stand up for what is right. I'd hoped Kingsley would make more of an effort. He was my best mate, but he was less reliable than a soup fork.

I scanned the alley again and sighed, then squeezed myself between two pallet stacks and slid down the wall until I sat on my heels, out of the muck and out of sight.

Time passed with me glancing at my watch every few seconds. He had five minutes. That's it, no more. I'd do the mission by myself if I had to—

"Chalia?" a voice called, echoing off the brick walls.

I peeked through the pallets and spotted Kingsley striding into the alley. He was a small lad, the top of his head barely reaching my nose, but he had a cocksure swagger. A Chihuahua with a lion's shadow, I always said. He hated that and would belt on anyone else who said it. Not me, though. We were best mates since birth, and that made us family.

Deciding to teach the kid a lesson about time management, I remained hidden behind the pallets as he passed.

"Chalia?" he called again, this time with uncertainty. "You here?"

He walked to the trash bins on the opposite side and peered behind the mounds of garbage. He kicked a bag, and its contents spilled out. "Always late, she is."

I crept from my hiding spot, doing my best to ignore the indignation of being called late by Kingsley, and pounced. I hooked one arm around his head and hugged it to my chest while I pushed my pocketknife to his throat.

"Dosh," I growled in as deep a voice I could muster. "Give it to me or I'll slice chips from you."

Kingsley froze, a split second perhaps, and then his shoulders heaved as he laughed. "You're dimmer than a drowned fish if you think I've quids for you." His voice didn't tremble, not a little. His knees didn't knock, and he didn't plead for his life. He was the smartest lad I knew, but sometimes it was wasted on him.

I pressed the knife harder against his throat. "Check yourself, boy. I've seen flea crap larger than you."

Kingsley stiffened like a long-dead dumpster cat, and my ears tingled a warning. Kingsley's temper was known throughout Barden, as was his sensitivity about his height.

I lowered the blade, unhooked my arm, and quick-stepped away.

Kingsley spun faster than a twice-kicked badger and launched a punch at my head. It might have clipped my cheek if he hadn't recognized me and pulled the swing.

"Chalia!" he said. "I almost ended you!" He straightened his jacket with a huff. "Then your mom would never cook me dinner again."

I pocketed my knife. "You'd need to have no taste to eat that slop . . ." My voice trailed off as I caught sight of his face. His whole left cheek was blacker than the ace of spades, and his eye looked a burnt Yorkshire pudding.

I clenched my fists. "I'll kill him," I hissed. I snatched Kingsley's arm and pulled him into a shaft of light so I could see better. The bruise ran down his neck and under his shirt, and I was willing to bet it shaded most of his body. I wanted to scream and run to the bar where I knew he was at. "I'll finish that bastard to death."

"Let off," Kingsley said, struggling in my grip. "What're you about?"

I didn't let go. I couldn't. "Thinks he's a big man, does he? Beating up on someone smaller than him?" My voice trembled. "How many times does this have to happen before we make him stop?"

Kingsley yanked free and poked a finger in my chest. "First off, I'm not that small! Second, you're not going to kill nothing. I fight my battles. He will get his own, I promise you that!" He turned and punched the brick wall. "It's just not worth the hassle right now. You don't know what it's like—"

"To be used as a boxing bag?"

"To have a dad!"

I spluttered, and my anger parted just enough to let in a wave of pain.

Kingsley gasped and spun back around, eyes wide. "I'm sorry," he gushed. "I didn't mean that. It's just . . . it's too much, sometimes, ya know?"

I sighed. "No. But I can imagine." I turned from Kingsley and rested my elbows and forehead on the pallet stack. My dad never mistreated me like Kingsley's dad. In fact, he was the perfect dad, until he wasn't. Maybe that's why I had so much anger boiling through me. Maybe that's why I latched on to any stability like an oyster to a rock.

Kingsley squeezed my shoulder. "Who needs them, anyway? Just you and me, Chalia. That's all what matters. Proper family."

I nodded. "It'll just be me if your dad does you in."

Kingsley chuckled. "That old drunk would run outta steam before he even gets close. Don't worry about me. I'll not let you rot in this place alone. Promise." He slid his back down the pallets and looked up. "Anyway, I skipped school to have fun, not chat about bell ends."

I joined him on the ground, draped an arm over his shoulder, and pulled him in. "You're not too sore?"

Kingsley shrugged. "Life is sore. Hanging with you makes it bearable. Anyway, what's this plan you've got, then?"

I handed him my bag.

He unzipped it, and his eyes sparkled. "Lush!" he said as he pulled out a can of black spray paint. "How many?"

"Enough for many more days like this," I said, standing. "But we have to be quick."

I grabbed his hand and helped him to his feet before leading him to the end of the alley overlooking Barden High School. A shiny Rolls-Royce was parked in front of the turnstiles, looking as out of place as the queen in a coal mine.

"See the Royce?" I asked.

"Hard to miss."

"That's the mayor's. He's in assembly now, giving his annual 'stay-out-of-trouble-and-you-might-not-be-a-drop-kick' speech. The poor fellow must be a right mess, driving that thing."

Kingsley raised an eyebrow. "What's wrong with a Rolls-Royce?"

"Don't you see? The manufacturers forgot to tint the windows! That's right embarrassing." I shook my can of paint. "Good thing we're here to help our beloved mayor."

It took a second, but eventually a crooked smile spread across Kingsley's face, and he shook his can too. "You know, sometimes I mistake you for a bland sort of lass," he said as he reached into my backpack and pulled out a second can. "Sometimes I'm wrong."

"You're too kind," I said as I scanned the street. "Listen, we get in and out, no mucking about. Got it?"

"Yeah, yeah, whatever."

"I'm serious." I narrowed my eyes. "If the mayor is here, so is his police escort. If I say run, you run."

"Okay! Jeez, relax, you're taking the fun out of skipping school—"

"Say it."

Kingsley rolled his eyes. "If you say run, I run."

I stared at him, and my ears burned. He wasn't in the right state of mind. He was angry, and that was never a good thing, not with him. "Listen, Kingsley, maybe we should—"

"*Screw the mayor!*" Kingsley shouted, then shot out of the alley with both cans raised like pistols.

A shiver sliced down my spine. A warning. It was not the right day to be babysitting Kingsley.

Chapter 2

- Chalia -

"Damn it!" I hissed, bouncing on the balls of my feet as I glanced up and down the road. It was deserted, but far from safe. "Going to get me killed one day!" I sprinted out of the Warrens and into the untamed wilderness of Barden. It was *supposed* to be a stealth mission, but Kingsley was about as stealthy as Prince Harry in drag. We might be okay, as long as he drew no more attention to us—

Kingsley reached the Royce and leaped onto its hood, sliding across it with his arms wide for balance.

My breath caught in my chest. "Get off there!" I shouted, but the Rolls-Royce's alarm sang the unmistakable anthem of a car-jacking. Everyone in Barden knew that sound, but the pigs, their ears were tuned to it like radar. We had minutes at most.

Kingsley turned to me with his crooked smile and shrugged. "Whoops," he mouthed.

The siren screeched, louder and louder, and lines of warmth flitted through my body, from my stomach to the tips of my fingers and toes, setting every hair on end. My breathing quickened. I should have ordered him to run. I should have run myself. There were many things I should have done, but in that moment, adrenaline and a fierce desire for control killed my sanity. In that moment of madness, I leapt onto the hood too, and my life changed forever.

Kingsley's smile touched his ears. "Welcome aboard the Renegade Express. Next stop: retribution!"

"Not if we're caught," I said, pushing past him and crouching over the windshield. "Hurry!" My hand was a blur as I sprayed an impressively large member of the male genitalia. I completed it with two devil horns and the same round glasses the mayor wore. I was about to write some choice words, but something inside the car caught my attention—

A face, eyes wide and mouth working soundlessly. It stared at me from the driver's seat with a look a stunned mullet couldn't pull off.

I froze, and the can fell from my grip to clink on the hood and roll away.

"You all right?" Kingsley asked, looking up from his own artwork. He followed my gaze to the chauffeur and whooped with surprise.

"Ho, now!" he said and dropped to his knees. "There's a chav trapped in the Royce." He rapped on the glass like it was an aquarium. "An ugly little fellow, isn't he? They must not be feeding him enough."

The chauffeur spluttered, and his face turned tomato. He fumbled with his seatbelt.

"*Ruuuun!*" I screamed, vaulting from the hood and hitting the ground in a sprint. Not once had the idea crossed my mind that a person was left in the car!

I bounded across the street in ten strides and dove into the Warrens. I reached the pallets before chancing a look over my shoulder.

"Damn it!" I said, digging in my boots and sliding to a stop. Kingsley hadn't run at all, but was on the Royce's roof, dancing out of the chauffeur's grip and spraying the man in the face every time he took a swipe at his feet.

"*Run, Kingsley!*" I screamed, hopping from one foot to the other.

Kingsley ignored me. He laughed and played like a kid with a new toy on Christmas Day.

I was about to call again but choked on my words. Two figures raced from the school turnstile, dressed in the telltale white shirts and black vests of cops. They had faces as sour as fermented trash juice. Pickering and Newlin, two of the rottenest cops in Barden. Pickering was more beluga than man, and Newlin a cheap toothpick. The mayor's security.

"Pigs!" I screamed, running back to the street. Kingsley glanced up and saw the pair. One can fell from his grip.

The chauffeur took his opportunity and caught Kingsley by the ankle. He tugged, and Kingsley crashed to the roof just as Pickering and Newlin arrived.

Pickering wrenched Kingsley from the car and slammed him against the door, sending Kingsley's head lolling about like a tetherball.

I had to help. I had to do something! But what? I was strong for my size and might have had a chance against one of them. But three?

I looked behind me into the Warrens. Five steps, that's all it would take, and I would be safe. Kingsley had brought this on himself; it would serve him right to get a few hours in the cells.

I shook my head. It wasn't the cells I was worried about; it was what his drunk father would do once he found out.

I raced back across the street in a low crouch and ducked behind the car in front of the Royce. I peeked over the trunk.

"Who have we here?" Pickering wheezed, his beady eyes sparkling. "Young Kingsley, of all people. Do you believe that, Sarge?"

Sergeant Newlin nodded, a grin on his lipless mouth. "It's a shame that I *do* believe it. Everyone knows the lad ain't got wits enough to tie his laces, let alone stay outta trouble."

"Pity him not, Sarge," Pickering said, slamming Kingsley against the door again. "If I know his old man like I think I do, he'll beat some smarts into him tonight, all right."

"Looks like he's been schooled already, if those pretty bruises are anything to go by. I don't think the lesson's been stuck, though. Do you?"

Pickering looked down his nose at Kingsley and shook his head. "Afraid not. Perhaps a broom handle will be a better teacher. Helped my grades, it did."

Newlin snickered, his gaunt eyes turning into slits. His laugh, however, was drowned out by Kingsley's own.

Pickering's face fell into a scowl. "Boy, you must got the bollocks of a giant to be laughing right now. What's so damned funny?"

It took a second for Kingsley to compose himself enough to speak. "I reckon you probably ate the broom handle before it could teach you anything, you fat bastard."

A laugh escaped Newlin before he could cover his mouth. Pickering, however, swelled like a bloated rat. He grabbed Kingsley by his shirt front and hoisted him from the ground.

"That mouth of yours just cost you, lad," he breathed. "Mark me, you'll never walk again, not after I'm done with you."

My lungs iced over. The pigs in Barden weren't like the pigs on TV. They were worse, far worse, and weren't above sending Kingsley swimming in the Thames weighing three bullets heavier. Pickering would kill Kingsley, and he would kill me if I tried to help. That's the way Barden was, always had been, full of corruption and greed, a real-life Gotham City. I looked back to the Warrens again. It wasn't too late; I could still disappear. What good would it do anyone if I was killed too? The hairs on the nape of my neck prickled.

"Over here, you slimy pillock!" I shouted as I hurdled the Royce's hood and launched into Pickering. I knocked him sideways to crash into Newlin, and we all fell to the ground in a tangle of limbs.

"*Run!*" I shouted as I rolled free and regained my feet.

But Kingsley didn't run. He pounced on Pickering's bouncing gut and smashed his forehead into Pickering's nose. The nose crumpled, and a fountain of blood sprayed Kingsley as Pickering's head smacked the pavement.

I grabbed Kingsley's arm. "Leave it," I said, trying to pull him away, but he shrugged free and rained blows into Pickering, mashing his face to strawberry pie.

Pickering squealed and thrashed, then gurgled and choked.

Kingsley didn't let up. "*Think it's fun to beat on kids?*" Kingsley roared with each punch.

Pickering tried to cower behind his hands, but they soon dropped to his sides, and he convulsed.

"He's not your dad!" I screamed at Kingsley. I tried to pull him free, but he was a lion with a gazelle in its mouth. *"Please,"* I begged. "It's not too late!"

Newlin slowly gathered his feet, blood trickling from a deep gash above his ear where he'd hit the curb.

"Please, Kingsley," I said. "We need to skip town—*Oomph!*"

I jolted forward as something crashed into the back of my head. White light exploded around me, and I collapsed to the ground. It wasn't hard, like usual. It was clouds. The brightness dimmed, and the last thing I saw was the chauffeur standing over me, tire iron in his hand.

"Kingsley . . ."

CHAPTER 3

- GEORGE -

The quarter moon reached for midnight over the sleepy British village of Belbury-on-the-Brook. Candles were cold and their wax hard once more, horses and cows dozed in stable and field, and George slept peacefully in his thatched cottage, duvet up to his chin and hot water bottle on his chest. His dreams had changed little over his long years. They weren't the ordinary dreams of a man living an ordinary life; no one in Belbury could ever claim such a thing.

A hammering on George's door cut his snore short. He sat up, spluttering, his heart pounding. *What on earth?* He wiggled a finger in his ear, tilted his head to one side, and listened. Rain lashed the windowpanes, and the old timber in his cottage groaned, but it was otherwise silent.

"I'm losing it," he muttered as he lay down and pulled the duvet over his shoulders. Belbury was not a place for visitors after the night log had been placed in the hearth. *Not unless you count that one time* . . . He shook his head. That was a long time ago—

Boom! Boom! Boom!

The door rattled, and George's eyes flitted open. He propped onto his elbows and his jaw stiffened. *If it was Bekka and Elanil playing one of their jokes again* . . . But as the cottage fell quiet, a chill swept down George's neck. It was storming fierce outside; whoever was knocking must be desperate.

"George!" a muffled voice shouted from the porch. "Open this damned door!"

George gasped. He knew that voice; he'd grown up with it his whole life. But only once since he'd returned from the second war had it ever interrupted his sleep. Only once, and the chaos that followed had almost destroyed the village.

George threw the duvet off and fumbled in the darkness to light the bedside lantern with fingers sore with age. The wick flamed to life, and he swung his legs out of bed and hurried down the hallway to the front door, crepitus crackling his knees like static on the old radios.

He reached for the handle and hesitated, fingers pulling away from the knob as though it were hot iron. Once he opened the door, there was no going back. His world changed the last time he answered a midnight call, and change was for the young. He hadn't been accused of that for a long, long time.

The door shuddered on its hinges, and George jumped.

"George! I see your light! Open the door, we need you."

George lifted his chin. Change would come, whether he wished it or not. He opened the door.

The village mayor, Arthur Princeton, stood on the hearth, rain beading off his tweed coat while his gray mustache twitched like a fly on a fishing line. He strode past George and hurried to the fireplace where red embers crackled and popped.

"Grab your coat," he said, holding his hands before him as he stared into the flames. "Hurry."

George squinted into the darkness of his front yard. The pear tree waved in the gale, the hedges glistened from the light of his lamp, but the road beyond was cloaked with night and rain. He closed the door. "It's happened again?"

Arthur rubbed his hands together but did not answer. He was a stiff man, rigid with pride, and held a firm gaze which the years had not robbed. They were both in their nineties, but Arthur was running out of haircuts on top. He turned to George, chewed his lip a moment, then nodded.

George leaned against the wall for support, the strength leaving his knees. More visitors had arrived? What did that mean for Belbury? "Are they the same?"

Arthur's lips pressed into a tight line. "I'll explain on the way. Hurry now, the other Founders have been warned and will be waiting."

George nodded, feeling every ache in his old body. He sighed and collected his trench coat before pulling on gumboots and placing his timeworn trilby hat over his gray hair. He opened the door and scanned the front yard once more and then stepped into the downpour. Arthur strode past him and set a blazing pace.

"They come from the water well?" George asked as they hurried along the muddy road that paralleled the brook to the village.

"Well, they didn't arrive by train, did they?" Arthur said.

George studied the mayor. Arthur was a composed man and not one to fluster easily. "What aren't you telling me?"

Arthur's boots squelched in the mud. They passed Moira's

cottage on the left before he spoke. "Belbury-on-the-Brook is doomed 'less we stop them."

The fear in Arthur's voice halted George in his tracks. "They are not the same as the other visitors, then?"

"About as different as rhubarb pie and boar crap," Arthur said, not slowing.

George buried his hands in his coat pockets and trotted after Arthur who turned onto the stone bridge connecting north and south Belbury.

"Can we send them back?" George asked. "Certainly, the others must know a way?"

Arthur stopped, his pencil mustache drooping into a frown. He looked at George a long moment. "I don't know," he sighed at last, shoulders sagging. "I—I've never seen anything like them, George. Not in the horror films we watched as kids. Not in the pages of novels or screams of nightmares." He turned to the brook and watched it a while, fingers tracing the lip of the parapet. "Almost seventy years since the first visitors arrived, and I'd hoped it'd be seventy more until the next." He chuckled dryly. "Remember earning your military medal in France? The hell you had to fight through to get it? Remember Daniel and Nicholas who got nothing ever again? I'll tell you one thing for sure, George, those days will seem like a trundle in the playground compared to what awaits us."

George glanced over his shoulder, almost expecting someone, or *something*, to creep up on him. He was not a fearful man. He hadn't shied from danger in his twenties, and he'd be damned if he shied from it in his nineties. "Well now, old chap," he said with a false brightness in his voice. "It is a good thing Belbury breeds them tough, as we know." He clapped a hand on the mayor's shoulder. "But let's get a move on—I find things aren't nearly as bad on second glance. Was anyone hurt?"

Arthur pushed off the stonework and continued along the bridge. "Bumps and bruises. Talgodge had the drink knocked out of him, but that's the worst of it."

George nodded. "Probably did him a favor."

"I'm sure he'll make up for it tomorrow."

"I'm sure everyone will make up for it tomorrow, if things are as bad as what you say."

The village square was to the right of the bridge. It was normally empty at such a late hour, but not this night. A handful of villagers crowded around the water well, each in varying states of night dress, steam rising from their rain-soaked bodies. Constable Oliver was clothed only in his cotton pajamas and boots as he struggled to shepherd the crowd along. There was something on the cobblestones next to his feet, a dark lump, like several sacks of potatoes.

George lifted a hand to his chest. "Oh, my . . ."

"Hmm," Arthur grunted. "You're wrong, George. It looks every part as bad on second glance, maybe even worse."

George hardly heard him over the pounding of his own heart. All his long years of life had not prepared him for what he saw writhing on the ground. He crept forward on numb legs. It was a beast from hell. A demonic fusion of insect and man. Eight feet tall with broad shoulders and green-tinged skin that shone like pressed metal. The creature spat and cursed and arched its back, trying to break free of the ropes coiled around it. One of its wings was cocked at an odd angle and buzzed uselessly. Its icy-blue eyes locked on George's, and George felt like a fawn in a wolf's stare.

George knelt in front of the creature, and it stopped struggling. He opened his mouth to speak, but snapped it shut as the beast spat in his face.

George didn't flinch; he was too old for that. He wiped the saliva from his cheek with his sleeve without breaking eye contact. "Why are you here?"

The creature's lips peeled into a grin, and it hissed a laugh. "You are old," it said in a voice of stones in a meat grinder. "Where I am from, only the smart live to see their wings fail." Its fangs were sharp and serrated. "Are you wise, old man?"

George looked to Arthur with eyebrows raised. The creature's use of English was flawless. Hard on the ears, but flawless. He turned back to the beast. "I believe so—"

"Then flee," it said. "Pack up and go. Ghultar is coming, and he will save us all. Any who stay will curse the day they were born."

George gasped. It had been many years since he heard Ghultar's name spoken, and it was never done in the dark of night. His stomach tensed. "We know that name, but we will not retreat. We will stand with your old enemies, united as one."

"Then you will not live," the beast said.

"We will see."

Arthur gripped George's shoulder. "Come and hear Talgodge's story."

George nodded but did not move. His old eyes scanned the hard platelike skin of the monster. The joints were shielded by ridges, and the organs might as well have been hidden behind armor. He reached out and rapped a knuckle against the beast's arm. Rock hard. Where was its weakness?

The beast snapped its head forward and gnashed its teeth,

trying to bite. George stood quickly and shook his head. "We have lived a long time, and we will live longer still." He turned and followed Arthur to the town hall, leaving Constable Oliver to deal with the creature.

Talgodge was seated on the steps, a black boar the size of a pony beside him. He was a stout man, wider in the shoulder than should have been possible, and had a long red beard that typically held more food than a dinner plate. A laceration on his cheek oozed blood, and a fat lip made it look like he was pouting. His eyes were also glazed, but George suspected that had more to do with the amount of ale he had drunk than from any injury.

All in all, Talgodge was a typical dwarf, one of the original visitors to emerge from the water well all those years ago, showing that not all who came were evil.

Arthur nodded to Talgodge. "He discovered them—"

"Them?" George asked. "More than one?"

"My word there was!" Talgodge grunted. He pointed to his face. "I wouldn't be looking like this if there was only one of them beasties."

George nodded. "Tell me what happened."

Talgodge's expression lifted. "Well, it all started this morning when I woke with a thirst to parch an ocean—"

"The shorter version," Arthur cut him off.

"Well then," Talgodge said, rubbing his chin. "I guess it all started when we finished lunchtime drinks—"

"Start from when you left the tavern tonight," Arthur said irritably.

"All right, all right," Talgodge said, patting the air in front of him. "Missing out on a delightful story, though. Well now, I was on me way home from the Pointed Ear, I was, just me and Bessie—" he slapped his boar's flank, "—when the termite bastards flew right out of the water well! Thought I was seeing things again, like after I tried old Stanthrop's ale at New Year's. But then I remembered I hadn't drunk more'n a dozen pints this evening, so I had no right to be hallucinating and all. And besides, the bastards clarified things when they spotted me back. The cowards attacked me—which speaks of their intelligence. *Me*—can you believe it? Fools, both of them. Me and Bessie gave them hell, chased one of them right back into the hole it came from, and I sat on the other one and hollered until Oli came to help."

George looked to Arthur. "One escaped?"

Arthur nodded, his lips pressed thin.

"But that means—"

"It knows we are here," Arthur finished.

"Bah! Let them come," Talgodge said. "Could use a bit of entertaining around here. Bit too quiet these days, if you ask me."

Arthur shook his head. "They will entertain you right into a grave, you foolish dwarf."

CHAPTER 4

- CHALIA -

Agony sliced through my brain like a broken bottle of London Pride. I groaned and pressed my hands to my temples but kept my eyes tight shut. How many puppies had I kicked in a past life to deserve such pain? I massaged my fingers in a circular pattern and after a long moment opened my eyes.

A fluorescent light flickered almost green above me, its diffuser stuffed with insects long dead. I was lying on something hard, a bench perhaps, and the room smelled of sweat and rot. I turned enough to see metal bars running floor to ceiling, and I cursed. How had I ended up in the cells?

The Warrens, they had something to do with it. I was there . . . but not alone—

"Chalia," a voice called. It was apprehensive, though cut the silence like a gunshot. "Are you—are you all right?"

"Mmm," I grunted, closing my eyes again, and then I remembered.

Kingsley's bloodied fists pounding Pickering's face, smashing it to mush . . . I-I couldn't stop him. I tried, but . . . but what if Pickering was—

No. I couldn't think like that. Pickering was alive. He had to be.

I opened my eyes and spotted the blurry outline of Kingsley two cells away. With a groan, I swung my legs off the bench and fought through a dizzy spell to sit. "Oh, Kingsley," I said, my gut tightening as I thought of the trouble we were in. Not with the law, but with the pigs, and they were two very different, and dangerous, things. "We should lie low a while." My eyes cleared enough to focus on Kingsley's face. I looked at him for a second, not sure what I was seeing, and then I gasped.

I rushed across the room and pressed my head between the bars. Kingsley's face looked a puffer fish with a water allergy. Giant welts colored it black and swelled it to twice its normal size. His top lip was split and crusted with blood, and thin slits were all I could see of his eyes. His shirt was tattered and stained dark, and he was nursing an arm across his chest.

"What did they do to you?" I asked, unable to comprehend Kingsley was somewhere in there.

Kingsley brushed aside my worry and smiled, revealing a missing front tooth. "Well . . . you know how teachers are twats, right?" he said with a lisp. "Like pretty much all of them? Turns out there is at least *one* good teacher out there."

"Kingsley, your face . . . what do teachers have to do with this?"

He stuck out his scrawny chest, winced, and then spoke. "I taught them pigs a lesson they won't never forget."

I sagged against the bars, feeling as though I'd just run a mile uphill. "Are they still . . . did you kill . . ." I tried but couldn't finish. I saw through Kingsley's bravado; he was scared and knew what he was in for. Talking about it would not help. I glanced down and spotted a dead cockroach next to my boot. It was on its back, legs in the air, and for a moment, I envied it. It no longer had to deal with the crap life threw at it. It was free, and no one could take that away. The room fell silent.

Kingsley cleared his throat. "Been a while since we've been here," he said in a higher voice than normal. "Three months?"

"Five."

"Five? Well, we're long overdue." He picked at the stain on his shirt then looked at his fingers. He flexed them a while, squeezing his hand into a fist then relaxing, before looking up to me. "I—I got them good, Chalia," he said in a barely audible whisper. "Pickering and the chauffeur—they won't be beating on kids no more."

I closed my eyes and fought back tears. "We've stuck our foot in it this time."

"And fist."

Kingsley was a smart lad, the smarts what made some kids nerds. He wasn't a nerd, just brilliant, and he knew what was waiting for him on the other side of court. "You'll get Borstal for this."

"I'm not scared of juvie—"

"Stop it!" I snapped, and a hot tear spilled onto my cheek. "This is real, Kingsley. Borstal will have you for years—you know what that place does to people! Remember Frankie? He wasn't released more than a month before he upped and swung himself to death."

Kingsley deflated. "I really bollocksed up, huh?" He pulled his knees to his chest and wrapped his arms around his legs. "But don't you worry about me, Chalia. I'm stronger than I look; Borstal won't hurt me like it does other lads. Besides, it doesn't own me yet—I've things what need doing first. And who knows, it might never get me at all."

The way he spoke, like the wits had been bashed from him, sent a shiver down my spine. "What things?" I asked, my throat burning. "We ain't had nothing what needed doing for years."

He rested his chin on his knees and looked past me. "You ever dream about getting out of here? Away from this rotting city? Away from *them*?" He didn't say as much, but I knew *them* to be adults and the hurt they brought with them. His dad. My dad. The pigs. The mayor and teachers. Everyone who thought they owned a right to order us around like sheep. "I do. I dream it every night. I dream of escaping and finding a dot on the map what's mine and my own, the one place I'll belong, rain or shine, and no one can take it away from me. I dream of finding that dot and scratching this place from memory."

In that moment, he looked an armless toddler hoping to become a bricklayer. It stung me, and I didn't have the heart to remind him miracles didn't happen for people like us.

"Where's your dot?" I asked with a mother's pity.

A wistful smile played across his face. "The Motherland."

I cocked my head. "Italy?" Kingsley's mother came from Italy when she was young, but Kingsley had never stepped foot outside of London, let alone England.

He nodded and closed his eyes. "Italy."

"You don't even like pasta."

"I like pizza double, though." He sighed. "I know it's a dream and nothing more. But I can see myself there—you know? I can smell it and taste it and hear it." He got to his feet and crossed the cell to poke his face through the bars. "I can see myself working there until I have enough money to buy some land on a hill. Think of it, views of the ocean on one side, an olive grove on the other. Pigs will be for eating, not for abusing us, and the lasses—oh, Chalia, the lasses will be fit as, tan and gorgeous and in love with my English accent—"

The door to the cell room burst open, and Newlin stormed in.

I jumped, heart in throat, and backed away.

Newlin strode to my cell, mouth twisted into a deranged smile, and clutched the bars between us.

"Look at him good, lassie," Newlin said. "Remember that ratty face of his. You ain't like to see it ever again, I promise you that." His eyes were wild, and his head twitched to one side like a horse's tail swatting flies.

I stepped back, feeling naked before the glint in his eyes, and looked to Kingsley.

Newlin followed my gaze and his smile spread. "Has he told you what he did? Not keeping secrets, is he?" He squeezed his face between the bars and the skin pulled tight. "Poor old Pickering's face can't rightly be called a face no more, not after your boyfriend was through with him. I've seen crap splatters on the pavement what looked more human than Pickering's mess of a head."

I shook my head. No. Newlin was exaggerating. He was trying to scare me; that's what pigs do, they scare people. But then Kingsley's shoulders drooped, and my knees trembled.

"*Look at me!*" Newlin shouted, rattling the bars. "Doctor just phoned, she did. Said Pickering might not see morning never again. Might not go home to his wife and kids. Might not never do nothing. All because your *friend* here is a looney. A mind-sick runt what needs ending before it infects everyone." Newlin's nostrils flared a moment then relaxed. When he spoke again, it was in a calm whisper. "Barden's finest get our own; don't think twice on it, lass. We are family at this station, and we look out for each other." He looked to Kingsley. "Your days are numbered, my sick little friend. We're coming for you, sure as night comes for the moon."

Kingsley took a step forward. "You're too daft to put a hit on me, Newlin. You'd probably end up necking yourself—"

"Keep making your jokes, boy, not many of them left—"

"Sergeant Newlin!" a voice boomed from the doorway. The inspector, a hefty man with a walrus mustache, marched into the room, palm resting on his baton. "Step away from the cage."

Newlin didn't move. He glared at Kingsley, smile twitching at the sides. "Enjoy these last moments, boy. Make them count—"

"*Sergeant!*" The inspector pulled free his baton and eyed Newlin beneath furrowed brows. "I'm warning you!"

Newlin spun and gave a curt nod to the inspector. "Of course, Inspector, right you are. I'm just trying to educate the young man some manners, is all." His raspy voice was light and conversational.

"That's not your place," the inspector said, still gripping his baton.

"Indeed. It's naught to do with me, but I'm sure his father will have much to say."

"That's not your business either. Get out of here—I won't warn you again."

Newlin looked over his shoulder to Kingsley and winked. "Yes, Inspector," he said in a greasy voice, and then strode out of the room.

The inspector waited until he was out of sight before letting his baton slide back into the holster. He sighed, sending his mustache tips billowing, and turned his gray eyes to me. He pulled out a ring of keys. "Your mother's arrived, Chalia," he said as he jiggled a key into the cell lock. "Come along, there's a mountain of paperwork to sort out before I knock off."

I looked to Kingsley, and for the briefest moment, I saw fear in his eyes. I couldn't leave him there by himself, not in the pigpen, not waiting for his father.

"If it's all the same to you, I'd prefer to stay," I said.

The inspector glanced to Kingsley. "It's not all the same to me. He won't be leaving until later tonight. If his bail is paid, that is."

"I don't mind—"

"This is not a bed-and-breakfast!" the inspector snapped. He yanked open the cell door. "Get out now or I'll drag you out."

"But—"

"Go on, you daftie," Kingsley said. "I'll be fine. Get out there before Newlin tries his luck with your mom."

I shook my head. "Kingsley, listen—"

"You listen," Kingsley said. "She is one of the good ones, Chalia. I know you don't think it, but she is. Look after her. Look after yourself."

I pressed against the bars as far as I could. "I won't leave you—"

"Always so dramatic," Kingsley said, and I could almost see him rolling his eyes beneath the swelling. He grinned, and I wanted to cry. "Find your dot on the map, no matter where it is. Swear it."

"I'll go to Italy with you—"

"Swear it. Escape here and find your dot."

At that moment, the inspector grabbed me by the arm and dragged me from the cell. I wrestled with his grip, but he was too strong. "Let me go!" I shouted, hooking my feet around the bars.

"Swear it!" Kingsley said.

"I swear!" I cried as the inspector pulled me across the room to the door. "Swear you'll come with me."

Kingsley didn't answer but lifted a hand and waved.

My throat burned, and tears prickled my eyes as the door to the cell room closed. "I swear," I whispered, and then I broke apart.

CHAPTER 5

- CHALIA -

The inspector guided me through the station with his hand pinching the crook of my arm as though he feared I might run away. He needn't have bothered; I wasn't going anywhere, not with Kingsley stuck in the cells.

Not with him going to Borstal.

As smart as Kingsley was, he wasn't smart enough to keep his mouth shut around people with fists the size of his head. He needed me, and I wouldn't let him down. An image of a hill in Italy flashed through my mind, and it brought with it a calmness. I wiped my eyes on my bomber jacket and straightened. We would skip town tomorrow morning, just me and him, and work our way to Italy. I'd seen TV shows of people who'd hitchhiked the world, it couldn't be that hard—

"Chalia!"

Mom raced through the crowded office toward me, her bird's-nest hair streaming behind her, while her filthy work apron bounced around her knees. She wrapped her arms around me and squeezed. "Are you all right?" she asked as she ran her hand over the back of my head.

I winced when she touched the spot where the tire iron had connected. "I'm fine," I said, pulling out of her grip.

She looked me up and down, kissed me on the forehead, then spun to face the inspector. "Call yourself police officers!" she said coldly, jabbing a finger in his chest. "Beating up children—and girls, no less—"

"We didn't beat your daughter, Mrs. Lainslade. A man named Gavin Darnell did—"

"Where is this *Gavin*?" Mom asked as she scrunched her fists and looked around the station. "I'd very much like to have a word with him."

"I have released him into the mayor's care."

"You're kidding," I said, stepping forward. "He bloods someone and is released? That's taking the Mickey, ain't it?"

"It is what it is," the inspector sighed. He lowered himself into a tattered office chair behind a desk piled with folders and paper and empty coffee mugs. "Now, if you please, Mrs. Lainslade, we have a lot of paperwork to go over."

"No, I do *not* please," Mom said. She planted a hand on his desk. "Who do you think you are . . ."

And so began a fifteen-minute tirade about what she would do to anyone who laid a hand on me again. By the end, every pig in the station had exited the room backward, hand on their taser, with eyes fixated on Mom's fury.

I was ready for bed by the time I completed the paperwork. I was drained, sore, and altogether fouler for it. A pounding headache bounced between my ears by the time we left the station and stepped into the lamp-lit streets. I held two documents. The first was a charge sheet, the primary charge being *assaulting or threatening to assault a person with intent to resist or prevent arrest*, but also included vandalism and destruction of property. The second was a summons sheet ordering me to appear in court in just under two months' time. I had no experience with judges or lawyers, but I imagined them as corrupt as the pigs we'd just left. My youth would earn a guilty charge the moment I stepped into the courtroom.

Not that I intended to show.

A short while later, I opened the shattered glass door to our government housing building and climbed the stairs littered with beer bottles and take-away boxes.

"Why can't you just talk to me?" Mom asked as we entered our one-bedroom apartment. She hadn't let up the whole way, and my ears were all the sorer for it.

I walked past her and shoved aside the dirty plates on the futon. My throat burned, and I didn't know whether I wanted to shout or cry. I was a pot of Mom's stew, all leftover ingredients boiled together with no idea how it would taste until I opened my mouth.

"Just once, tell me how you feel," Mom said. "Tell me how your day was. Tell me what you want for dinner. Tell me anything. Please . . ." Her voice trailed off, and she ran her fingers through her messy hair.

I stared at my hands. The nails were cracked, and more than a few scratches lined my palms. I made a small, bony fist, and the image of Kingsley pummeling Pickering flashed through my mind. I opened my hand again in a hurry.

Mom sighed and gripped the small statue of Mother Mary she kept in the kitchen. Her lips moved silently for a moment, and then she released the statue and kneaded her eyes. "Chalia, I love you more than anything. But this city, this . . . everything . . . it isn't good for us—"

My blood heated. "Isn't good for us?" I said, looking up. "What isn't good? What aren't you happy with? Tell me, Mom— how am I ruining your life?" *Say it*, I thought. *Tell me how you blame me for Dad leaving.* I knew it was how she felt because that's how I felt too.

"My life?" she said. "It's been seven years since I've had a life! Two jobs, Chalia! Two jobs so I can put you through school. Feed you. Clothe you. Everything I do, I do for you, but it's never good enough—"

"You think you're the only one Dad hurt when he left?" I said, jumping to my feet. "I've eaten macaroni and cheese every night for the last week. I live in a house—if you can call it that—with more rats than the *Titanic*. I'm wearing clothes from three years ago, Mom. Three years! And my best friend just got beaten bloody by the cops." My lips trembled, and I collapsed back to the futon and buried my head in my hands. "I can't do it anymore. I just can't."

Mom rushed from the kitchen. "Oh, Chalia," she said, wrapping her arms around me. "I'm sorry. I know it's difficult."

I fell into her, and tears streamed down my cheeks unchecked. "They got Kingsley, Mom. H-he'll go to Borstal . . . I'll never see him again."

"Hush, dear," she cooed as she stroked my hair. "I'll see what I can do to help him tomorrow. We will get through this, I promise. It's this city—it rots everything it touches. We should never have come."

I sniffled then pulled away. "Why, then?" I asked, watching her face. "Why did you move us here if you hate it so much?"

Mom looked at her feet and chewed her lip. "Because it gave me you," she said eventually. She looked up and searched my eyes, then gave a small nod as though deciding on something. "Chalia, there is something I've been thinking about for a while. This apartment, the police, the city, all of it—it's killing us. I want to—"

"No—"

"I want to ask your great-grandfather if we can move in with him in Belbury-on-the-Brook—"

I pushed away from her until I was against the far side of the futon. "No," I said again. "No way—I will not live in some cow farm in the middle of nowhere. Kingsley needs me here."

"Maybe . . . maybe he can come too. Please, Chalia, there is a better life waiting for us."

"You think a village is a better life?" I asked. "Where the only friends I'll have are sheep and the only thing to do is pick up cow crap from the lawn?"

"What other option do we have—"

"Staying," I said, standing and setting my jaw. Mom could do what she wanted after I left for Italy, as long as she left me out of it.

Mom reached for my hands, but I pulled away. "Please," she said. "All I want is to see you smile again. What will it take to make you happy, Chalia? Tell me and I will do it."

I looked at her and shook my head. "Not all stories have happy endings." Then I walked to my bedroom and flung myself onto the bed.

What *would* it take for me to be happy again?

A miracle.

I laughed. It was hollow and self-pitying. Barden didn't grant miracles, and Belbury-on-the-Brook would not grant happiness.

CHAPTER 6

- CHALIA -

Riiing-ring! Riiing-ring!

Our phone screeched in the night, its high-pitched trill cutting the darkness like an air horn in a cemetery.

I jolted awake and clutched my chest. The sky outside my window was pitch black. What chav would call so late?

Riiing-ring! Riiing-ring!

A flicker of hope rushed through me. Maybe it was Kingsley wanting to get an early jump out of Barden.

Riiing-ring! Riiing-ring!

My heart stammered. I sat. Kingsley would never call in the middle of the night if he knew Mom was home.

Riiing-ring! Riii-click—

"Whozzit?" Mom mumbled from the kitchen, voice slurred with sleep.

Silence. Goose pimples prickled my neck. I pulled my duvet up to my chin as the walls pressed in on me like a coffin.

Mom gasped, and a glass smashed on the tile floor. "No . . . oh, please, no . . ."

I couldn't make out the words on the other end of the phone, but I knew that mousy voice. It didn't make any sense. Why was she calling so late?

Mom whimpered. "No, it can't be true . . . Oh, Maria, how?"

The silence doubled, and the air grew hard to breathe. My chest convulsed, squeezing a whine from the back of my throat.

"I'm so sorry," Mom said. "Listen, I'll come right over . . . no, it's okay . . . you sure? It's no trouble . . . Okay, if there's anything I can do . . . I understand, thank you for letting us know, I'll tell her . . . Okay, Maria, please don't hesitate . . ."

Click.

I stared at the door handle. Why was Kingsley's mom calling us in the middle of the night? I grew old a hundred times in the seconds it took Mom to open the door. She found me sitting, tears trickling down my cheeks, and rushed forward to throw her arms around me where she broke into sobs.

That's when I knew for certain.

No. I'd known before that.

I'd known the moment I left Kingsley in the cell.

"What happened?" I asked, my brain numb as though it was floating in a gutter of winter runoff.

Mom pulled away from me. "He . . . ah . . ." she gulped, and then gushed, "there was an a-accident and he . . . he—"

I didn't need her to finish. "His dad?"

Mom shook her head. "Once Kingsley was out of the cells, his dad took to beating him. Maria tried to stop it, but he ended up beating her too. She thought she was going to die, and K-Kingsley must have too. He stabbed him—oh, Chalia, he stabbed his dad and killed him." Her lips trembled as though recycled sticky-tape held them on.

I thought back to Kingsley in the cell. He'd warned me—said he had things what needed doing. I should have known. I should have talked him out of it. He had never planned to go to Borstal. From the moment he was caught, he was going to set his dad straight, even if it meant the end of him.

"The neighbors called the police when they heard scream-ing," Mom said from somewhere a million miles away. "Kingsley ran . . . but he still had the knife. T-they shot him. He . . . he's dead—"

"No," I said, my eyes losing focus. I was having a nightmare. I would wake soon, and I would get Kingsley out of Barden be-fore anything could happen. "Maria is confused. She must've been drinking—"

Mom shook her head, and tears splashed to my sheets. "Maria asked me to tell you . . . she knows how much you cared for Kingsley—"

"*Care*," I said, climbing out of bed. "I *care* for Kingsley. Maria is wrong—"

"Chalia—"

Maria was drunk, that made sense. I would set her straight be-fore she hurt someone. I ran from the room and bounded down the stairs into the cool night, where my bare feet pounded the pavement. I wore only my extra-large Oasis shirt and should have been freezing. I felt nothing. Heard nothing. Saw nothing but the road in front of me.

It was near a mile to Kingsley's apartment. I'd traveled there so many times I could do it blindfolded. I passed the Occidental Bar and turned left onto his street where the angry flashing of red and blue caused me to falter.

No. That proved nothing. Kingsley's neighborhood was dangerous, and the cop cars could be there for many reasons.

And the people lining the sidewalks, they were just going for a stroll. Yes, they wanted to lose some weight for summer.

The breeze blurred my vision and brought tears to my eyes. I slowed to a walk. There was marking tape in front of Kingsley's house. Sunshine yellow in a black-and-white world. I tripped up the gutter, drawn to the tape like a fly to a lamp.

You could buy marking tape at the corner shop if you wanted . . .

"Lass, get back to your house," someone ordered from the road. I ignored them.

A stain colored the footpath.

It was dark and glistening in the police lights and wide enough to water the grass on either side.

I collapsed to my knees in front of it, fingers digging through the woody weeds to the dirt, and screamed. It wasn't a word, but a complete history of emotions. Anguish. Contempt. Rage. Guilt. Resignation. These and a thousand more. Truth answered back. It clawed at me until I was nothing but the shreds of a girl, torn and tattered and lost.

Kingsley was dead, and I was dead too.

I have no recollection of the rest of that night. It's wiped from my memory, lost like a pencil to an eraser. Mom thinks the grief was too strong for my body to bear, so my head took matters into its own hands. All I know is Kingsley took more than a small part of me when he left, and I would never get it back.

CHAPTER 7

- GEORGE -

Lightning flashed across the night sky in Belbury as rain lashed the cobbled roads in swirling sheets, sending torrents of water streaming through the alleys to cascade into the muddy brook. May was in full swing, summer almost come, not that anyone would know, going by the weather.

George, his stomach growling, was longing for a warm meal by his toasty hearth. Maybe even a swill of his finest whiskey to warm his bones. Time had taught him the best things in life were often the simplest, such as dozing in a comfy chair in front of a fire dancing to the pitter-patter of rain on the windows. Instead, he was making his way to the Pointed Ear Tavern to discuss matters that had no place outside of a nightmare. He pulled his coat tight to ward off the chill, shuddering as he did so. The vision of the aurocan still played across his mind, the cold insanity in its eyes, the promise of death.

Don't be an old fool, he berated himself. He needed to be strong, for the Belbury's sake. The gworth he was riding snorted and shivered, snapping George out of his dark thoughts. Not naturally found on Earth, gworths were beasts resembling bulls in an if-you-had-too-much-to-drink kind of way. They were much sturdier, with coats of thick wool, and had six legs, the middle two ending in great claws. It was easy for humans to mistake them for monsters, which is why none was allowed outside the borders of Belbury.

George squinted skyward as his gworth, Bessie, carried him across the bridge and into the town square. "Fitting," he muttered, blinking rain from his eyes, thinking the stormy night a perfect symbol of the dark times they were facing. Bessie belched in reply, and George rubbed her woolly neck. "I'm glad you agree."

They passed two sentries standing next to the newly erected warning bell beside the water well. Their longbows were strung, their stance at attention, and their gaze alert.

"Hoo-loo, George," the sentry named Tirathiel shouted over the pouring rain. Water beaded off his angular face, though it didn't bend the smile from his lips.

"Hoo-loo," George shouted back. "About as dry as the tavern's toilet seat on payday, huh?"

Tirathiel laughed. "I believe we have Gormer to blame for that. But I suppose nothing makes a fire more magnificent than a cold, wet night. Unless, of course, you have a barrel of Hrathenir's sweetest winter wine."

"Indeed," George said with a tip of his hat, having tasted the wine only once in his life, but remembering the syrupy drink with great fondness. All elves had a similar attitude toward life, and George appreciated it. Too often grown men grumbled about things of no consequence.

George carried on and passed the town hall before turning

right at the intersection. A slight incline carried him to the tavern, where the windows glowed, warm and inviting. He pulled into the stables and steered into one of the few remaining stalls. "Won't be long," he said, scratching Bessie's ears. *Hopefully.*

He pushed open the heavy door to the Pointed Ear, and a wave of warmth greeted him. Just as he expected, the smoky tavern was bustling. Patrons filled every table and bar, with a few jostling for prime position around the circular fire pit in the center of the room. The aroma of smoke and roasted meats and ale-soaked floorboards tickled his nose. He breathed in deeply, and the tension in his shoulders disappeared.

"They're waiting out back," a gruff voice said beside George.

George startled. He turned to find Arthur standing by the wall, still as a hat rack. His face was unshaven, and dark bags lined his eyes. *He hasn't slept since the aurocans arrived,* George thought. He did not envy the mayor his role in what was to come and was glad he no longer held that position. George forced a smile, hoping to lighten the mood. "Hoo-loo, Arthur—"

"Yes, yes, hoo-loo, hoo-loo," Arthur said, brushing away the greeting as though it were a mosquito. "Come along, much to discuss." He stalked past George and crossed the room, shoulders hunched.

George hung his coat on a spare hook and made his way through the crowd and into the conference room. Eleven of the twelve Founders sat at the long table in the center; those with weapons had them leaning against a storage cupboard at the far end of the room. They all greeted George as he entered, and George smiled in return as he found his place between old Mr. Higgleglade and Mrs. Smitherson. Arthur, seated at the head of the table, drummed his fingers impatiently. They were the four humans in the room; the other seats were occupied by four elves and four dwarves. Collectively, they were the Founders.

"Let us begin," Arthur said as soon as George's bottom touched the seat.

"Not darned likely!" the dwarf named Gormer said with a thump of his heavy fist on the table. "Talk is only half as good without ale, and George here is dryer than a sunburned rock."

The other three dwarves thumped their near-empty tankards in agreement. The elves shook their heads, knowing it was inevitable the dwarves would want to make a party from the meeting. Arthur, however, frowned.

"Thank you," George said with a smile. Truth be told, he needed a drink more than ever.

Gormer winked and scuttled to a voice pipe attached to the wall. "Barkeep!" he yelled into the mouthpiece. "The vet has a thirst for ale! Might as well make it five, seeing as us dwarves are near done. I swear, your tankards get smaller with each drink!"

Payne, the bartender, delivered the drinks in short order, and the room grew quiet. George's stomach turned as he looked around, a nervous energy radiating through his lungs. In a few seconds' time, he would cause a ruckus among them, and he did not know how it would resolve. He had rehearsed his speech, wanting to polish it until it shone and was bulletproof, but each time his words came out awkward and unreasonable. But he had to try, if not for his sake, then for Valerie's.

Arthur cleared his throat to speak, but George got in first.

"Before we begin," George said. "I'd like to raise a topic."

Arthur pursed his lips. He looked as though someone asked

him for his last shilling. He leveled his gaze at George for a tense moment and then gave a curt nod. "Be quick."

George's heart fluttered. He took a gulp of ale to wet his dry mouth and then stood. "I received a letter on Thursday from Valerie—"

There was a sharp intake of breath at the table. "*The* Valerie?" Gormer asked, tankard halfway to his mouth. "Yer granddaughter?"

"Who else would it be?" the elf named Talien asked as he leaned forward. "How is she?"

"Not well," George said honestly. He pulled out the folded letter from his breast pocket and held it up for everyone to see. "She lives in a terribly dangerous city. It is full of murder and rape and corruption. She fears for the safety of her daughter—"

"As she should!" Gormer exclaimed. "I visited Cheltenham once, and what a nasty, horrid place it was. All those people and the cursed loud things carrying them places. Nope. It's no place for a young lady, and ye tells me Barden is even bigger? Bah, but I don't believe it."

Mutters of agreement sounded from the table, and while there were sympathetic faces looking up at George, there were just as many indifferent ones. He expected as much; they may all love his granddaughter, but not all of them would rally behind a lawbreaker, especially not the law Valerie had broken.

"Valerie's daughter, Chalia's best friend was murdered, and he was only fifteen," George said, his gaze swinging to each Founder. "Valerie fears the same fate may find Chalia, unless they escape soon." George swallowed, and a knot found his throat. "Now, I'll be the first to admit Val has made mistakes, but who here has not? Are her crimes worth the death of her child?" He turned to

Arthur, the moment upon him. "I am requesting permission to bring Valerie back to Belbury-on-the-Brook."

The effect of his words was immediate. The table burst into hushed conversations, but George only had eyes for Arthur.

The mayor shook his head, mouth in a grim line. "George, you're my oldest friend, and I will always do what I can for you. But this? We evicted her for life. What precedence would we be setting if we allowed this crime to go unpunished?"

George squared his shoulders. "She was young, little more than a girl when it happened, and she has paid the price for *fifteen* years." He thumped his hand on the table. "I say it is punishment enough. Forgive her the mistakes of youth and let us move on. For all I've done for this village—let me see my granddaughter again before age steals my sight."

An uncomfortable silence fell upon the room as the Founders looked to one another, no one willing to be the first to speak. George's stomach churned, and a dizziness found him. He sucked in a deep breath and focused on Arthur's eyes.

Finally, Arthur sighed and shook his head. "George, understand—it is dangerous to let her return. Think of what it might say to the others who wish to follow her lead. We simply can't allow it."

George's legs trembled. The image of him hugging his young Valerie again, after all those years, faded from his mind. He felt old, empty, like a toothpaste tube squeezed dry. He sat back in his chair, suddenly too heavy to stand, and looked down to his hands. *Why couldn't they see reason?*

Gormer stood, sloshing beer from his tankard, and George looked up. "Bah, let her come back, says I! She should never've been booted in the first place. I said it long ago, and I'll say it today. Such an absurd rule I've never heard!"

The candles in the middle of the table flickered. Chairs groaned as their occupants shifted their weight. Then, a quiet voice said, "Hear, hear." It was a dwarf seated across the table.

A spark ignited in George. Could it be?

And then the remaining two dwarfs slammed their tankards on the table and cried, "Hear, hear!"

And George's spirits soared. Thanks be to the dwarves' ever willingness to bend the law!

"I've always been fond of Valerie," Mrs. Smitherson said beside George. "Bring her home, and let's be done with this nonsense." Her toothless smile reached her eyes, and George wanted to pick her up and wrap her in a hug, but he doubted either of their backs would survive such a bold movement.

Arthur's mustache jerked. He turned to Talian. "And you?" he asked hotly. "Your voice has power here, seeing as you were most affected."

Talian, the speaker for the elves, placed his two index fingers together and rested them on his lips. After some time, he spoke, voice somber, and everyone in the room understood why. "Time will not return my son to me, and holding on to resentment will do little but burn my hands." He looked to George. "If you believe it safer in Belbury than Barden, bring her home. But do not make this judgment without thought, not with the dangers of the water well upon us."

George chewed his lip. Belbury was certainly facing difficult and dangerous times, but it must be safer than Barden, going by all reports. Or was that just wishful thinking? Would he place Valerie and Chalia in danger just to see them again?

He shook his head. No. He would never do that. Every time he journeyed to Cheltenham for supplies, Barden was always in the newspapers for some nefarious event or another. It was better the lasses were by his side, where he could protect them. His gaze hardened. "Thank you, Talian. I will not forget this."

Talian bowed.

Gormer raised his tankard. "A toast!"

But George turned to Arthur, heart in throat. Without the mayor's blessing, the Founders' votes would mean little. He alone had the power to remove Valerie's eviction.

Arthur's brows knitted as he turned from Talian to George. His jaw ground like he was chewing cud. "So be it," he said. "But it is on your reputation, and her actions your responsibility. One toe out of line—from Valerie or this daughter of hers—and I will remove them from the village for good."

George sucked in a breath and melted into the chair, his sight blurring. *She was coming home! At last, she was coming home.* "T-thank you," he stammered, unable to say more. He looked away to rub his eyes.

"To old family and new beginnings!" Gormer shouted, eager for a toast almost as much as he was eager for a drink.

Tankards crashed together, spilling ale over the table. Arthur, refusing to take part, looked at the wet tabletop with a shake of his head. "Unless anyone else has other matters to discuss—" he glared at them all, daring them to speak, "—let's move on.

"Last week we received our first visitors in seventy years. From what the elves and dwarves have told us, this Ghultar and his horde are a threat to our very existence." His gaze fell on Talian. "Last Wednesday, the magical defense of Belbury-on-the-Brook was tasked to the elves, along with the provision of offensive magics. Do you have a status update of this?"

Talian stood. "I have divided our community into two task forces, one for defense, the other for offense. We have placed hindrance wards and traps on many buildings, but our biggest challenge is creating the magical barrier at our borders to restrict the invaders from escaping into greater England. This task will take time, because of the area requiring the shield."

Arthur nodded. "Any progress adding wards to the water well?"

"No," Talian said with a shake of his head. "The portal between the worlds consumes all magic we cast upon it. It is like trying to drown a dwarf with ale—no matter how much you pour in, there is always room for more."

Arthur chewed his lip. "And offensive spells?"

"It's been a time since elves have needed such magic, but we still remember. To ensure we realize our full capability, I have issued orders for the community to practice. When the time comes, we will be ready."

Arthur almost smiled. "Good, good," he said, sounding like a proud father praising his child. He turned to Gormer. "And the dwarves?"

"We're not naturally gifted in magics like the red-ears, but some of us have the gift. The termites won't know what hit 'em when me boys pull out their spells."

Arthur's jaw tightened. "I'm more interested in your blades and hammers."

Gormer's eyes twinkled. "Thirstier than ever. They'll drink their fill of aurocan blood before this is over, have no doubt."

Arstand, an elf with cropped silver hair, snorted. "Do you

still remember how to use them? Dwarves aren't known for their memory."

Gormer barked a laugh. "Once a dwarf learns to swing an axe, it'd take the loss of his head before he forgets it."

"I'd hardly call that a loss," Arim, an elf with large, amber eyes, remarked. The table chorused with laughter.

"Enough," Arthur said. "Let's carry on." He looked to Gormer. "Keep the forge fired and drill your dwarves—we may have need of every man, woman, and child to bear arms before this battle is over."

Gormer acknowledged the order with a nod, and Arthur turned to George. "As beastmaster, I tasked you with preparing the creatures. What news have you?"

George placed his beer on the table. "Five of the gworths are battle trained and ready. I have increased their diet to add power to their frame and exercise them as much as possible. Their skill will be a great asset in the fight to come—"

"Five?" Arthur asked. "Is that all we have?"

"There are more, but they are too green for battle."

Arthur frowned. "Reserve the battle gworths for our best warriors and do everything you can to get the green gworths up to scratch. Tell me of the other beasts."

"Seven snarzis, all with fangs and claws sharp enough to mold steel."

Talian coughed. "Are we certain they'll attack aurocans and not villagers?"

"No," George said. "Even I can't control them once they smell blood. It would take enough sedative to knock the trunk off an elephant to calm them."

Arthur sighed. "I expected as much. Keep working them; there may come a time when we need to risk them in battle. What of those bat things?"

"The vraps breed like mice," George said. "It won't be long before my barn is full of the nasty buggers."

"That's a good problem to have," Gormer said.

"Indeed," said George. "I watched one take down a white-tailed eagle as though it were a sparrow. Release a few hundred of these when the aurocans are in flight, and the vraps will tear them to shreds. They are aggressively territorial."

"Keep breeding them," Arthur instructed. "If all else fails, they can be fodder while the elves and dwarves prepare for the fight."

The meeting carried on long into the night. The candles burned low, and tankards piled high by the time they were done. George, bones aching and mind exhausted, was craving the comfort of his bed. He was the last Founder to leave the room.

Or so he thought.

Huddled in the storage cupboard, cramped and regretting their decision to spy on the meeting, were Duke and Elanil, a dwarf and elf, both fifteen-year-old lasses with well-earned reputations of getting themselves into trouble they couldn't get out of. That night was no exception.

Duke blew a breath once George left. "Did not expect that," she said, wiping curly hair from her face.

Elanil cracked open the cupboard door and stepped out, her muscles numb from hours of sitting still. She made her way to the open door leading to the main bar. "I've heard Father talk of aurocans, and never in a good way. This is bad, Duke. This is really bad." When Duke didn't answer, Elanil turned and groaned.

Duke was at the table, draining a tankard of its remaining ale. She burped and wiped her lips and looked to Elanil. "Aurocans? Bah, sound like a bunch of cats if you ask me."

"You hate cats."

"Not in a soup," Duke said with a laugh.

CHAPTER 8

- CHALIA -

The days after Kingsley's death were the darkest of my life, and there was a time I didn't think I was strong enough to see them through. I was beyond comforting, in a terrible place where despair and hopelessness were my only companions. It hurt to be outside—everything reminded me of him. The Warrens, the school, the roof we used to sneak onto to catch glimpses of the sun. I spent most of my time curled beneath my duvet, staring at the scorch marks on the wall and wondering how long the pain would last.

In the end, I didn't put up a fight when Mom gave me a ticket to Belbury-on-the-Brook. She guided me onto the National Express bus to Cheltenham station at twenty past ten the morning following Kingsley's funeral. Tears sparkled in her eyes when she promised she would follow as soon as she sorted out her jobs and the apartment. I didn't cry. I couldn't. The hollowness in my soul swallowed all emotions. Snuffed the life out of them until they were mild sensations of no consequence.

First Dad.

Then Kingsley.

I'm cancer.

The journey was long and boring and had a way of making my mind wander further than the coach; not a good thing when thoughts were grim. To distract myself, I thumbed through the magazine I'd lifted from the station. The cover was a photo of Venice and its winding canals. If only I had the power to jump into that photograph, to transport away from the world I was living in, my life would be so much easier. I flicked open to the centerfold and tried to read the article about Venetian tourism, but the words twirled and jumbled, turning into a thousand scurrying ants. Giving up with a sigh, I settled for resting my head on the window and watching the smog and chaos of the city give way to rolling green farmlands.

It was early afternoon when the coach hopped to a stop outside Royal Well Bus Station. The other three passengers exited, leaving me alone. My chest squeezed. I was about to see him again, my great-granddad. It had been ten years, and now the old kook thought he could look after me? He would probably have a stroke when he saw my bullring and half-burnt bomber jacket. Probably ain't never seen a pixie haircut either, not all the way out there among the livestock. With a sigh, I grabbed my bag and exited. I glanced up and down the station and quickly realized it was deserted. Empty. No other buses, no cars, no cranky old man waiting beside a rusty Volvo to pick me up. No one.

"Great," I muttered. He probably had dementia or something. I took a seat beneath the shelter and closed my eyes. A hill popped into my mind, spotted with citrus trees. An imaginary breeze cooled my face, carrying with it the smell of wood-fired pizza. A

cute lemon-yellow house was perched above stakes of rose tomatoes, and waves crashed in the distance. It could all be mine, I just
needed to find that dot—

Clippety-clop. Clippety-clop.

My eyes snapped open. What the hell was that?

Clippety-clop.

I turned to find an ancient horse-drawn cart steering onto the
station road. It looked something out of a Robin Hood movie,
which made me almost smile, thinking I'd caught the bus to the
twelfth century. A wrinkled man guided the cart along the road,
rocking side to side with a smile. He gave a tilt of his trilby hat
when he spotted me.

I looked away, hoping to avoid any accidental conversation. I
was not in the mood to talk to anyone, especially someone driving
a cart. Despite my efforts, the old man steered the horse right to
before rolling to a stop. He leaned down.

"Hoo-loo," he said, his smile deepening his wrinkles, making
him look like a forgotten potato.

Hoo-loo? What drugs was he on? "Yep," I said, crossing my
arms and looking to his Clydesdale, hoping it would trot on.

"Chalia, I'm guessing?" the man asked. "Couldn't be anyone
else, not from Valerie's description."

I looked to him to find him beaming down at me. My lips
pursed. How did he know Mom?

"Few in these parts who can get away with all them rings in
their face, but you've hit it for six. Come along, lassie, bag in the
back and bum on the bench. We've a way to travel, and in these
times, it'd be safer to get there before dark."

My bag slipped from my knees to slap on the ground. "You're

George?" I asked, dumbfounded, looking over the cart and horse again. Surely he was joking, one of those old man jokes young people couldn't understand. Where was his car?

"I am, though you might not remember it," he said with a wink. "Now hop aboard—like I said, these are dark times, and a hearth would go a long way to brighten them."

I stared at him without the faintest idea of what to do. He was a nutter, surely. One without too much spark between his long ears if he couldn't even drive a car. The coach's squeaky axle screamed behind, and I turned to watch it pull out of the station. I was left alone with George and his enormous horse. I scanned the car park once more. Maybe I could hitchhike back to Barden, find a temporary job to save enough money to get to Italy. I shook my head. No. I could never step foot in that place again, not without Kingsley.

The old man grinned when I turned back to him. He reclined in his seat and looked like a person with all the time in the world. I shook my head as I scooped my bag and tossed it into the cart. What else could I do?

George held out a hand to help me onto the bench. His grip was firm for someone so old, and he smelled of wood fire and aftershave. "Nice to see you again, lassie. Must be ten years since you were last out this way."

I brushed my fringe from my face. "Give or take," I said, hoping he would not talk the whole way.

"Well, I am glad I finally get to spend some time with you. Call me Pop. I have never much liked George," Pop said as he gathered the reins from his lap and gave them a flick. The horse stepped forward, pulling us along. "Umbrella by your feet, if you have a need for shade. We are not completely without comfort, you know."

"Clearly," I mumbled, adjusting myself on the wood bench, certain broken glass was more comfortable.

"How's your mother?" George asked. "Letter said she had to stay in Barden for a couple weeks?"

"Yeah, she needs to sort out some things." I fished a letter from my pocket. "She asked me to give you this."

Pop raised a bushy eyebrow as he accepted it. After a moment, he tucked it into his woolly vest, unopened. We turned out of the station and onto a street lined with cars. "Heard you went through a tough time in the city," he said as he crossed a leg over his knee.

I fingered a hole in my bomber jacket. I'd burnt it in the last week. The threads were crispy and black and unraveled. I couldn't remember how I'd done it. I couldn't remember much of anything.

"Death is a terrible thing to live through," Pop went on. "It holds power to bring people closer together or send them to the opposite ends of the world, never to speak again."

I ground my jaw. "What do you know of death? You're a hundred and still alive."

Kingsley was only fifteen.

Pop chuckled, though there was a sadness to it. "Oh, dying is the simple part of death. It's the people who carry on who do it the hardest. Time will never let you forget, though it dulls the pain. You seem a lass with your head on straight, even if you've had your trouble, so I don't doubt you'll come out the other side stronger."

I crossed my arms and turned away. "You know nothing about me."

Pop sighed and gave a click of his tongue, sending the Clydesdale into a trot. He didn't say another word for some time. In fact, we'd left Cheltenham far behind before he made any sound at all. A whistled tune, the type you only heard from old men. I was a Metallica fan, but quite by accident I found the sound removing the edge of my bitterness.

The farmland surrounding us was dotted with cattle and sheep and divided by waist-high stone walls. Farmers on horses were hard at work, shouting orders to their dogs. Before long, the warm sun and gentle sway of the cart lulled me to sleep.

"Look sharp, Chalia," Pop said sometime later, startling me from my dreams. "We are at the gate."

I sat up straight and wiped drool from my chin, taking a moment to remember where I was. A wall of mossy stones cut the path to our front. A timber gate barred the road, and a weathered watchtower overlooked us on the far side, narrow window slits climbing the three stories with battlements on the top.

Pop leaned in and whispered. "You were too young last time to remember the peculiarities of the folk of Belbury, but please try not to stare. I'm sure they will extend the same courtesy."

"Why would I stare?" I asked. "And what's up with the gate?"

Pop chuckled. "If these folk do not make you want to stare, then nothing will." He looked ahead. "The gate is to stop anyone accidentally wandering in."

At that moment, four people emerged from the watchtower and trotted through the gate. My eyes widened. Two of them were the height of children, but both with shoulders wider than Dwayne Johnson's. The other two were normal height, but their hair sparkled in the sun like glitter. The four divided into two groups, the stocky ones walking to my side of the cart, the sparkle-hairs to Pop's.

I couldn't close my mouth if I wanted to. The man's beard was thick enough to hide a dog in, and he wore the most absurd clothing I'd ever seen. A wide-brimmed straw hat shaded his face, suspenders held up black trousers over a blue plaid shirt, and for some unknown reason, he had an axe slung across his back. The woman, no less ridiculous, wore a white bonnet and black dress and carried a sledgehammer with a nasty point on one side. Both looked me up and down beneath thick eyebrows.

Pop placed a hand on my shoulder. "Don't mind them, they are Amish folk, settled in Belbury from Scotland," he said, as though that explained everything.

The woman snorted. "Bah! Don't be warning the lass about us and forgetting about them no good red-ears!" She jutted her square chin at the shimmering-haired couple beside Pop.

In comparison they looked almost normal; tall, dressed in jeans, boots, and flannel shirts. In fact, the only thing that gave them away as weirdos—apart from their hair—was the curved swords on their belts. Oh, and the fluffy red earmuffs covering the sides of their heads. Who on earth would wear earmuffs on such a warm day?

"Papers?" the golden-haired man asked.

CHAPTER 9

- CHALIA -

The shimmering-haired man's beautiful face held a hard edge to it when his gaze flicked to me. He looked me up and down, and his mouth pressed into a tight line as though he'd just eaten the skin of a large lemon. I crossed my arms. What was his problem? He was the one wearing earmuffs on a hot day; maybe I should be staring at him like he was gutter scum.

"Oh yes, the papers," Pop said and rummaged through his pocket. He pulled out a folded piece of paper and handed it over. "Any news, Alamril?"

Alamril held my gaze for a second longer, then accepted the paper and ran his eyes over it. "Nothing yet," he muttered. "Though I suppose that is news in itself." He looked to me again. "Valerie's kid?"

"Indeed," Pop said.

Alamril chewed on that for a moment, then handed the paper back. "I have questions before I let you through."

Pop leaned forward. "I've already gone over this with Arthur."

Alamril pulled a notebook from his pocket. "And it's on his

orders we ask the questions." He licked the tip of his pen and put it to paper. "Has Chalia visited Belbury-on-the-Brook before?"

"You know she has," Pop said, dropping the reins.

"When?"

"Ten or so years back."

Alamril's pen raced across the notepad. "How long will she be staying?"

"Indefinitely."

"That seems a possibly long time."

"Perhaps even longer."

Alamril scribbled another note.

A fire sparked in my stomach. It was one thing to be handed off to Mom's relatives in a village in the ass end of England, but it was another thing to suffer the disapproval of a typical adult jerk-off I'd never met. I leaned past Pop and glared at the man. "Don't worry, I won't be staying in your rubbish town longer than I have to."

Alamril gave a curt nod, eyes never leaving the notepad, and wrote without saying a word.

Pop laid a hand on my shoulder and squeezed. "Pay him no mind, lass, he is just following orders."

"He can shove his orders up his ass," I muttered, turning away. They didn't matter, both the shiny-haired freak and Pop. All that mattered was Italy, and how I was going to get there.

A groan behind me stole my attention. I swiveled on the bench and looked down to find the little Amish pair rolling around on their stomachs in the midst of an arm-wrestle. They grunted and groaned and cursed, but eventually the woman slammed the man's fat hand down. She cheered and jumped to her feet, arms spread wide in a V. The man cursed and punched the dirt.

"Ye cheated, ye did!" he spat.

The woman laughed, loud and raw. "Maybe if ye spent more time drinking ale than tending your veggie patch, ye'd have half a chance!"

The corner of my mouth twitched up, but then a snippet of Pop's conversation reached me. The word *secret* had been said, and it hung in the air like cloud full of rain.

"How much does she know of the *secret?*" Alamril had asked.

I leaned in a little.

"None of it," Pop said, and he sounded irritated by the question. "Not that it will matter before long."

Alamril snapped his notebook closed and slipped it into his jeans pocket. "Good. I've been asked to remind you it must remain that way. She'll be evicted if she learns more than should be known, and as it is your second offense, you will follow. Understood?"

Pop tensed. "Perfectly." He snatched up the reins and turned away from Alamril.

"It's not forever, Georgie-boy," the Amish man said as he dusted dirt from his beard. "Don't take it personally—once we sort this other mess we'll have a welcoming ceremony for the lassie, and she'll know all." He looked to me with a toothy smile. "Knew your mom, I did. Wonderful girl, even if she had more'n her share of cheek. Your father was a good man too, considering his kind and what not."

Pain stabbed through my chest at the mention of Dad. "He was a scumbag," I said, trying to deflect from the guilt I felt at him abandoning me.

The Amish man's eyes flicked to Pop's, and then he choked an awkward cough. "Well, family can be tricky. I grew up with that thing for a sister." He nodded to the woman beside him. "She used to fart louder than a mob of boars. Almost blew the thatch off the cottage, it did."

His sister punched him in the arm, sending him crashing into the cart, which jolted under his weight. "Bah! I did it to cover the stink of your breath!"

I smiled before I could help it. They were different from other adults, I realized. They didn't talk down to me, not like everyone in Barden. The pain in my chest dimmed.

The man rubbed his arm as he glared over his shoulder at his sister. He turned to me and extended a hand. "Me name's Stanthrop."

Fat calluses covered his palm, and his fingernails were filthy. After a second, I took it. "Chalia."

"Hoo-loo, Chalia. I'm sure I'll be seeing you around the village. I've a daughter your age, and I'm sure you'll hit it off."

Pop stiffened. "Sounds like trouble to me."

Stanthrop laughed and slapped his belly. "Aye, but let them get it out of their system while they're young!" He leaned in, resting an elbow on the cart, and spoke to Pop. "I've a day in Belbury to-morrow, I'll swing by to check on the progress of the . . . erm—" he looked at me from the corner of his eyes, "—packages in the barn."

"That works fine," Pop said. "Sooner we finish with them, the better—"

"Thank you for your time, George," Alamril cut off the conversation. He stepped away from the cart, and his companion swung open the gate.

"Indeed," Pop said. He smiled to the Amish siblings then gave the reins a flick.

We trundled in, leaving the tarmac at the gate and taking a dirt road winding westward over valleys and hills.

"Don't mind Alamril," Pop said after a while. "He's been at the outpost too long. Never a smile on his face these days."

"Hmm," I said, finding Alamril was too basic to waste thoughts on. The secret, however . . . "What's the secret you talked about?"

Pop went rigid. The axles groaned as we continued our slow roll downhill. "It wouldn't be a secret if I told you," he said at length. "And they would kick us out of Belbury if I did. Not sure I could survive that, not at my age."

"Aw, come on," I pressed. "It's just us two here. No one will know." I gave him my most innocent smile.

Pop snorted a laugh. "Your mother used to look at me like that when she wanted something. She ought not to have. It worked far longer than I care to admit, but I eventually wised up." He smiled. "I can tell you the secret to love, the secret to life and happiness, but I can't tell you the secret to Belbury. It's not the right time, and it's not safe. I will not endanger you for want of a story."

"I'm not a kid—I don't need you look after me."

"Course not. I fought in a war when I was near your age—I've not forgotten the power of youth." He was silent for a long while, and just when I thought he would say no more, he spoke softly. "I destroyed lives the last time I broke Belbury's laws. I'll not cause such pain again, not by choice nor force."

I turned away. It didn't matter I was family to him. He would treat me the same as every other old bastard just because I was young. Well, I didn't need him; I didn't need anyone no more.

Pop sighed and pulled a pipe from his pocket. He filled the bowl with tobacco from a leather pouch and sparked it with a match. "You've some anger inside, Chalia, and I expect it with the life you have had. What's important is when you let it out, you let it go. Don't kennel it, for it is like to bite you more than anyone else." He took a long draw and chewed it for a moment before exhaling.

Who was he to give me life advice? I hadn't known him two seconds, and already he thought he knew me? No, it didn't work that way. I watched the pine trees roll by, and my mind wandered. I thought on the strangers at the gate. The Amish people with their weird clothing. "The man back there, Stanthrop, he said he knew Mom?"

"Of course," Pop said with a wide smile. "Most in Belbury do. She was a popular lass, so happy and loving and always getting into mischief. Everyone grew spurs on their feet from how she kept them on their toes! Your father too, they were just as cheeky as each other, and inseparable since birth."

I didn't answer but looked to the west, where the sun was midway down the sky. Obviously Pop didn't know who Dad really was, the man who betrayed me and Mom. He hadn't lived through the hell Dad left me in when he deserted me. He hadn't lived with guilt all those years.

We didn't speak for a long, long while. I was lost to anger until we rolled out of a dense forest and rounded a ridge to spot a village squeezed between a hill and forest with a stream cutting it in two.

"Welcome to Belbury-on-the-Brook," Pop said.

CHAPTER 10

- CHALIA -

Looking down on Belbury-on-the-Brook was like looking at someone who was slightly cross-eyed. Something was out of place; I could feel it in my bones, but couldn't put a finger on it. It wasn't until we rolled past the first of the village's wild hedges and narrow laneways that the oddity became clear—the entire village looked like it was from an *Oliver Twist* set.

Thatched cottages lined the highway, buried beneath cloaks of ivy, and free-spirited gardens grew right to the doorsteps. Wild herbs and fruit trees grew here and there, and brambles spotted with plump black fruit ran beside the road. People tended wheelbarrow planter boxes and sprinkled feed to their chickens as we passed. Every one of them looked up from their work and offered a "hoo-loo" and an overeager wave of their hand or tilt of their hat.

A two-story stone building on the right marked the end of the dirt road and the beginning of cobbled streets. Laughter and shouting carried through the open door as smoke drifted skyward from a large chimney stack.

"That's the Pointed Ear Tavern," Pop said, sounding like a tour guide. "The best Sunday roast in town."

Two men sat on a bench beneath a towering oak tree in the front yard, a small glass of beer in their hands. Great folds of skin hid their eyes, and the wrinkles on their faces looked older than time. In a slow manner, they both tipped their hats to Pop, who returned the salutation with a smile.

"Henry and Anthony," Pop whispered. "They served in the second war too, and have been served day and night at the Pointed Ear ever since. Steer clear of them, less you have a want for stories changed by time and failing memory."

We continued down a slight gully and turned left before the next rise. I kept my eyes peeled for any sort of entertainment; a skate park or cinema, an arcade or pool hall, but all Belbury offered was bumpy roads and old people.

A church with a graveyard to its front was on the right of the road, while a village square opened up on the left, reaching down to the brook.

"Hoo-loo, lads," Pop called to two Amish folk standing beside a water well in the center of the square. Both held axes and looked quite disgruntled. "Any movement?"

"Naught but our churning stomachs," grumbled the first.

"And the rest of the village wending their way to the Ear to fill theirs," muttered the other as he picked at a notch in his axe.

Pop was still chuckling as we crossed the brook on a stone-arch bridge and turned left onto a dirt path. His laughter died when two lasses appeared to our front, both sprinting toward us like they were being chased by the Blinders.

"George!" the Amish girl panted when she reached the cart.

"Save us! Old Mrs. Moira has gone bonkers!" She was fifteen or sixteen and had a broad face hidden beneath a mane of curly hair.

"Completely insane," said her red-earmuff-wearing friend, looking over her shoulder. "And for not much reason, neither!"

Pop pursed his lips. "For no reason? I find that hard to believe with you two—"

"No time to explain," said the red-ear as she vaulted into the back of the cart and lay flat, hiding from view.

The Amish girl made to follow but crashed into the side, rocking us about. She attempted again, her legs kicking wildly, and pulled herself in.

"You haven't seen us," the red-ear said.

"Today or yesterday," added the Amish.

"Actually, the full week. To be safe."

Pop clucked his tongue. "What have you done to poor Mrs. Moira?"

"Not much more than usual, to be telling the truth," the Amish girl said.

The red-ear nodded. "She's in a foul mood because someone nicked the carrots from her patch."

Pop tilted his head. "And I suppose that someone wasn't you two?"

"Of course it was," the Amish girl said. "But that's no reason to be carrying on the way she is! Hers aren't the only carrots we've borrowed, and no one else acts a danger like her."

As peculiar as the conversation was, I found I couldn't much concentrate on it because I was caught off guard by the red-ear. She was the most beautiful person I'd ever seen. It was the type of beauty what made others look like mold-covered tuna in comparison. I was surprised to find a part of me wanted to run my fingers over her lips to see if they were really as full as they looked. Another part of me wanted to punch her annoyingly perfect nose, just to bring her down a notch.

Her enormous amber eyes flicked to mine, and we shared a gaze. My heart froze. She was perfect. What on earth was happening to me? I'd never felt that way about a lass before. Men were trouble . . . but a lass? My mind must be muddled from the long trip.

The red-ear blinked her long lashes, then turned to Pop. "Who's the weirdo staring at me?"

I spluttered and looked away, my cheeks burning.

Pop flicked his reins, and the cart lurched forward again. "Elanil, this is Chalia. Chalia, meet Elanil and Bekka—"

"Duke," the Amish girl corrected. "My friends call me Duke."

"Hi," I said quietly, suddenly shy.

"Welcome to Belbury!" Duke said. "Anything you hear about us is a lie, of course."

Elanil looked me up and down, eyes flowing from the seven rings in my ears to the bullring in my nose, and finally to my torn and burnt bomber jacket. She crinkled her nostrils, rolled onto her back, and looked up to the sky without a word.

"Here comes Mrs. Moira," Pop said. "Hush now."

I balled my fists and turned back to the front. A large shape was charging toward us weirdly, like a drunk pony. It drew nearer, and I gasped. Had I somehow gotten drunk? It made little sense! An Amish lady, bonnet and all, was riding a giant galloping pig. Her hair bounced around her face in a frizzled mess, and her black dress flapped behind her. She skidded the pig to a stop in a cloud of dust to our front. Her eyes were wild as she scanned the brook.

"You seen 'em, George?" she grunted as her boar pawed the ground, its tusks the length of my forearm.

Pop smiled. "Good evening, Moira," he said. "I'm assuming you're talking about Bekka and Elanil?"

Moira's eyes hardened on Pop's. "You have seen 'em, then?"

"Indeed," Pop said. "They almost ran straight into my cart while crossing the bridge. What have they done now?"

Moira cursed. "What haven't the buggers done? Made away with half me spring veg, for a start. And if that weren't enough, they pinched me mulberry pie from me sill as it cooled!"

Pop blew out a breath and shook his head. "Those rascals will never learn. Though in their defense, I've tasted your pies, Moira, and I can hardly blame them for the acquisition."

Moira's scowl faded somewhat. "Yes, well, thank you, George dear. But that's not the worst of it. I'm sure it's them what's been teaching me parrot to cuss! I can't have a friend over for tea, for fear its tongue will be sharper than its beak!"

Behind me, Elanil and Duke muffled their laughter with hands pressed tight to their lips.

"Surely not," Pop said, raising a hand to his heart.

"Afraid so," Moira said, casting a suspicious gaze over me as though I was guilty. "Well, I best be off—me boars are hungry, and they'll be dining on Duke and Elanil tonight, if I can find them." She steered her pig around our cart and kicked it into a gallop.

Pop flicked the reins, and we trundled on. After a while, Elanil sat out of the tray and leaned between Pop and me. "The absurdity of it all. We would never steal her pie."

Duke joined her. "Not the whole pie, anyway." She plunged her hand into her dress pocket—the one not overflowing with carrots—and pulled out a handful of what looked like mashed cobbler. Purple juice ran between her fingers to drip in the cart. "Hungry, George?" she asked, holding it beneath his nose. "We owe you at least half for saving us."

Pop recoiled. "No, no, dear, it's quite all right."

"How about you, Chalia?" she asked, swinging it toward me, her fingernails caked with mud and muck.

"Thanks, but I . . . uh . . . I'm not hungry."

"Suit yourself," she said with a shrug and slurped some of the juice. "So, this is your great-granddaughter, huh?" she asked Pop.

Elanil elbowed her in the ribs. It was subtle, but I caught the movement. Pop drew his eyebrows together. "How do *you* know she's my great-granddaughter?" Pop asked. "As far as I was aware, there were select few in Belbury who knew she was coming to stay at all."

Duke's eyes widened. She stammered, and pie fell from her mouth.

"You both look the same," Elanil said quickly while fixing Duke with a stern look.

Duke nodded. "Yes, yes, that's it. You could be brothers. Or— or sisters. Or, you know, relatives in some way or the other."

"Hmm," Pop said, staring at her. "If I learn you've been sneaking into the Founders' meetings again, Moira won't be the only person after your hides."

"Yes, sir, don't worry about us doing that again," Elanil said, shaking her head. "We learned our lesson last time."

"And the time before that," Duke added.

Pop glared at them for a moment longer before facing back to the front. We passed several cottages on the right before turning onto a driveway that carried us through a garden of tangled shrubs and trees that almost hid the thatched cottage from view.

"Woo-up, girl," Pop said, parking the cart in front of a barn at the end of the driveway. Moss covered its timber boards, and it was at least five times the size of the apartment I grew up in.

Pop stood and stretched, arching his back with hands on hips. After a groan of satisfaction, he looked down to me. "Well, there's scarcely an hour of light left, so we'd better start on your chores if we're to get them done."

"Huh?" I asked, surprised. I'd only just arrived, and he was talking about work?

"Chores," he said. He climbed out of the cart and walked around the horse to my side. "Life isn't easy in these parts, and work needs be done to survive." He turned to Duke and Elanil. "You two sticking around to help?"

"Gee, we would love to, George," Elanil said as she jumped from the cart.

"Very kind of you to offer," added Duke.

"But I don't want our folks to worry about us."

"And as you said, it's getting rather late."

"We best be off home."

Pop looked heavenward. "God forbid you fail to be home on time for the seventh day this week. All right, away with you both."

The two dashed down the driveway. "Thanks again, George," Duke called over her shoulder. "Nice to meet you, Chalia."

They disappeared around the hedge and left me staring after them, still very much undecided on whether I wanted to get to know Elanil better or punch her in her beautiful face.

CHAPTER 11

- CHALIA -

After Duke's bouncing hair vanished behind the hedge, I turned back to find Pop watching me with a small frown as though he'd seen a scratch on his cart. He quickly smiled, though it seemed forced, and when he spoke, his voice was unnaturally bright.

"Good kids at heart," he said. "But it would be wise to give them space, even for a while, until you learn more of Belbury. People are different here, with different ways and rules; it is a big tablet to swallow in one go."

My first reaction was to laugh at the old man for telling me what to do. I found I couldn't do that, not after he—an adult—helped two people my age. Perhaps he wasn't as bad as the rest.

"Elanil is a spoiled brat," I said, hoping he wouldn't prove me wrong. "I'd rather hang out with a three-mouthed pikey."

Pop chuckled and relaxed. "Famous last words."

I climbed out of the cart, massaged my bum, which was stiff from the hard bench, and looked around. The backyard was as wild and overgrown as the front. It wasn't messy, just free. It was calming and didn't look an awful place to spend some time.

I shook my head. My time in Belbury was limited. I was there to earn money, then leave, with zero time for relaxing. I needed time to think of a plan for how to get my dosh over the next days. I hadn't ruled out nicking it from someone who had enough to spare.

"What're these chores?" I asked Pop, wanting to get them done so I could figure out what to do. "Need help packing the horse away?" I asked, moving to the barn doors.

"No!" Pop said, rushing forward. He grabbed my wrist and spun me to face him. "I don't have many rules, Chalia, but the *one* rule I have is, you must *never* go into the barn. Never. It doesn't matter if it's on fire and you need to enter to save it. Steer clear of this place at all times."

I backed away a step. "All right, jeez," I said, pulling free of his grip. "What have you got in there, eighteenth-century porn or something?"

"Just promise."

"Why?"

"Chalia—"

I groaned. "Fine, whatever," I said, rolling my eyes. "I won't go into your stupid shed. What are my chores if not the horse?"

He smiled. "Follow me." He led me around the side of the barn and into the sprawling backyard. An apple tree towered in the center, its branches fanning wide. Smaller fruiting trees and garden beds flanked it, these sprouting an array of vegetables. A mossy path led to a chicken coop pressed against a waist-high stone fence at the back of the yard, beyond which grew a dark forest.

"Here we are," Pop said, stopping in front of a chopping block with an axe leaning against it. He collected a footlong log from a pile and balanced it on the block. "Ever chopped wood before?"

I snorted. Was that a real question? "Yeah, all the time, after I've finished churning butter."

"Good," Pop said, missing the sarcasm. He clapped a hand on my shoulder. "This shouldn't take long. Split a couple dozen—that should last until the end of the week—and stack them with the others." He nodded to a neat pile of split logs against the shed. "Then toss the chickens two scoops of feed. I'll see to the other animals and get a start on supper. Shout out if you need any help." He disappeared back around the barn.

I picked up the heavy axe, a mix of bitterness and resignation flowing through me at the situation I was in. "*Go to Belbury*," I muttered, mimicking Mom. "*I think you'll actually enjoy it.*" Yeah, right! The only way the place could get any worse was if the village sacrificed children to a lion-headed god in a cult ritual. I smiled. That might even make it a little more exciting.

I squared up to the log, lifted the axe over my head, and swung with all my might. The blade caught the side of the wood and bounced into the dirt. I huffed and reloaded. Another swing, another miss. It took five minutes until I sliced off a sliver of wood. I let out a yip of excitement. It was only a small piece, but it was progress.

After twenty minutes, blisters had formed on my hands, my back ached, and I couldn't feel my arms. I wiped sweat from my eyes and looked at the three logs I'd split. It wasn't the couple dozen Pop asked for, but it was what he was getting. I looked over my shoulder to make sure he wasn't watching, then walked to the back fence and stared into the woods, done with chores for the day.

As I stared at the deepening shadows, my mind drifted to the dilemma at hand—how to earn enough money to get to Italy. My first thought was pinching it, but that could be a disaster in a small town like Belbury. No. I would try for a job first thing in the morning before I risked stealing.

"Your mother used to spend her evenings sitting out here in this very spot," a voice said behind me.

I jolted and turned to see Pop winding his way through the backyard. He leaned against the fence beside me and pulled out his pipe. "She was always reading one book or another or talking to her hens—she named them all, you know. Black Beauty, Merrylegs, Mrs. Blomefield. She loved animals—the weirder the better."

"Hmm," I said, not much in the mood of talking about Mom.

Pop filled his pipe from his pouch, then sparked a match and lit it. He puffed a few times, staring into the forest, before he pulled it out. "I saw your nifty work with the axe," he said. "I thought you knew how to chop wood?"

I tensed. "The axe was too heavy." Was the old bugger going to lecture me about it now?

"Indeed," Pop said, eyebrows raised and eyes sparkling. "You know, Chalia, there is no shame in not knowing how to do to something—I'm yet to meet a person who knew how everything worked without being taught. What is important is if you don't know how to do it, *you ask*. All of our actions—or inactions—have consequences."

I opened my mouth to argue, but Pop silenced me with an up-raised hand.

"Take, for example, these chickens. If you agree to feed them, you should, because if the chickens don't get fed, they won't lay eggs, and if they won't lay eggs, we won't have breakfast, and there is great shame to be found in a family who have no eggs for breakfast." He looked down at me and smiled. "I'll ask many things of you while you're here, and if you're unsure about any of it, ask. You're almost a woman now, Chalia, and that means having the moxie to take ownership of your actions. Fair?"

I chewed my lip. He wasn't yelling. He wasn't ordering. He was doing something far stranger; he was asking, talking to me as though I were an equal.

I nodded. "Fair."

"Good! Let's get these chickens fed and watered, and I'll show you around the house. You'll have your mom's bedroom until she arrives. I hope you don't mind pink," he said as he messed my hair. The look of revulsion on my face made him laugh.

CHAPTER 12

- CHALIA -

It was dark the following morning when something snatched me from my sleep. My heart raced as I opened my eyes and scanned the unfamiliar room. Something—or someone—had made a sound. I glanced through the darkness to the door; still closed. Whatever it was could be in my room. Maybe some sort of rabid country animal—

Cock-a-doodle-doo!

I bowed my head and groaned. A rooster? I was scared of KFC? I collapsed back to the mattress and looked out the window. Faint pinks colored the dawn sky, pushing away the night. It was early. Too early for me to be awake. The rooster crowed again, and I held a pillow across my face.

My first night in the cottage was an experience in time travel. There was no power. No lights, TV, PlayStation, or refrigerator. The timber muttered and moaned and smelled of smoke and meat and soil. If the cottage were a person, it would be a geriatric gardener wearing well-worn gumboots, patched denim overalls covered with compost, who was rarely seen without a scone and cup of tea. It wasn't a terrible night—I slept like a baby—but it was weird.

Pop had cooked his "world-famous" beef stew for supper. It was a far cry better than the macaroni and cheese I grew up on. Much to my surprise, I had a laugh with the old bugger as he told me stories of the trouble he caused when he was my age. Before long I found I didn't despise him as much as I thought I would.

Cock-a-doodle-doo!

I groaned again and threw my pillow off my face. I had one mission that day: find a job. The sooner I started, the sooner I left for Italy. I rolled out of bed and slipped into my jeans, Metallica shirt, and bomber jacket. After brushing my teeth and running my fingers through my short hair, I stepped outside into the crisp, foggy morning, and crossed the front garden, where I turned left onto the path beside the brook.

I passed some cottages with glowing windows and smoke billowing from their chimneys, though most were still dark with sleep. Mist rolled across the water as I crossed the bridge, hands buried in my pockets to fight the cold. I startled when I found two Amish men asleep beside the water well. They sat back to back on the cobbles, their beards flapping in the breeze while their hands were fixed on their axes.

I scoffed and shook my head. Those people took personal safety to the next level. I was about to turn away when the water well drew my eye again. It was the only structure in the square, not counting the bell, and looked centuries old, with its circular stone base and bucket dangling from the spool. Why did the village need a water well when there was a brook not a hundred feet away? And how deep did those things get, anyway? I looked over my shoulder to make sure no one was watching, then I crept past the sleeping lads and looked inside. Pitch black. I couldn't see nothing past a foot or two. I looked around my feet for a rock to toss in, when a cold uneasiness tingled my ears. I froze.

Something was wrong.

I spun as someone grabbed my jacket and yanked me away from the water well. I tripped and crashed to my bum. Hot pain shot up my tailbone like lightning. I plunged my hand into my jacket and gripped my pocketknife, ready to cut my attacker, but I stopped when I recognized Duke.

"What were you thinking?" she whispered, eyes wide with fear. "That's not safe, what you did. Not safe by a long shot! Are you all right?"

I scowled and released my knife. "It's not safe what *you* did," I snapped, thinking of how close I was to making potato salad from her cheeks.

"Shh!" she hissed, looking to the Amish men asleep on the ground. "I'm sorry about that. I just didn't want you to get hurt."

"Don't apologize," a curt voice said behind me.

I looked over my shoulder and spotted Elanil. She looked about as happy as a vegan at a Brazilian barbecue.

"You saved her," Elanil said as she crossed her arms. "She should thank you."

"Saved me?" I asked, locking onto her annoyingly stunning eyes. "From what? You think I'm clumsy enough to fall into a well?"

Elanil looked me up and down, then shrugged.

"It doesn't matter," Duke said in a rush. "It's my fault, I'm sorry. Here—" She held out her hand.

I brushed it aside and got to my feet myself. "You could've just said it was dangerous—"

"Shhh!" Elanil hissed, eyes darting to the men, one of whom had just muttered something in his sleep.

Duke nodded. "Better these louts don't know you were playing with the well. Come on." She grabbed my wrist and tugged me across the road.

I tried to shake her free, but she was so strong, her grip like a vise. Eventually I gave up and allowed her to lead me to the grassy area in front of a teahouse on the brook's bank.

Duke faced me. "Listen, I'm sorry I scared you—"

"You didn't," I said as I rubbed the numbness from my wrist. "I just wasn't expecting to be attacked today. I'm busy and don't have time to be crept up on."

Duke raised her eyebrows. "Oh? What're you up to? Going to raid a garden? That's what we're doing—have to get in quick before everyone wakes. Want to join—"

"Damn it, Duke," Elanil said, stepping forward. "Her fat feet will get us caught for sure!"

I snorted and looked at her red earmuffs. "And you think you're the picture of a ninja? Pretty earmuffs, dumbass."

"They're not pretty," Elanil said as she took a step closer and balled her fists. "They're functional."

I smiled, welcoming her to throw a punch. I had just seen who she was; read her like a book. She was a tomboy. She was gorgeous in a way that made other women spiteful, but she hated being attractive. Or at least hated being judged by it. That was interesting.

Duke patted the air between us. "It's all right, lasses. So what if Chalia has fat feet or Elanil has stupid earmuffs—"

"I don't have time for this," I said, turning away from them. I looked down the road, wondering where I should start. "I'm job hunting today."

"Job?" Duke asked, sounding as though the word was foreign. "Like, actually do things and get paid for it?"

"That's the idea."

"Doesn't sound anywhere near as fun as raiding gardens. Where were you thinking?"

My eyes rested on the sky-blue teapot sign hanging above the teahouse. "There."

Elanil laughed. "Figures. You'd look good in an apron. The makings of a little housewife."

"I look good in anything."

Duke snorted and clapped my shoulder. "You have a sharp tongue, Chalia, but your head is blunt if you think the teahouse is a fun place to work. We can't let you embarrass yourself like that on your first day. Why not the abattoir?"

"No!" Elanil said, poking a finger in Duke's chest. "Not bloody likely."

Duke roared with laughter this time and slapped her belly. I looked from one to the other, not understanding what Elanil was angry about. The abattoir was a hell of a lot more appealing than than serving idiots in a cafe. At least then I could do some actual work.

Duke wiped tears from her eyes. "We can put in a kind word for you. Elanil's mom owns it."

"And your mom runs the pitch house," Elanil said. "Ask her to hire this girl."

Elanil's ears turned red, and I smiled on the inside. She was a prat, but I could have some fun with that. "The abattoir it is. How do I get there?"

Elanil's nostrils flared. "Accidents happen at abattoirs."

I shrugged. "Accidents happen everywhere." I looked to Duke. "Is she always this sour?"

"Sour?" Duke asked. "This is the happiest I've seen her all year!" She hooked her arm in mine and pulled me along the bank of the brook, back past the bridge. "The abattoir's a little way out of town, so you can tell me all about the outside world. I've heard so many crazy things—from George especially—but they can't all be true. Do metal horses really exist? Motor-hikes, or something?"

"Motorbikes?" I asked. "You really never seen a motorbike?"

"You mean they exist?"

I looked over my shoulder to Elanil. She stared after us with a small frown on her face, and once again I was struck by how beautiful she was. It was a dangerous beauty. "Yeah."

CHAPTER 13

- CHALIA -

The abattoir lay on the northern side of the stream, about a mile east of town on Banquet Road. The road followed the brook haphazardly—sometimes it climbed knolls to offer breathtaking views of the countryside, other times it turned inland to thread the pine forest, but always it returned to its home by the water, like it couldn't stomach being separated too long.

We stumbled across a mob of deer on our trek. They were grazing beside the road, unbothered by our passing, and looked as tame as any dog I'd ever seen. Rabbits bounded from warren to field like wads of cotton, and shrews scuttled here and there in search of breakfast.

It would have been an enjoyable walk—much better than treading the filthy streets of Barden—if it weren't for Elanil. I wasn't sure how I offended her, but she couldn't stomach the look of me.

Duke, in comparison, was the most interesting lass I'd ever known. She knew as much of the world beyond Belbury's borders as I knew about medieval Antarctica. I was beyond intrigued. Sure, never hearing of famous bands like Oasis and Led Zeppelin was understandable, given how she lived in a backward village, but her not knowing the basics of electricity was beyond me.

"It powers things, like TVs and toasters," I explained.

"TV?" she said, scratching her chin. "I don't know—it sounds made up, if you ask me."

"You're kidding," I said. "You watch things like sport on it."

"Why not just watch it in real life? We have a football field in Belbury. Maybe you need one where you're from?"

I resisted the urge to tell her Wembley Stadium could fit the whole of Belbury inside it. "It's not the same. Electricity does other things, too, like warm food—"

"Like a fire?"

"And cool you down—"

"Like a paddle in the stream?"

"And let you play video games—"

"You play games? How old are you again?"

I threw my hands up in defeat, frustrated she had an answer for everything. A family of ducks paddled upstream toward the rising sun. The last chick in the group became separated and chirped.

"Were you happy?" Duke asked.

"Huh?"

"Back in your village—were you happy?"

I thought on it, and try as I might, I couldn't rightly say I was. I had moments with Kingsley when I felt less miserable, but that was different from being happy. "No, not really."

"Well, I'm happy," she said as she skipped away. "I smile and laugh and steal carrots and I'm happy. I don't need no eclectrity. I have the sun and grass and Mrs. Moira's mulberry pies."

I stopped and watched her bounce down the road. She had a

point, but it raised another question: where did happiness come from if not TVs and games and toasters? Before I had an answer, Elanil drew my attention as she passed, balancing on the stone fence beside the road. Her shoulders were slumped, and she dragged her feet. I watched her a moment before catching up with Duke.

"And Elanil?" I asked. "Is she happy?"

Duke looked over her shoulder and sighed. "She smiles more when it's just the two of us. You should have seen her when we drove a flock of sheep into Constable Oliver's cottage. A smile from ear to ear, she had. She's like that—happy when you can make her forget everything else. Her father . . . well . . . it's complicated."

I fidgeted with the burnt hole in my jacket. So, Elanil had family problems, same as me, same as Kingsley. Was that why she hated me? Because my family situation made her remember her own? I almost smiled. Far from being discouraged, I felt drawn to her, as though our family issues connected us as so few would understand.

"We're here," Duke said when we rounded a bend.

The abattoir, unlike most buildings in Belbury, was built on stilts. It hovered above stockades and had two ramps connecting it to pens outside. The whole thing looked older than the forest surrounding it.

A woman loaded crates into a cart in front of the stairs. She noticed our arrival and waved. And then, as though catching herself doing something wrong, quickly reached into her pocket and pulled out a pair of red earmuffs and put them on.

"What a pleasant surprise," she said breathlessly when we arrived. "Hello, dear," she said to Duke. "Staying out of trouble?"

"Always, Mrs. Zinvyre," Duke said with a grin which screamed *guilty*. "This is Chalia, George's great-granddaughter. Chalia, this is Elanil's mother, the one you have to impress."

Either I misheard, or Duke was having a laugh. There was no way Mrs. Zinvyre was Elanil's mom. She was stunningly beautiful and didn't look a day older than twenty-five. Unlike Elanil, Mrs. Zinvyre had a ready smile, and it brightened her face and gave it a glow that Elanil was lacking.

"Nice to meet you," I said, shaking her hand.

"You too, dear," she said before turning to Elanil, who was leaning against the cart, looking uninterested. "I'm happy you're finally making new friends—"

Elanil groaned. "You're so embarrassing." She jutted a thumb in my direction. "She needs a job, and I know you need a hand. Can she work here?"

Mrs. Zinvyre looked me and tilted her head. "I don't know . . . working the abattoir is hard, and no offense, dear, but you don't look the type to enjoy the messy work. Have you much experience?"

My gut wrenched. I needed that job. I needed money. I needed Italy. "I've worked plenty," I lied. "Used to be a hand in the old supermarket, stacking shelves in the deli."

Mrs. Zinvyre smiled. "What I mean is, this job's torture on the body. You'll leave here with your back screaming and a smell on you which is hard to forget."

"I can handle torture," I said, puffing out my chest. "I chopped wood yesterday."

Elanil and Duke snorted, but Mrs. Zinvyre's face was kind. "Oh? That is tough work. May I see your hands?"

I hesitated, not wanting to show her the blisters that had formed on my palms. They were evidence I wasn't suited to tough work, and would give her a firm excuse to say no. But I was trapped, so with a sigh, I held my hands forward.

Mrs. Zinvyre grabbed one with a gentle touch. "Hmm," she said as she ran her fingers over the bumps. "Do you know what blisters tell of a person?"

I looked at my feet. Here it comes, her rejection. "That they're not suited to hard work?"

"No," she said, lifting my chin with a finger. "It says you are determined, and you can push past pain to get the job done. If you are willing to give this place a try, I would be a fool to turn you away."

I grew light, and a smile spread across my face. "Thank you so much!" I gushed. This was it, my first step to escaping to Italy. For the first time in my life, I was taking ownership of my future, *and it felt amazing!*

Mrs. Zinvyre stooped to pick up another crate. "You can start immediately. I have a busy day, and it is a blessing you arrived." She dropped the crate into the cart. "Elanil, I need you to help Chalia clean the second chamber—"

"What?" Elanil asked, bouncing off the cart. "No! Duke and I had plans to go to the White Tree later."

"You can go another time," Mrs. Zinvyre said. "I need to run this load to the Pointed Ear. I'll be back before lunch."

Elanil glared at Duke. "Happy now?"

Duke laughed. "More than you will ever know."

"You're helping!"

"I can't," Duke said with a shrug. "I just remembered Mom needs help to separate the new resin." She turned to Mrs. Zinvyre. "Don't suppose you have a spare seat for little old me?"

"If you help load the rest of the crates, I'm sure I could squeeze you in."

Elanil looked to me with pursed lips. "You haven't been here a day, and already you're the most annoying person in Belbury. Come on, the drain won't clean itself." She turned and stormed up the stairs without a backward glance.

"You're in for a right treat with her in that mood," Duke said. "Stick it out, she'll come good."

Hearing Elanil's curses, I found I wasn't quite as convinced.

Perhaps a slaughterhouse wasn't the smartest place to work, after all.

CHAPTER 14

- CHALIA -

The abattoir had an overwhelming smell about it. Not rancid, like Barden's bin juice or a rotting alley cat, but it had a coppery tang so rich it was like I was sucking on a handful of pennies. I pinched my nose and followed Elanil past pens on the left, the timber floorboards squeaking beneath us, until we reached the three rooms at the end. Elanil turned to me, saw my expression, and rolled her eyes.

"You best get used to the smell quick, because you're going to need both hands for cleaning."

If her frown could get any darker, I would die of shock. She would be a nightmare to work with if she didn't change her attitude soon. I got a sudden idea and decided I should change her attitude for her. I crossed my eyes and put on a nasally voice.

"*You're going to need both hands for cleaning,*" I mocked her.

Her lips pressed into a tight line. "What?"

"*Clean chamber good, smile baaad!*"

She narrowed her eyes and ground her jaw but couldn't stop her lips from twitching upward at the edges. "You're going to find it hard to clean when you're hung by your ankles on hooks."

"*Not the hooks!*" I cried, shielding my face with a hand and backing away. "*Give me fire, give me sword, give me anything but the dreaded hooks!*"

I dribbled a little.

And Elanil broke.

Her mouth curved into a smile, and a spluttered laugh escaped. A moment passed where the smell of blood disappeared and Elanil was happy. And even after she regained control and fixed her misbehaving lips into a straight line, it didn't seem as firm, nor her eyes as hard.

"Urgh, come on," she said, opening the door to a chamber. "I can see this is going to be a long day."

The chamber housed a narrow pen on the left wall, a chute opening at the rear, and several hooks and pulleys suspended from the ceiling. The floor was layered in congealed blood, dark and richly sweet, and an array of tools were laid on a table beside the door.

I gagged.

"All right, softy?" Elanil asked as she collected a hose from the wall.

"I'm fine," I said, pinching my nostrils again. I tiptoed into the room, doing my best to avoid stepping in all the filth. Trying to sound anything other than repulsed, I added, "I thought there would be more blood."

Elanil shrugged. "It was a quiet morning." She passed me the end of the hose. "You can have the easy job since it's your first day. Spray everything down, but be careful; it's slippery in here."

"Obviously," I said as I started toward the chute. "I'm not completely useless—*woooaaaaah!*"

I hadn't taken two steps before my leg slipped from under me and I skidded on one foot, arms windmilling, until I crashed to my back into the clotted blood. It gave way beneath me like custard.

I froze, hands in the air, too shocked to move. Blood soaked my hair and seeped into my jeans. I stared wide-eyed at the ceiling.

Please let it be a nightmare! Was there any hope Elanil hadn't seen?

Elanil laughed, unrestrained. It was loud and free. I struggled to my feet, gripping the wall for stability, and glared at her. She was bent double with tears streaming down her cheeks.

"Yeah . . . funny," I mumbled as I scooped blood from my hair, wishing I could disappear down the drain.

"*Bloody* hilarious!" Elanil wheezed.

"Glad you think so."

"Oh, don't be grumpy all your life," Elanil said. She straightened and wiped her eyes on the back of her hand. "I can't count the number of times I've slipped in here. Bend over—let's get the blood off you."

She ran the hose over my head. The cool water sent my skin to gooseflesh, which was made even bolder by her touch as she combed her fingers through my hair, leaving trails of warmth to fight the cold. I closed my eyes.

"It's different," she said after a moment. "Your short hair— I've seen nothing like it in the village."

"Belbury isn't exactly up to date with the latest trends."

"And these?" she asked as she traced her fingers over the seven earrings in my left ear.

Shivers raced down my neck. I wasn't sure I liked the shortness of breath her touch brought. I straightened and stepped away, fighting the feeling in my gut which begged me to kiss her.

"More common in my city than here," I said as I squeezed the water from my hair. "Thanks."

She shrugged and handed the hose back. "You're welcome."

Mrs. Zinvyre returned just before noon. She was happy with the work we'd done, and unlike Elanil, she sighed when she heard of my mishap. "You would best be finding some better clothes if you wish to work here. I'd hate for your nice ones to get ruined."

She brought lunch back with her. Salad rolls and scones with clotted cream and strawberry jam. We sat on the stockade rails outside, enjoying the fresh air while watching a few sheep graze in the pens. I'd never realized how noisy Barden was. I mean, yeah, I knew there was traffic and sirens and shouting, and a thousand other sounds all at once, but until I heard the quiet of Belbury, I'd never appreciated how deafening it was.

We chatted about this and that, and I decided I could like Mrs. Zinvyre, regardless of her being my boss and all. She had the feeling of a nurse about her, friendly and caring, and was smart about most things. But as for life outside Belbury, she was just as clueless as Duke.

"Nothing for us folk out there," she said, hair sparkling in the sun.

"But haven't you ever wanted to know what the world offers?" I pressed. "Hasn't anyone here?"

Mrs. Zinvyre looked to Elanil, and Elanil gave a quick shake of her head. Mrs. Zinvyre sighed and turned back to me. "Well, there was one of our folk who left a while back. He was young and curious and didn't much like the law. He left and had a rough and sad time of it, and no one has followed since. The outside world isn't ready for us Belburnians, and we are not ready for the outside world. We are happy here, and will stay as long as we are welcome—"

"Or as long as *here* exists," Elanil muttered.

"Hush, Ela!" Mrs. Zinvyre scolded.

"What do you mean?" I asked. "Does that have something to do with the secret?"

Mrs. Zinvyre looked to Elanil with furrowed brows.

"What?" Elanil protested. "I didn't tell her."

"I heard Alamril talking to Pop about it at the gate," I said. "Won't you tell me about it, Mrs. Zinvyre? No one else will."

Mrs. Zinvyre sighed and shook her head. "It's not my place to say. I'm sorry, Chalia, but you will know when the time is right. Until then," she sprang lightly from the rail. "I need you and Ela to de-muck the pens."

Elanil gave me a shrug and followed her mom inside. I tossed the last bit of scone to the sheep, no longer hungry. I would get to the bottom of the secret. I had a whiff of it now, and I wouldn't stop until I knew it all.

I finished work at four forty-five, filthier than Homeless Harry, but I was happy. It was my first proper day's work, and knowing I was moving toward my new life in Italy brought about a sense of achievement I'd never known. Kingsley would be proud.

Mrs. Zinvyre gave me a lift home in her cart, and we passed the time with her teaching me a red-ear song. It sounded French, with the words running together pleasingly. I'd learned the first few lines by the time we pulled up in front of Pop's cottage.

"Will you be back tomorrow?" Mrs. Zinvyre asked as I jumped out of the cart.

"Of course," I said. "We can't trust Elanil to get the job done right."

Elanil groaned. "Just go already."

"See ya," I said, giving her a wink.

And she smiled.

I walked around the side of Pop's cottage and tossed two scoops of feed to the chickens. "Lay us some breakfast," I said, and then made my way to the chopping block.

CHAPTER 15

- CHALIA -

I was at the chopping block for half an hour and had a growing mound of split wood to show for it. My shoulders burned and back ached, but I felt seven feet tall and invincible.

"Not one to let a bit of wood make a fool of you, I see," Pop said from behind.

I turned and watched him approach. "Not two nights in a row," I said, brushing the sweaty hair from my face and accepting the glass of water he offered.

He smiled. "Be careful, that attitude will take you places." He then crinkled his nose and stepped back. "What stinks of spoiled cheese?"

I laughed and leaned on the block. "Cheese? That's being nice."

His eyes took in my muck-stained clothes, and he shook his head with a small laugh. "You look a lass with a story to tell. But first, a soak in the bath is needed. I'll heat the kettle."

It was dark by the time I stacked the wood and entered the cottage. The bath was full and steaming, and the room was lit with candles on the windowsill. I groaned as I lowered into the tub. The water washed away the aches of the day, and the scent from the sprigs of lavender floating on the surface caused my eyelids to droop.

I flexed my hands, enjoying the sting of water on my blisters, and thought of Elanil snickering when I'd shown them to Mrs. Zinvyre. Elanil was a blister, I realized. She was a pain, and she popped off with anger regularly.

But there was a small part of me, a part I'd not known was there, that wondered if I might catch her after I put in some hard graft.

I thought of her eyes, the flecks of gold coloring the light brown. They had a power I was sure Elanil did not understand. They could trap you, like in a trance or something, and hold you prisoner and steal your breath.

I sat out of the bath, splashing water on the floor, and shook my head to clear it. The tub was hotter than I thought. Why was I thinking of Elanil like that? Lads had never given me such a reaction. It had to stop. That twisting feeling growing inside me like . . . like a cancer . . . begging me to do things to her I'd never imagined.

Besides, I was leaving Belbury soon, and I didn't need an anchor chaining me to the brook.

I dried and dressed and found Pop in the kitchen, puffing on his clay pipe as he fished two Yorkshire puddings from the oven. A chunk of roast beef was resting on the bench, setting my stomach to growling.

"I was about to send some lifesavers in to make sure you hadn't drowned," Pop said once he noticed me.

I grabbed two plates from the cupboard. "I didn't want to waste the hot water."

"Good lass." He carved the roast, its juices flowing onto

the cutting board. "Be a darl and load some vegetables on the plates, please."

We ate in the armchairs by the fire. I didn't have time to talk—I was too busy playing a game of seeing how much food I could fit in my mouth at once. When I was done, I licked the plate clean and fell back into the chair, my stomach bulging.

Pop topped up his pipe. "I was happy to find you missing when I woke this morning."

I laughed. "Gee, thanks."

"I feared you were going to spend the entire day in your room and miss out on all Belbury offers. You proved me wrong, and I couldn't be happier." He blew a smoke ring. "What did you get up to?"

"Found a job," I said, silently praising myself.

"Well, now—that *is* something!" Pop said, leaning forward. "Congratulations, my girl. Who hired you?"

"Mrs. Zinvyre at the abattoir."

Pop snorted and choked on his smoke. "I know Tanelia well. Lovely lady, but you couldn't find dirtier work in Belbury if you tried. Why the abattoir?"

"Oh, you know—playing with blood is a hobby of mine."

Pop rested his feet on a fraying footrest. "It wouldn't have anything to do with a certain Elanil, would it?"

I stammered. "What? No! She's a nightmare, she is. I'd get less headache if I head-butted my way through a brick wall."

Pop looked at me beneath bushy eyebrows, his expression turning somber. "Listen, Chalia . . . I have to warn you of something." He placed his pipe down and stared at it for a moment. "You have seen the different people in the village, yes? You know of the Amish and the 'red-ears'—or so they are named. Well, there is more to them than their appearance; there are *cultural* differences too, and rules which go with them. By law, only Amish are to mingle with Amish, and red-ears with red-ears. I noticed the way you looked at her yesterday, and I must caution against acting on emotions—"

"Eww, Pop, no!" I cried, recoiling from him as though he were diseased. My cheeks burned. "Stop before you say something I can't forget. I'm not falling for a red-ear. Or an Amish, for that matter!"

"All right, all right," Pop said, patting the air in front of him. "I just wanted to make sure." He reclined once more and picked up his pipe. "I've made mistakes in the past, Chalia, and I'd be a nasty bugger to make them again."

I rested my feet on a stool and willed my breathing to return to normal. "Besides, I'm going to be too busy earning money to be doing anything else."

Pop blew another smoke ring and watched as the hearth's hot air took it on a bumpy journey. "What is the money for, if you don't mind me asking? If there is something you need to buy, I may be able to help."

I stared at the bouncing flames and wondered if I should tell him. Would he try to stop me leaving England? No, I decided. I would trust him so long as he treated me as an equal; he had earned that, at least. "I'm moving to Italy."

Pop froze. The fire crackled and sent a flurry of sparks flying up the chimney. "Hmm," he said. He raised his pipe, took a long pull, held it, and exhaled. And then he did so again. "Interesting," he said in a light voice. "Valerie must have forgotten to mention it."

"I haven't told her; she would try to stop me."

"She wouldn't be your mother if she didn't." Another puff of his pipe. "Why Italy?"

It surprised me at how calmly Pop was taking the news. It was most unadultlike. Before I knew it, I told him the complete story of Kingsley and his dad, of the police and the murder, and finally the dot on the map what once held Kingsley's name.

Pop sat in silence, puffing now and then while staring into the crackling fire. When I finished, he shook his head sadly. "I'm sorry for your loss, Chalia. No one deserves what Kingsley went through in his brief life. Valerie had not mentioned half of what you told me."

"Thank you," I said, feeling better. I couldn't tell Mom those things, she just wouldn't understand.

"His dream was a beautiful one," Pop continued, "but it is not yours to take. Living another person's dream is like looking through someone else's photo album and saying you had a significant life. A dream is as individual as your memories and should be owned as such."

I tensed and felt my walls being rebuilt around me. Pop's words made sense, but they went against everything I had planned for my future. I couldn't accept that.

"Thanks for the advice," I said, standing and collecting our plates. "I'll ask for it next time if I want to hear it. If the dream was good enough for Kingsley; it is good enough for me."

CHAPTER 16

- CHALIA -

I was so exhausted that night that sleep found me not long after my head hit the pillow. I wasn't sure what I dreamed of, or if I dreamed at all, but when I woke the next morning, I felt I'd slept a week. I was so excited to begin the day that even the crowing of the idiot rooster didn't annoy me.

I dressed in the dark and left my room, where I almost tripped over a pair of gumboots and denim overalls outside my door. I flushed with guilt as I realized Pop left them for me, and I regretted the way I'd spoken to him the night before. He had my best intentions at heart, but he was wrong about Kingsley's dot on the map—I was certain of that. What he was right about was me not getting too close with Elanil. Not because of whatever law nonsense he'd mentioned, but because she would make it all the harder to leave. And so, when I stepped into the foggy morning, I knew I needed to distance myself from her.

Two men fished from the bridge as I passed. Both greeted me with surprised hoo-loos, which I returned, the word awkward in my mouth, before carrying on down Banquet Road.

Elanil waited for me inside the abattoir. She sat in a pen with a cow, humming while she scratched its neck.

"Morning, loser," she said as she spotted me.

She looked different; her hair was braided down one side, and I couldn't be certain in that light, but I swear she was wearing mascara. It took a moment for me to realize she'd said something else.

"Huh?" I asked awkwardly.

"I said, I thought you'd given up after yesterday." She climbed out of the pen and stood before me, hands on hips.

I smiled. "I'm your mom's best employee—I can't just abandon her."

Elanil raised an eyebrow. "Oh, really?"

"I didn't want to bring this up," I said, "but she said she wished her daughter put in as much graft as me." My pulse quickened, and my plan of distancing myself failed miserably. There was just something about being around the lass that made me ignore common sense.

"Well, that's it then. Mom's gone insane."

I patted her on the shoulder. "Jealousy's ugly, Ela."

"So are your clothes."

I looked down at my mismatched clothing and laughed. It really was hard to make denim overalls sexy. "All I need is a pair of those ridiculous red earmuffs, and I'll be a complete Belburnian."

At that moment, Mrs. Zinvyre walked into the room from the first chamber, wheeling a barrow filled with cuts of meat. I dropped my hand from Elanil's shoulder.

"Oh, good morning, dear," Mrs. Zinvyre said, lowering the barrow. "Bright and early, I see. I like that."

"Morning," I said. "I figured you couldn't trust Ela to do all the work, so here I am."

Mrs. Zinvyre laughed and looked to Elanil. "You need more friends with this attitude. Please don't scare her off like the others."

"I give her two days before she disappears like a stink in the wind," Elanil said.

Mrs. Zinvyre rolled her eyes then looked to me. "Ela is in a foul mood today. First she was angry because she couldn't find the jeans she wanted, then she snapped at me because I didn't have time to do her hair properly—"

"*Mom!*" Elanil snapped. "You're *so* annoying!"

I smiled inwardly. Elanil was putting in a lot of effort to look good, for someone working the abattoir. "Well, I think you did a great job with her hair."

"Ugh!" Elanil moaned. She grabbed my hand and pulled me away. "Come on, the animals in the rear stockade need feeding."

Mrs. Zinvyre waved goodbye. "She is only acting tough because you're around."

"I know," I said as my spirits soared.

Three sows, one stag, and two lambs were enjoying the morning sunshine in the stockades. Most pens were empty, however, and I supposed it was because there couldn't be more than a few thousand people in the village, so demand wasn't high.

Underneath the building were three concrete basins about as tall as I was. Metal tubing ran into each from the abattoir floor, and all had a tap on the bottom.

"That's where the chambers drain," Elanil said, noticing my curiosity.

"So, they're full of blood?"

"And water. Come on, I'll give you a tour." She led me beneath the floor, over a layer of dried animal dung, and to the vats. "We churn the contents before we drain them; that way we break up any solids." She rotated a crank on the side, making the vat slosh and slurp. "Then we connect the hoses and send the liquid to the drying bed downhill a little way. The water evaporates, leaving us with plant feed."

"You feed blood to your plants?"

Elanil shrugged. "It's good fertilizer."

"Remind me never to eat broccoli again."

"If that worries you, don't look inside the off-cut wagon. That's where we keep the scraps that are fed to the animals."

"The parts no one wants?"

"Yeah."

"Guess that's where you found your personality."

Elanil laughed and punched me in the arm. "That's where George will find your body if you keep being a pest." Then she turned and walked to a shed attached to the stockade.

The shed was filled with barrels of oats and bales of hay and odds and ends like tarp piles and hose coils.

Elanil filled a bucket with oats and handed it to me. "So, you don't normally work here?" I asked.

"Not when I can help it," she said as she collected two more buckets. "But Dad works away a lot, and Mom struggles to run this place, even though she pretends she doesn't. I don't know—I give her a hard time about it, but I'm always here to help if she needs it."

Remembering what Duke told me the day before, I pressed Elanil about her father. "Duke said you have some problems with your dad," I said in an offhanded sort of way.

Elanil stepped past me with her two buckets. "Duke is a frog. Small body, enormous mouth."

"Reckon a frog might be taller," I said as I followed.

Elanil emptied her buckets into a trough in the sow pen. "Reckon you're right."

I waited for her to say more, to talk about her dad, to tell me he was a scumbag like mine. But I was disappointed. I emptied my buckets into the trough, and we didn't speak again until the animals were fed and watered. Then I tried a different tack and asked about fun things to do in Belbury. This broke Elanil wide open, and she spent most of the morning telling stories of the fun she has, such as shaving the constable's mustache while he sleeps. Apparently he is convinced he goes to sleep-shaving at night now.

The morning fell away in the blink of the eye, and not once did I grow tired of hearing Elanil's voice or watching the sly grin play across her face as she talked about breaking the law.

We'd just finished our tasks and were heading back inside when I spotted movement on Banquet Road. "Who's that?"

Elanil turned and saw it too. "That's our frog."

After a few seconds, I made out Duke racing toward us on a large black boar with her hair flapping in the wind behind her, bonnet barely holding its place. She held a tether connected to a second boar.

"Hoo-loo!" she cried as she skidded the beasts to a stop in front of us. She jumped down. "Will your mom mind if you come to Maisey's for lunch?"

Elanil shook her head. "Nah, I'll tell her I wanted to take Chalia out—she'll love that. For some reason, she likes the kid." She hopped up the stairs to the abattoir.

"You can take Gunther," Duke said, passing me the tether to the second boar, whose tusks looked like they'd have no issue tearing holes through sheet metal. It nuzzled my arm, leaving a trail of snot.

"I'd like to, but . . . um . . . I've never ridden a pig before."

"You're kidding!" Duke said. "Like, ever?"

"Never."

"Not even to get fresh milk?"

"Nope."

She blew a low whistle. "You outsiders are so weird. Okay, well you can mount up with Elanil then. She is a slow rider. Most elv— ah . . . red-ears . . . are."

CHAPTER 17

- CHALIA -

"*Ruddy hellllll!*" I screamed, clinging to Elanil for dear life as the boar galloped with the speed of a thousand caffeinated horses. I squeezed my eyes closed to stop them blowing to the back of my head, and I thought of happy things: ice cream and chicken nuggets and Italy.

It wasn't until I heard Duke laughing that I realized we'd stopped. I forced open my eyes to find we were parked on the grassy bank in front of Tilly's Teahouse beside the bridge.

Duke offered a hand to help me down. "Looks like you've seen a ghost," she said with a toothy grin.

"I almost *became* a ghost," I grumbled as I slid from Gunther.

Elanil's teeth flashed as she jumped down. "I've never heard anyone scream so much. Poor Constable Oliver will think there's been a murder."

A tinkling bell sounded from the teahouse.

A woman with newly graying hair and a sunny yellow apron waddled out to meet us. "Why, hoo-loo, Bekka and Elanil!" she said in a bouncy voice. "Lovely to see you again! And my—who's this?" she asked as she adjusted her glasses, eyebrows raised so high they were at risk of disappearing into her hairline.

"Hi," I said. "I'm Chalia."

"Chalia?" she asked, raising a finger to her chin. "I've never heard of no Chalia in Belbury. Are you sure, dear?"

"She's George Brownhill's great-granddaughter," Elanil said, fighting a smile.

"You don't say!" the lady exclaimed as her magnified eyes widened. "I was good friends with your mother," she said, wrapping a heavy arm around my shoulders and leading me to a setting beneath a massive elm tree. "It was back a ways now. She was a few years younger than me, mind, but old for her age, in a young kind of fashion—if you get my meaning. Oh, and when she started going with your father! Oh my! It caused such a stir, him being so gorgeous and all!" Her eyes glossed over, and she stared over my shoulder for a long moment.

I looked to Duke to see if the lady normally behaved in such an odd way, and she was chewing her fist to stop from laughing. Elanil wasn't much better—her bottom lip had disappeared into her mouth as she battled a snicker.

"Oh, my!" the lady said after a moment. "But look at me babbling like a swan on the brook. Here now, I'm Maisy, if you like. I work at Tilly's Teashop, if you've not guessed. Is there something I can get you to eat and drink?" She pulled three menus from her apron pocket.

Duke ordered without reading the menu, a salad with extra lettuce. Elanil ran her eyes over the pages, sighed, and ordered two royal sandwiches.

My stomach growled as I read the lunch items. I'd just decided on a roast pork roll when I realized I'd left my money in Pop's cottage. My stomach went from barking orders to churning uncomfortably.

Maisy looked down at me expectantly, her notepad open with pen to it.

I closed the menu and handed it back. "A glass of tap water will be fine." I looked over the brook, hoping the others couldn't see me blush.

"What?" Duke asked. "You've been working all morning, lass. No wonder you're skin and bones. Order something."

"Nah, it's okay," I said, taking a sudden interest in some ducks waddling across the lawn. "I had a big breakfast—"

"Make that four royal sandwiches, thanks, Maisy," Elanil said, cutting me off as she handed back the menu. "With the works. Put it on Mom's account."

Maisy scribbled in her notebook. "Sure thing, dear. The tea will be out shortly." And then she disappeared inside.

I rubbed the back of my neck, unable to meet Elanil's eyes. "You didn't have to," I muttered.

"Course I did," she said, and I glanced up. She was smiling. "When we clean the chamber this afternoon, I'm on hose duty, so I need you to have squeegee energy. And nothing gives you energy like a royal sandwich."

Duke slapped Elanil's shoulder. "You tart, always wanting to be on a *hose*." She made air quotes around *hose*. "Have something on your mind?"

Elanil's cheeks turned bright red. "No! The cleaning hose—the one at work, to clean the chamber—"

"The *cleaning hose*," Duke said with a sly wink to me. "Is that what you call it?"

Elanil stuttered, blushed harder, and then shoved Duke from the bench and dived on top of her.

The pair rolled on the grassy bank, locked in a wrestling match. Kingsley would have loved it. Hell, all the lads in Barden would have.

Duke gained the upper hand early, her weight pinning Elanil down. But Elanil, in a catlike fashion, twisted herself out of the knot and wrapped an arm around Duke's neck. She squeezed, and Duke's face turned red.

"Always the same with those two," Maisy said as she returned with a tray laden with china cups, sugar, cream, and a teapot.

"They're always like this?"

"Well, normally there is a lot more cussing," Maisy said as she placed the tray on the table. "I guess they are behaving because you are here."

Duke's fingers clamped around Elanil's arm as she tried to un-hook it from her throat. "Tea's here," she wheezed. "That's a draw."

Elanil released her. "Like hell—you were done in."

The argument lasted through lunch. It wasn't until I'd devoured my cucumber-and-egg sandwiches and was onto my second cup of tea that Duke changed the subject.

"That'll be me, one day," she said as she nodded to a constable walking across the bridge in his black-and-white checkered hat. He was guiding a horse-drawn cart and seemed in a hurry.

"A horse?" Elanil asked. "You're already halfway there." Duke threw a tomato wedge at her.

A darkness found me as I watched the constable. I was back in

Barden with Pickering and Newlin and the rest of the corrupt bastards. A knot formed in my chest, and my jaw ached from biting down so hard. I remembered that footpath, drowning in blood.

"Police officer," Duke clarified as she watched him disappear into a lane. "I'll be an inspector if I can. Wanted to be one ever since I was a little lassie."

"You're better than a pig," I muttered, unable to stop myself.

"Huh?"

"They are scum, Duke. You are better than that."

Elanil cocked her head. "All right downer, what's got you cheesed off?"

I looked away from the spot the constable had disappeared. "Nothing," I said. It was still raw, and I couldn't bring myself to talk about Kingsley, not yet.

Elanil placed a hand on my wrist. "You sure?"

"Yeah, it's fine," I said and forced a smile.

Duke crossed her arms. "All right then, Ms. I'm-Too-Good-to-Be-a-Police-Officer, what are you going to be when you finish school?"

"An olive farmer," I said without hesitation, surprising myself. I'd not once thought of it, not consciously, least of ways. But there it was, and I supposed it made sense.

Elanil snorted tea out her nose. "An *olive* farmer? You? That'll be the day!"

I narrowed my eyes. "What's wrong with that?"

"Chalia, you're a city lass—what do you know of farming?" Elanil asked.

"I know there is no shame in not knowing how to do something."

Duke stuffed a leaf of lettuce in her mouth. "Yes, but, why a farmer?"

"Long story—"

"We have time," Elanil said as she leaned in.

I sighed and after a moment's hesitation, gave in. I told them of my belief that everyone owned a dot on the map, and Italy was my dot. I didn't mention my trouble with the pigs, or Kingsley, just my dot and how I planned to move there as soon as I could afford it. When I finished, an uncomfortable silence greeted me.

"I see," Elanil said at length. She placed her teacup down and turned the handle inward. "Belbury is a layover for you."

"Listen, Elanil, I still have weeks here—"

"It's fine." She stood. "We should go. Don't want to keep Mom waiting." She made her way to the boars, who were lapping at the brook.

Duke sighed. "Oh, Chalia, you really are thicker than a bowl of porridge, aren't you?"

"Apparently," I said, watching Elanil.

"Why would you tell her you were leaving, right when she was liking you?" Duke stood and walked to her boar.

I sat a moment. I *had* to leave; I owed it to Kingsley to follow his dream, no matter how much it hurt me. I couldn't let nothing get in the way of that, not Elanil, not Pop, not nothing.

"Coming, loser?" Elanil called, sitting on Gunther. She smiled, though it looked strained.

My breath caught in my chest as I watched her sparkling hair, and I knew it was going to be a lot harder to leave than I planned.

CHAPTER 18

- CHALIA -

Mrs. Zinvyre was loading her donkey-drawn cart with cuts of meat to deliver to her butcher shop when we returned.

"A customer's picking up offcuts later," she said, adjusting her earmuffs. "Once you have helped him—and if the chamber is cleaned—you are welcome to finish early."

A flicker of excitement ignited within me. Maybe Elanil could show me around Belbury. It would be my chance to hang around her so much that I got sick of her, like eating too much chocolate. That would make leaving Belbury all the easier.

I thanked Mrs. Zinvyre and followed Elanil to the chamber, fighting my churning stomach as I waded through a layer of blood to the squeegee.

We made quicker work of the chamber than the day before. Squeegeeing was oddly satisfying, much the same as popping a pimple; gross, but you couldn't help feeling happy once it was done. I was wiping down the last of the hooks dangling from the ceiling when it happened.

"Chalia," Elanil called.

I looked to her and caught a jet of water to my face.

"Bitch!" I said as I spun and gasped for breath as the hose washed over me. "You having a laugh?"

"I'm always laughing at you."

Water pooled into my overalls and filled my boots. "Regular comedian, aren't you?" I said, and then turned and ran into the stream. I caught Elanil in a hug and spun her to the ground in a puddle of water. She struggled, but I pinned her hands beside her head.

"Payback is going to be oh so sweet!" I said as I contemplated the best way to exact revenge. Wetting her would be too easy, so I thought about rubbing a bit of blood on her face. That's when I noticed her earmuffs and came up with another idea. "Why do you weirdos wear earmuffs, even when it's warm?" I asked and made to pull them off.

In a sudden frenzy, Elanil thrashed and bucked beneath me. "Don't touch them!" she shouted, panic in her voice.

I moved a hand closer. "Or what?"

"Please . . . don't . . ."

I let go of her left wrist and grabbed her earmuff—

But before I could pull it off, her free hand snatched the front of my shirt and yanked me down. Her lips met mine, and my strength flowed away down the drain. Her lips were full and soft and amazing. Everything I thought they would be and more. My thoughts disappeared, my stress and worry, and I kissed her back, knowing I would never kiss a lad again. This was right, and very wrong, all at the same time.

She flipped me over, so she was straddling me, and pinned my arms down.

She panted into my ear. "I win—"

"*What the heck is going on here?*" a voice bellowed from the doorway.

I looked up to find Pop striding into the chamber, his face livid.

Elanil rolled off me quicker than a whip and jumped to her feet. "We were just mucking around."

Pop's eyes bore into mine. "What did I tell you just last night?"

"What's the big deal?" I asked through gritted teeth. Who did he think he was, speaking to me like that?

"*What's the big deal?*" He threw his hands in the air. "Respect is the big deal! I told you this was not to happen!"

"Respect?" I asked with a bitter laugh. "Who I kiss has *nothing* to do with respect! And it has nothing to do with you. You're not my dad; he abandoned me long ago—"

Elanil stepped forward. "He is right," she said, unable to meet my eyes. "This can't happen."

"What?" I asked, my voice catching. "Don't say that. Elanil . . . look at me—never mind what he says. He doesn't matter."

But Elanil turned to Pop. "I'm sorry, Mr. Brownhill. It will never happen again. Please don't tell my parents."

My bottom lip trembled. Surely I misheard. The Elanil I knew would never say something so hurtful. The burning fire of passion and excitement in my stomach had turned into a sinking rock of regret and pain. "Don't say that—"

"It was a mistake, Chalia," she said, still looking at Pop.

Pop looked from Elanil to me, and gradually his face softened. "Elanil, you know why this will never work, right?"

Elanil nodded.

"Then I need you to promise this will never happen again."

"I promise," Elanil said without hesitation.

The words cut me like a knife, and I felt I would collapse to the chamber floor, the abattoir having claimed another victim.

Elanil picked up the hose and aimed it at the floor. "I can finish cleaning, Chalia. Help Mr. Brownhill load his cart, and then you are free to go."

It was hard to breathe. I had opened myself up in a way I'd never imagined. I was exposed and vulnerable and felt like a piece of meat hanging from one of the butcher hooks.

Pop stepped forward. "Come on, lass," he said, placing a hand on my shoulder.

I shook it off and stormed out of the chamber. I wouldn't cry. I wouldn't let losing another person hurt me again. I had shed enough tears for Dad and Kingsley; Elanil deserved none of that.

But when I got to the stairs, I stumbled as my eyes blurred with shame and anger.

CHAPTER 19

- GEORGE -

George hurried from his kitchen, snatching his trilby hat as he passed the coat rack by the door, and stepped into the night. He winced as his left knee complained at the unreasonable pace, but he didn't slow. The mayor had sent orders for an urgent Founders' meeting in the church. Arthur must have information about *them*, what other reason would he call for a late-night rendezvous? George looked longingly to his barn, where his gworth, Bessie, was stabled. What he would give to ride her instead of walk, but he could not risk Chalia seeing the beast, not yet.

George heard a great deal of shouting from Moira's house as he passed. Moira was furious at her partner, Torrock, for fishing too long into the night and missing supper again. A metallic clang rang out, sounding suspiciously like a thrown pot crashing against the wall. George shook his head. That's what living together for over three hundred years did to a couple.

He had only been living with Chalia a week, and already the cottage was thick with tension.

George cringed as he remembered his argument with Chalia.

The night after George caught the lass with Elanil was one for the books. Chalia shouted until she was blue in the face and her voice was a hoarse whisper. George had never been spoken to that way, not even from his ex-wife. He took it with as much stoicism as he could muster, knowing in his heart he deserved it. He was shocked when he caught Chalia and Elanil and had lashed out before he had time to think. His only consolation was he acted out of fear and love, not anger. But he supposed that made no difference to a teenager.

Since that night, Chalia had barely spoken a word to him. She accepted dinner and helped with chores but did so with an icy indifference, and George could almost see her counting down the days until she left the village.

With a sigh, George crossed the bridge and spotted the Founders gathered on the church steps. Some of them, at least. Talien and the elves were leaning against the wall, talking in whispers, and Arthur was standing by himself, arms crossed and his foot tapping impatiently.

"Hoo-loo, Arthur" George said as he hobbled up the stairs.

Arthur uncrossed his arms. "Evening," he said shortly.

"I suppose I don't need to ask whether it is good or bad news—not these days."

"More bad than good," Arthur said. His cheeks were a carpet of stubble, and his shoulders had a slump to them George had never seen.

George looked Arthur up and down and noted his scraggly appearance. He was about to ask Arthur how he was doing—how he was *really* doing—but was cut off by a shout from the road.

"Hoo-loo, Georgie-boy!"

Gormer and his three dwarves strode toward them, smiles on their faces as though they'd won a raffle at the Pointed Ear. "Sorry for our tardiness, but I had to resupply me lads out there by the well and bell," he said, nodding to where two dwarf sentries stood with foaming mugs.

"Damn it, Gormer!" Arthur said. He jabbed a finger at the sentries. "They need their wits about them when they're on duty!"

"What you mean to be saying," Gormer said as he pulled a deep-bowled pipe from a pocket and filled it with tobacco, and perhaps something a little stronger, "is thank you."

"Thank you?" Arthur asked, his mustache twitching.

"You're welcome," said Gormer, and the elves laughed. "Nothing gets a dwarf's fighting blood heated like a nice warm ale, mark me words."

Arthur looked to the heavens. "Give me strength for the idiocy of dwarves!" He took a deep breath, calmed himself, and addressed everyone gathered. "Mr. Higgleglade and Mrs. Smitherson will not be present tonight, so let's get this over with." He led the way up the stairs and into the church.

Inside, the church was dimly lit by a haunting glow from the candelabra; the dancing flames cast bouncing shadows on the stone walls and stained-glass windows. Two rows of thirty pews faced the chancel, where a group of six dwarves huddled by the altar.

Arthur walked between the pews. "We have been attempting to *coerce* information out of the aurocan since his capture. The good news is, we have finally succeeded. The bad news is, it is not good news at all."

They climbed the stairs and found the aurocan chained to

the altar top, his face a bloody and puffy affair. Many lacerations hashed his body, many of which still oozed blood, which dripped to the floor, and he looked dazed and weak.

George gasped and rushed forward. "What have you done?"

"What I needed to," Arthur said, motioning for the dwarves to give them space.

"There is *never* need for torture!" George snapped as he took in the pitiful creature. "Or have you forgotten?" The creature's glassy eyes slowly turned to him.

"I will do *everything* I can to ensure no harm comes to the village—not while I'm in charge," Arthur said, his voice stiff. He faced the others. "The aurocan cracked just after supper. The main aurocan force has been routed from their home by another army on Hemoertha. They are desperate and looking to follow the elves and dwarves to Belbury to take it as their own. At the moment, they are licking their wounds and preparing for battle, but they will come, and sooner rather than later."

"How many?" Gormer asked as he passed his pipe to another dwarf.

"Six hundred, if it tells the truth."

George sank and closed his eyes. *Six hundred!* Belbury could handle six hundred men—but six hundred beasts? What had he brought Chalia into?

"That's less than took our city," Talien said.

"Bah! And it'll be less still once me boys're done with them!" Gormer said. "We won't be caught off guard like we were seventy years ago—we'll be ready." He looked to Arthur. "Don't you worry your gentle little head, me mayor friend. Us dwarves are bred for battle, and battle we shall have."

Talien looked from Gormer to Arthur. "The first thing we need to do is close the tavern to ensure the dwarves are ready to fight."

"Blasphemy!" Gormer spat, and the other three dwarves made their voices heard. "You close the tavern, and I'll join forces with the cursed termites!"

Talian's face cracked, and he smiled. "Two beasts with one stone—"

"The news is not all bad," Arthur said, cutting them off. "The elves have worked their magic and reinforced our borders with a shield to keep everyone—and everything—contained in Belbury. Nothing can leave, and nothing can enter."

"Mighty fine!" Gormer cried. "Keep them trapped in here with me boys, and we'll cut through so many of them, our axes will be naught but blunt clubs by the end."

But George frowned. "Nobody can enter?"

"No."

"Even Valerie?"

There was an awkward silence, and the elves shifted on their feet. Arthur sighed and shook his head. "I'm sorry, George, but it is safer if Valerie stays in Barden for a while longer—I'm sure you understand. Be content with Chalia for the time being." His expression softened. "How is she, anyway? I've seen her around, always covered in blood. Nothing to worry about?"

George's head spun as he realized he might not see his Valerie before the end. He leaned against the altar for support. "Chalia is working with Tanelia in the abattoir," he muttered.

Gormer snorted. "More like working with Elanil."

An unpleasant silence followed, where the only thing that moved was the skittish shadows. George narrowed his eyes at the dwarf. He liked Gormer, but at times—especially after a few drinks—he said things best left unsaid.

"Huh?" Arthur asked, looking between the two.

"It's nothing," George said.

Arthur's lips pressed into a line. "George, I must remind you the consequence of Chalia learning more than she should—"

"Leave it," George said as he flexed his fists. He hated the law decreeing it illegal for human, elf, and dwarf partnerships. It was outdated and segregated the community. More than that, he despised keeping secrets from his great-granddaughter. He looked at Arthur with cold eyes. "If we survive this, things are going to change in Belbury."

Arthur's left eye twitched. "Things will change when I say they change."

But George was already storming down the stairs. He left the church without another word.

CHAPTER 20

- CHALIA -

It was early morning, the idiot rooster yet to call the sun, and I was sitting on my bed, staring at a thick envelope in my hands. A tingling sensation swirled my insides. I couldn't decide if it was excitement or dread, happiness or sadness. The envelope held a stack of twenty-pound bills; my first paycheck. Another one of those and I would be free to travel to Italy, to leave Belbury forever . . .

To leave Elanil and Duke and Pop.

Perhaps there was a little sadness.

Despite my inner turmoil, I was overjoyed with the weight of the envelope. Not because of how much cash was in there—though it was a pretty penny—but because it held more than quids; it held pride. My first paying job. I'd slaved away for over a week at the abattoir, day in, day out, and I now had the paper to prove it.

My insides swirled again at the thought of leaving. It was awkward in the small cottage with Pop, but the idea of leaving him didn't sit right. The fight with him had rattled me more than I wished to admit. I'd taken a chance and let my walls down for the first time since Dad abandoned us. I'd fooled myself into believing Pop was different from the other jerks. While he wasn't as bad as the worst of them, he wasn't as good as I needed him to be. I didn't hate him—I couldn't imagine anyone hating the old bugger—but I didn't trust him anymore, and I doubted I should ever trust again.

And so, in the week following the incident, I focused on making my remaining time in Belbury-on-the-Brook as painless as possible. I'd say my good mornings and good nights, I'd chop the wood and feed the chickens and help with other chores, but beyond that, I offered little more in conversation than a storefront mannequin.

Besides, I had bigger issues to worry about than pleasing the old man; I still had to work with Elanil.

I'd dreaded returning to work the day after the kiss more than I'd dreaded anything in my life. How would Elanil behave toward me? How would I act toward her? She was the first girl I'd kissed, and her rejecting me felt like she'd put my heart through the mincer and tossed it down the off-cut chute.

However, when I turned up the following morning in my gumboots and overalls, eyes downcast like a guilty dog, Elanil greeted me with a wet sponge to the face. I stood there, shocked for a moment, before I had the wits to pick it up and pelt it back. The ensuing water fight was one for the ages, and just like that, any awkwardness that should have been ruling the abattoir was washed away.

With a sigh, I picked up my backpack, pushed aside the black spray-paint cans, which I'd kept to remind me of Kingsley, and dropped the envelope into it.

I left the cottage and took two steps before I spotted Duke and Elanil lying under the pear tree.

"Morning, 'Alia," Duke said between a mouthful of pear. "Breakfast?"

I caught the pear she tossed at me. "What are you doing here?" I asked, looking at them suspiciously. Not since the day I arrived had they been at Pop's cottage together.

"Don't look at us like that," Elanil said, standing. "Mom gave us the day off."

"Really?" I said. "The entire day?"

"No," Elanil said, rolling her eyes. "Just the next five minutes. Stop asking dull questions—we'll be late if we don't leave soon."

"Late for what?"

"For proper breakfast, of course," Duke said, dropping her pear core and hopping to her feet. She held a large bundle wrapped in a cloth. "All the finest foods Belbury offers—mulberry pie, carrots, sponge cake, lettuce, cheese, and fresh-baked bread."

I narrowed my eyes. "You've been stealing from Mrs. Moira again."

Duke groaned and started down the path toward the brook. "Well, we didn't bake it ourselves. We ain't much of cooks. But permanently borrowing things, now *that's* our forte. Tell George we said thanks for the eggs."

I couldn't begrudge them stealing Mrs. Moira's food. I tasted her carrot cake a few nights earlier, and it was the most delicious thing I'd ever eaten. I followed them as the sky lightened in the east.

We reached the path running to the village, where I spotted a group of people walking toward us in the darkness.

"Who are they?" I asked. Few people made it past Pop's cottage.

Elanil followed my gaze and groaned. "It's Thomas and his cronies."

"Who?" I asked, noticing the lad in the lead. He was about sixteen, tall and handsome, and carried a bow. Two red-ears, an Amish, and three normals flanked him, all around the same age.

"Thomas Princeton," Elanil said darkly. "The mayor's great-grandson. Thinks the sun comes up just to hear him crow."

Thomas stopped short and smirked. "Well, well, well, look who it is. Duke and Elanil—the village cretins."

"Lovely to see you again, Thomas," Duke said. "Your ugly mug always makes me feel sexy."

Thomas's face dropped for a moment, then he forced a smile. "I'm surprised you can see anything above my knees, dwarf."

The mood changed instantly. His entire crew tensed, one girl gasped, and Duke nodded in my direction. It was short, but I caught it and wondered if she had a twitch.

"Real original," Elanil said, stepping forward. "Making fun of her height. Hilarious."

Thomas didn't look at her but grinned at me. "So, *you're* the illegal kid?"

"Huh?" I asked, taken aback. Did everyone know about my jail time in Barden?

"The vet's great-granddaughter?"

"Yeah, I'm Chalia—"

"The illegal kid, then," Thomas said. "Fine lot of friends you've found here. Peas in a pod, I'm sure."

"Leave her out of this," Elanil said.

"Or what?" Thomas sneered. "You're going to fight us? You're outnumbered."

Duke stepped forward. "I could put you to sleep until the end of summer, if you want to play."

Thomas bent over so his head was at Duke's level. He opened his mouth to respond, but one of his red-ears placed a hand on his shoulder.

"It's not worth it," she said. "Come on, we need to get started."

Thomas glared at Duke for a moment, his square jaw grinding. And then, as though he were a different person completely, his lips turned up into a charming smile. "I wouldn't waste an arrow on you." He straightened and pushed past us to continue down the road, his gang in tow. They disappeared into the forest at the end of the path.

"What's his problem?" I asked.

"Problem?" Elanil asked. "As in singular? He is more problem than person."

Duke laughed. "Doesn't help that your folks don't get along with his."

"Doesn't help that he is a snotty-nosed brat who thinks he runs the town because he is related to the mayor."

I looked into the forest's deep shadow. I'd heard stories of giant panthers living in forests around England when I was a kid. I knew they were make-believe, told to scare children, but I couldn't shake the feeling that something dark lived in the forest beyond Pop's plot. "Where are they going?"

"Camping, I'd guess," said Duke. "They go all the time, trapping rabbit and hunting deer. It grinds me to say, they're nifty with their bows and magi—" she paused, eyes widening as though she'd said something she shouldn't have. "—magazine reading," she finished with a look to Elanil. "Excellent at reading magazines, they are."

Elanil turned away and walked to the brook, where a small jetty jutted out from the bank with Pop's rowing skiff tethered at the end.

"Jump in," Elanil said to me. "You're most likely to tip it if you get in last."

I didn't move. "That's not ours to take."

"Course it is—it's George's, so yours by inheritance."

I didn't feel comfortable taking Pop's boat without permission, but the idea of asking him to borrow it was even worse. I looked toward his cottage, where the windows were still dark.

"Stay behind, then," Elanil said after a second.

"No, I'm coming," I said, stepping past her and hopping onto the skiff. It wobbled dangerously.

Duke stepped in next and loaded the two oars into the oarlock before sitting down. Elanil untied the rope and jumped in.

"Hold on tight," Duke warned. "I'm going to put some steam in this thing." She pulled both oars, and the skiff cut a path to the center of the brook, water sloshing at the sides as her strong shoulders made easy work of the rowing.

CHAPTER 21

- CHALIA -

As the skiff gained speed, wind tousled my hair, sending it bouncing on my forehead like a flag. The oars splashed in a gentle tattoo, and it wasn't long before I relaxed in my seat, any tension I had fading away with the night. This was what life should be—calm, free of idiots, a beautiful red-ear watching the world pass by with her captivating eyes.

Over Duke's head, the sky was changing from its pastel pinks and purples to a lighter blue, filled with the promise of a nice day. I needed a nice day. I needed a nice week if truth be told. I shook my head. No, I *wanted* a nice week; I *needed* a terrible one, which would make leaving the village all the easier.

"Hoo-loo, Chalia," voices cried. It was Torrock and Glenn in their usual fishing spots on the bridge. They lifted their lines for us to pass.

"Hoo-loo, lads," I shouted back. "Any luck?"

"Aye, being away from Moira is luck enough for me," Torrock said. He was an Amish man, married to Moira, which meant his belt was under immense stress.

"Well, you best be catching something soon, lest Moira bakes you into one of her pies."

"She'd have to catch me first! I may not look it, but I'm a world-class swimmer."

Glenn slapped Torrock's belly. "Don't listen to him, Chalia—all he does is float and bob, as a bag of hot air is like to do."

We passed beneath them, and Duke smiled at me. "You mean you have other friends in Belbury? I feel cheated on."

"You'll always be my favorite," I said, and Elanil stiffened slightly. She still liked me, I could tell, but she hadn't let her guard down since that day in the abattoir. It was better that way, for her, me, and Pop.

On the other side of the bridge, beyond Tilly's Teahouse, the brook swept to the left in a bend. I'd not traveled so far west before, and it startled me to find the village sprawled further than I'd thought.

"That's my home down there," Duke said, pointing to a stone cottage on the south bank. In contrast to Pop's house, with its wild gardens and many trees, Duke's yard consisted of rocks—cobbled and sculpted—leading from the back door right down to the water's edge in multiple tiers. All the houses in her neighborhood were styled much the same.

"Never mind the weeds," Duke said, nodding to the tiniest patch of greenery growing between the seating area and the jetty. "I've been slack since Dad's been away for work, but I'll get round to cleaning it up."

"I think the grass helps soften the rocks some," I said, thinking an entire forest wouldn't be enough.

Duke looked over her shoulder at me. "You're bonkers, you are."

Elanil giggled and tucked a few loose strands of shimmering hair under her earmuffs. "Telling an Amish to grow grass in their yard is a sure way to lose friends. Rocks are in their heart. And head."

Duke nodded, not knowing she'd been insulted, and then dropped an oar and pointed beyond her cottage to another village square. "Mom's resin shop is out back. Cursed place it is, especially when it's waterproofing time—the resin sticks to everything." She showed me her hand, which had patches of black covering it.

"What's resin?" I asked.

"Pine resin," Duke said, picking up the oar again. "We mainly use it for waterproofing, but it has a bunch of uses. Like ruining all my clothes."

We passed the same family of ducks I saw on my first day. I counted the chicks and was happy to see all seven were together again.

"I live over there," Elanil said, pointing to the north bank. "Further up the hill a little way."

The north was as different from the south as apples and concrete. Magnificent parks of towering elms and oaks outnumbered the cottages five to one. Manicured flowerbeds colored the streets rainbow, and one of the sweeping lawns played home to a herd of grazing deer.

"Pretend you like it," Duke whispered over her shoulder. "They are sensitive about their yards."

"It's amazing," I breathed. Kingsley and I used to hang out in the park in Barden sometimes, just to relax a little. In comparison, the Barden parks looked like a sewer dumps.

"Good acting," Duke whispered.

We rowed along the snaking brook for near an hour. I spent most of the time laughing as Elanil and Duke teased each other nonstop. Forests came and went, and eventually we bumped into an island in the middle of the brook and disembarked. It was about half the size of a football field and was dotted with shrubs and the odd tree.

"Welcome to Dukanil Island," Duke said, hoisting the skiff up the bank. She placed her hands on her hips and breathed in deeply, savoring the air.

Elanil groaned. "She named it."

A ring of stones marked a fireplace on the shore, with a bundle of wood stacked beside it. Duke set about layering some twigs into a teepee.

"I have a light," I said, unslinging my bag. I dug deep until I found the lighter, but when I pulled it out, it surprised me to see a fire already crackling as though it had been burning for hours.

I knelt in front of the fire. "How did you do that?"

"What?"

"Light the fire so quick?"

Duke looked from the fire, to me, to Elanil who shrugged, and then back to me. She raised her resin-stained hands to her face and wiggled her fingers. "Magic."

Elanil groaned and shook her head. "Resin," she explained. "It's more flammable than a balloon of Duke's farts."

"Only after I eat that rubbish red-ear food," Duke protested. "That reminds me—" She fetched her bundle from the skiff and pulled out a saucepan, which she balanced on two stones over the fire. After a moment, she dropped in a nob of butter, which glided on the hot surface, and six fat sausages.

I helped by slicing the loaf of bread while the smell of garlic and rosemary filled the air and the bangers popped and sizzled.

"What does your dad do for work that sends him away for so long?" I asked Duke, trying to distract myself from my growling stomach.

"He's a village guard," Duke said, not looking up from the sizzling sausages. "Most the townsfolk are in some respect, but he does it full time. I saw him the day after you arrived, after I left the abattoir, but he's been away since. He said he met you at the gate?"

I cast my mind back. "Stanthrop?" I asked, remembering the friendly man.

"That's him," Duke said. "He and my aunty Illy work the gate in shifts."

"He was different from the other jerks," I said. "Nice, even."

Elanil raised her eyebrows. "Jerks? You had trouble with people in Belbury?"

I thought on it, of Mrs. Moira and her delicious puddings and pies, of Torrock and Glenn, the eager fishermen, of Maisy the aloof-though-friendly teashop worker, and even Henry and Arthur, the veterans who had taken residence at the Pointed Ear. "No," I said, and was surprised. I'd been so busy with work and planning my trip to Italy, I'd not considered that Belbury-on-the-Brook had a larger number of all right population than I was used to. "Only Pop."

Duke groaned and used a piece of buttered bread to pick up a sausage from the pan. She handed it to me. "Still crying about that?"

I paused with the sausage halfway to my mouth. "What do you mean *crying*?"

"You've been sooking about it like a baby. So what, he broke up your smoosh time—"

I glared at Elanil. "You told her?" My cheeks burned hotter than the pan.

Elanil blushed and looked away. "She got it out of me."

Duke snorted. "Bah! I couldn't shut you up about it. Anyway—" She grabbed another sausage and gave it to Elanil. "—all I know is, you both like each other. Perhaps George didn't handle things as well as he could have, but there is good reason for it—"

"What reason?" I asked. "Because we're both lasses, and he is too prehistoric to understand that?"

"No," Duke said. "Because—"

"Just let it go, Chalia," Elanil cut Duke off. "Let's move on. There are things which you don't understand."

"Let it go?" I said, the words tasting sour. "You're good at that."

Elanil smiled, and I hated myself for thinking it the most beautiful thing I'd seen that morning, and then she threw a piece of sausage at my head.

I stared at her dumbstruck. "What did you do that for?"

"Because you're being boring. Let's have some fun before you leave Belbury. Think you can handle that?"

I looked at her, unsure whether I wanted to tackle her to the ground or kiss her all over.

"I'll toss you in the brook if you don't snap out of it," Duke warned between cheeks stuffed with sausage.

I laughed before I could stop myself, and my anger burned away. "You'd have to catch me first, little lady."

"I ain't no lady!"

CHAPTER 22

- CHALIA -

I found it funny how when working the abattoir, time dragged on like a scolding from a teacher, but it disappeared faster than mulberry pie as soon as I was having fun. The morning on Dukanil Island flew by in a haze of food and laughter, and I couldn't be happier.

We ate our breakfast and took a well-deserved nap beside the fire as we waited for the sun to climb high enough to warm our bones. Duke snored. It sounded like the brook was about to erupt in a volcanic explosion larger than Pompeii. Even though it should have been impossible for me to find sleep, once I curled around the fire—my feet touching Elanil's just enough to find a tingling sense of comfort in my toes—I slowly drifted away.

It was almost midday when we roused enough to play a game of football. Or at least, that's what Elanil and Duke called it. It was closer to an all-in brawl than anything. I was a decent player in Barden—I was light on my feet and had a balance even Kingsley couldn't match, but the few times I stole the ball, I only held it for seconds before Elanil would take it back with a grace which made me feel a bumbling drunk.

It was two thirty when we called it quits. We were hot and sweaty and planned to travel back to Belbury to clean up before meeting at the Pointed Ear for supper. I climbed into the boat first, then Duke at the oars—I wasn't complaining—and finally Elanil after she pushed off.

Before Duke began rowing, I was gripped with a sudden urge. "Budge over, loser," I said to Elanil as I stepped over Duke. "I can't handle another trip staring at the back of Duke's head."

"Loser?" Elanil asked with eyebrows raised. "You understand you were the only one not to score today?"

"The day's still young," I said with a wink.

"Touché," Elanil said and made room on the bench.

Duke heaved the oars. "You two are cute together."

"Shut it," I said, but my heart fluttered.

No one was near as talkative on the return journey, which had more to do with exhaustion than us having nothing to say. Halfway home, Elanil rested her head on my shoulder and closed her eyes. A silly grin spread across my face, and I lost track of time. In some ways, Elanil snuggling up to me was more intimate than our first kiss, and I wondered all sorts of absurd things, like what if I didn't leave Belbury? What if I got serious with Elanil? What would Mom think? Would Mrs. Zinvyre approve? Would Pop disown me? Would I know what it was like to be happy?

After a while, Duke caught my eye and smiled, broad and genuine. Her bonnet was askew and her face sweaty, and I realized I loved her like a sister. It was an unwelcome thought, as I knew it was going to make my leaving even more difficult.

Regardless, I smiled back, knowing I would not have the courage to say goodbye to the lasses once the time came to leave. If there was one thing I learned from Dad, it was how to run. I closed my eyes and forced the thought from my head as the sun beat down . . .

"Hoo-loo, Mom!"

I jumped awake, heart thudding in my chest. Duke was waving to a lady in the rock garden of her home. Duke's mom was setting up tables and chairs on the top tier but stopped when she spotted us. She shouted something back, which my sleepy ears couldn't quite hear.

"I'll be home soon," Duke shouted. "Put the kettle on!"

Under the bridge we went and arrived at Pop's jetty. I tethered the skiff and helped Elanil and Duke disembark.

"Meet you at the Pointed Ear around six?" I asked, still holding Elanil's hand.

Elanil laughed. "Six? How long does it take to have a bath?" She looked over my shoulder and dropped my hand. "Who's that?"

"Dad!" Duke shouted as she pushed past me and ran toward an Amish man emerging from the barn. She reached him and threw her arms around his neck.

"Hello, me darling girl!" Stanthrop said as he lifted her easily from the ground and swung her around, almost clipping Pop.

Elanil and I looked at each other, both wondering if Pop had seen us holding hands. With a shrug, we crossed the path to meet them.

"When did you get back?" Duke asked.

"'Bout mid-morning. I was going to surprise you, but you were nowhere to be seen."

"None of them were," Pop said, locking the barn and turning to face us.

"Mrs. Zinvyre gave us the day off," I said. "I hope you don't mind we borrowed your skiff?"

Pop looked from me to Elanil, a crease forming on his brow. It didn't take a genius to guess what he was wondering. After a moment he smiled. "Of course not—I'm happy you are exploring the village. Where did you get to?"

"First island downstream," Elanil said, sounding relieved.

Duke coughed pointedly. "You mean *Dukanil* Island."

Elanil groaned, but Pop chuckled. "And I suppose you took a piece of Mrs. Moira with you?" he asked, raising his eyebrows at the purple mulberry stain around Duke's mouth.

"Perish the thought!" Duke exclaimed, and everyone laughed.

"Your timing is perfect," Stanthrop said as he placed a heavy hand on my shoulder. "I wanted to invite you lasses to a dinner party we're having tonight. There'll be a good mix of villagers there—probably half the town, knowing how excited Darna gets with these things—and the mayor said he will make an appearance, if he can."

My stomach plummeted at mention of the mayor, and it cast me back in time to that footpath, Kingsley's blood, and an anger sparked inside me.

Something of my thoughts must have shown on my face, because Stanthrop spoke again. "Of course, if you've other plans, I understand—"

"No, no," Pop said. "We would love to come." He looked at me and raised his eyebrows.

"Oh . . . Y—yes," I gushed, not wanting to offend Stanthrop. "That sounds great, thanks."

Stanthrop's eyes crinkled as he smiled. "Glad to hear it!" He messed Duke's hair then, and said, "Well, we should be off. Going by the smell of me daughter, it'll take a while for her to scrub herself fresh. See you at five thirty, George?"

"Indeed."

Stanthrop and Duke mounted a spotted brown boar tied to the side of the barn and raced away with waving hands.

Elanil fidgeted for a moment and then said, "Well, I'd better clean up too. See you at dinner." She left with quick strides.

Pop placed a hand on my shoulder as we watched her disappear down the lane. "Come on, lass. The kettle's on, and you smell like a yearlong bath wouldn't be enough to wash away the smoke, sweat, and passion."

It took a second for his words to sink in. *Passion.* Did he know I hadn't given up on Elanil? I looked up at him, but he didn't take his eyes from the road. He didn't seem angry.

"It will take more than soap and water to wash those away," I said.

"I know, lass. I know."

CHAPTER 23

- CHALIA -

"**G**et a wriggle on, Chalia," Pop called as he rapped on the bathroom door again. "If you take any longer, there will be no feast left, especially if they invited Torrock."

But I *still* wasn't ready. No matter what I did, my hair wouldn't sit right. It had never bothered me before—I used to be of the opinion that hair was hair and not worth much of a thought. But something changed, and I stared into the mirror with disgust. Had I always looked so messy? I ran my fingers through my fringe one more time, hoping to coerce it into behaving, and then, with a sigh, opened the door.

Pop's hand was raised to knock again. His eyes flitted to the mop on my head, and then slowly crept down to take in my clothes. I was wearing my nicest Metallica shirt, my bomber jacket, which had more burn marks, and my least holey jeans. He smiled. "Looking sharp, lass. You know the queen's not invited, right?"

"Oh, shut up," I said, though I felt better for the compliment. "All my other clothes are dirty."

"Of course." He chewed his bottom lip. "You know, when I was a young lad—"

"Surprised you remember that long ago."

Pop's eyes gleamed. "You have your mother's wit, Chalia. Now, when I was a young lad, I learned the power of a nice drop of spice. That's how your great-grandmother first caught me— oh, she was a looker, never you mind that, and she smelled of the sweetest rose and it drew me to her like a bee to nectar. Here, wait just a second." He scurried out of the hallway and disappeared into his room. I heard him fishing through a drawer for a moment, and then he returned with a small perfume bottle. It was one of those vintage ones, with a squeezing bulb attached. "This was hers. Your mother loved playing with it when she was a kid." He offered it to me.

I gave the bulb a squeeze, and a mist filled the air. It did smell of rose, and perhaps a little citrus. It was nice, but I'd never worn perfume before, and I wasn't sure I was the type of lass who could pull it off. "Thank you."

"A little goes a long way," Pop warned and turned to leave. "The cart is ready when you are." He walked down the hallway, and I heard the front door open.

What just happened? I looked at the bottle suspiciously. Why was he helping me smell nice if he knew I liked Elanil? Had he given up controlling me? Or was he simply implying I stank?

I found Pop sitting in the cart when I left the cottage a short while later, the smell of rose following me on the breeze. We pulled onto the road with six large bottles of Pop's home-brewed pear cider rattling in the back.

At first we traveled in silence, the only sound the clopping of the Clydesdale's hooves and chink of glass. But when we passed the bridge, Pop spoke, and his voice wasn't as bouncy as usual. "I've taken to thinking on our argument last week—"

I froze. "I'd rather not talk about it," I said. I'd let go of the anger, and I didn't want to find it again.

"I owe you an apology."

The cart swayed, left and right, and the Clydesdale's tail swished back and forth.

I looked to Pop to see if he was having a laugh, but there was no smile on his face. Instead, his somber eyes found mine, and I was speechless.

"I don't know what I was thinking, trying to stop young passion with old words." He turned to face the road. "Truth of the matter is, I know what it is to love—"

"I don't *love* her," I blurted.

"Perhaps. But I should have known better than to yell without listening." He coughed and cleared his throat but still kept his eyes fixed ahead. "It's been some time since I last saw a young couple fall in love. He was a cheeky red-ear with too much charm for any lad to have, and she had too much heart to resist it. I watched as love caught them, and I did nothing, though I should have."

I somehow knew who he was talking about without him saying so. I knew it to the marrow of my bones, and I couldn't for the life of me explain how. "Mom and Dad?"

Pop nodded. "Once the villagers discovered Valerie was pregnant with Alastair's child, they had no choice but to follow the law and evict them. I pleaded and begged as I've never done before, but the law was the law, and they were banished as an example to others. What was left of my heart was broken that day, and I was alone."

I grew light-headed and fell back against the bench. Not once had Mom mentioned being kicked out of Belbury. I assumed she ran away from home with Dad, but the truth was much more shocking. I thought of the hard life she endured in Barden, of the trouble I caused her, especially after Dad left, and I felt miserable.

"I've been trying to persuade the villagers to revoke the eviction ever since. Unfortunately, their fear of mixed relations has held the decision firm."

"What changed?" I asked. "Why is she allowed back now?"

Pop gave a bitter chuckle. "There's nothing like context to change an opinion. Compared to the troubles Belbury has faced lately, your parents' breach seems frightfully insignificant."

I looked over the brook without responding. Mom deserved to be in Belbury with people like Pop who loved her. I hoped she'd arrive before I left for Italy. I wanted to give her a hug, a big one, and it had been a long time since I felt that way.

"We're almost here," Pop said. He looked at me with cloudy eyes. "I have one last thing to say before we arrive. I see what is going on between you and Elanil, and I will not stand in your way—" I opened my mouth, but Pop held up his finger for silence. "I *will*, however, caution you this: tread with care, for my sake. It would not do to remind the villagers of old crimes, not when I am so close to having my Valerie back. Can you do that? For me?" His eyes had turned glassy.

My heart ached for the poor old bugger. The pain that shook his voice cut me. I had to do everything in my power to give him his request. "I can," I said. "I'll put aside my feelings for Ela. You and Mom deserve to be happy again."

"Thatta girl," he said, dimples deepening as he smiled. He messed my hair. "You are a good lass, Chalia. But now—we look like we have come from the morgue. Smile on your face, if you will. You are about to enter a party the likes of which you've never seen."

We parked in front of Duke's stone cottage, and Pop collected his cider from the cart. I knocked on the large timber door, and a moment later, an Amish lady opened it with a gleaming smile.

"George!" she cried as she wrapped him in a hug, the tip of her bonnet barely cresting his shoulders. "It's been a ruddy long time! You're well?"

"As well as I have any right to be," Pop said. "This is Chalia, my great-granddaughter."

"Bless me, why of course it is!" the lady said, wrapping me in a bone-crushing hug. "I'm Darna, Bekka's mom. It's so nice to finally meet you. Come on, come inside." She linked an arm through mine and guided me through her cottage. "I've heard all about you—Duke hasn't talked about anything else, to be honest. Suppose I owe you a thank-you for keeping her out of trouble this last week."

I suppressed a laugh, thinking on how much food Duke had stolen since I arrived. If that was her behaving, I'd love to see her on a bad week. "Oh, it's nothing."

Darna snorted. "Bekka out of trouble is nothing short of a miracle. Well, here we are."

We walked past the kitchen and through the back door and stepped onto the stone garden leading to the brook. A table large enough to fit a school of children filled the top tier. It was laden with bowls and platters of food. "Help yourself to nibblies," Darna said. "The main course won't be ready for a few hours yet. Bekka and Ela are here somewhere—please do go and have fun. I must be off to the Pointed Ear to collect some more drink—Stanthrop invited half the village again."

I looked away from the food and took in the rest of the yard. It was divided into three terraces; the top terrace held the table, the second the barbecues, and the third led to the brook's edge. About twenty people were gathered in small groups, a mix of red-ears, Amish, and normals. They chatted animatedly, and most held tankards of ale or wine. Puppies and piglets raced around their feet, chasing and yipping after each other.

Pop placed his cider on an elevated garden bed of stones. "They're probably by the water—"

"George!" an old man cried from the middle terrace, interrupting Pop.

Pop turned and cursed under his breath. "Hoo-loo, Frank," he said unenthusiastically.

Frank hurried to our terrace with ale dribbling from his beard. "Tell me about these war gworths I've been hearing so much about!" he said as he clapped Pop's shoulder.

"Not here!" Pop muttered. "How many times . . . ?"

I left them to their conversation and searched for Elanil and Duke. I'd just stepped onto the second terrace when someone shouted my name.

I froze, trying to remember where I'd heard that bitter voice before.

CHAPTER 24

- CHALIA -

Alamril, the red-ear from the gate, was standing in a small circle of people beside a charcoal barbecue. He wore a frown as he motioned me forward with a finger.

I watched that finger and realized I wanted to be anywhere other than talking to him. I hadn't forgotten how he treated me at the gate. I was about to turn my back on him, when I recognized another figure by his side.

"Hoo-loo, lassie," Stanthrop said, opening his arms wide in welcome. "Glad you could make it."

I couldn't help but smile at his broad grin and gravitated toward him. "Thanks for the invite," I said as I passed open-aired rotisseries. "Pop hasn't shut up about how awesome your parties are."

Stanthrop puffed out his chest. "Well now, our shindigs have earned the reputation fairly, let me assure you."

Alamril gave a small cough, and all eyes turned his way. He surveyed me over his pointed nose, and I felt as though he was trying to see through me. "You are curious, Chalia," he said. "You are the one person in Belbury-on-the-Brook who I've heard more of than I've seen."

I looked into his pale eyes without blinking. "That's unfortunate for you; my looks really are my best asset."

A silence fell over the group. Alamril's eyes narrowed and bore into mine. I wouldn't look away. I couldn't let him win that battle. The rest of the group shifted on their feet.

And then Stanthrop laughed, a clap of thunder, and he slapped Alamril on the shoulder, knocking him forward a step. "But aye, she has a dangerous wit to match her looks."

Alamril didn't smile. "Indeed," he said. "I hear you have been entertaining my daughter with your 'wit.'" He did not sound impressed.

"Daughter?" I asked. Since I arrived in the village, I'd only hung around Duke and Elanil.

My mouth fell open.

"Elanil?" I asked, looking to Alamril's red earmuffs.

"You two have barely been separated, by all accounts," Alamril said.

An uncomfortable knot twisted in my gut. Had Pop told him about our kiss? Would they kick me out like Mom if he knew? I wasn't ready to leave, not just yet—

"Leave Chalia alone," Mrs. Zinvyre said as she joined the group and placed an arm around Alamril's waist and squeezed. "I couldn't have run the abattoir without her help—she's been a godsend!" She handed Alamril a tankard of ale. "You mind your tongue and don't scare her off, or you will sleep with the pigs tonight."

"Wish I could sleep with the pigs every now and then," Torrock grumbled. "They don't complain near half as much as Moira."

The group burst into laughter, and any tension evaporated.

Torrock glanced fearfully over his shoulder to the top terrace where Moira was talking to a few other ladies. "Hush! Moira will hear me having fun and do what she can to fix it!"

This only made everyone laugh harder, and when they were done, many were wiping tears from their eyes. Though Alamril hadn't laughed like the rest, his lips had curved up to reveal his white teeth, and when his eyes found mine again, they were no longer hard. "My wife speaks highly of you, Chalia, and that is enough for me. I must admit, I had my misgivings after I learned of your trouble in Barden, but I am proven wrong. For that you have my thanks." He held out his hand.

A blow to my head from a flying sheep couldn't have surprised me more. I shook his hand, not comprehending what was happening. An apology *and* a thank-you all in one day? The world was mad.

"Ela speaks highly of her too," Mrs. Zinvyre said, giving me a wink. "Never seen her so eager to work before. I told her to take a few days away from the abattoir earlier in the week, that Chalia and I could handle the work ourselves, but she was having none of it."

I looked to Mrs. Zinvyre with surprise. "Really? She never misses an opportunity to complain about how it's my fault she's stuck working on school holidays—"

A hand grabbed my arm and yanked me back a step.

"What *are* you doing?" Elanil hissed.

"Chatting," I said with a shrug. Feeling like having a bit of fun, I added, "Your mom told me the craziest thing. She said you *love* working with me. Isn't that funny—*whoa!*"

Elanil pulled me away from the group. "You are being lame—don't talk to them."

Laughter followed us as Elanil led me to the lower terrace by the water.

"What was *that* about?" I asked, pulling free from her grip.

Then I gasped.

Elanil no longer looked a country girl in jeans and boots. She was a model about to step onto a Chanel runway. She wore a light-blue off-the-shoulder sun dress that brushed the top of her knees, and tan sandals with straps that crossed their way up her calves. Her hair bounced past her shoulders in waves, and her eyes . . . I wasn't sure what she did to them, but they stole my breath. My pulse raced, and for a moment, I forgot how to speak.

"Well?" Elanil said. "What are you staring at?"

"You're beautiful," I stammered.

And she blushed.

"You only just working that out now?" she asked, fidgeting with her dress. "You look nice too. I see you washed your boots."

I looked down to my boots, and my stomach lurched. I *had* given them a rinse to wash off the grime, but they were tattered and looked at odds next to Elanil's sandals, like meat pie beside a high-tea tray.

"There you two are!" a voice said. Duke hurried down the terrace toward us. She was wearing a tan dress which, at first glance, gave her the appearance of being naked. It would have been a pleasant change from the black dress she always wore, except it was already stained down the front with food. "You wouldn't believe it, but old Talgodge has brought fireworks!" she said, face alight with excitement. "Come see."

I'd never seen a proper firework before, not up close, anyway. Sure, Kingsley and I had stolen some bungers a few years earlier and had some fun with them. But Talgodge's were *real* fireworks. Ones you stuck in the ground and lit and ran like hell. We poked and prodded them as the sky turned a fiery red before falling to darkness.

As the evening progressed, the guests grew rowdier as stories were told and drinks were drunk. The empty bottles piled high, and the smell of roasting meats and veg set everyone's stomachs to rumbling. Torches were lit around the terraces, and an impromptu band comprising Glenn the fisherman on guitar and Talgodge on harmonica and vocals began. Before long, seats were cleared, and they made a dance floor. I'd never danced before, and I'd never intended to, but when old Henry the veteran moseyed up to me and held out his withered hand, I couldn't refuse. He was an excellent dancer—I assumed—because not once did he step on my feet, and I found I actually enjoyed it. The song ended, and Henry bowed before finding a spare seat and patting his brow with a handkerchief.

I was ready to find a chair also, but after Henry had his fun with me, it was Stanthrop's turn, and his dance moves were far more Godzilla-like than the slow-moving veteran's. He smashed his feet on the ground with each beat as he swung me this way and that. I was twirled so much I felt sick, and my feet ached. Just as the song ended, and I believed I would find freedom, another man held out his hand for a dance.

If Elanil hadn't stepped in, I would have been stuck on the dance floor all night. She grabbed my hand and dragged me to the brook.

"You're welcome," Elanil said as she led me upstream a little way.

I was lightheaded. "That was actually fun."

We sat on a cushioned bench two cottages up from the party. The music was muffled but still loud enough for us to hear.

"They like you, you know," Elanil said. "All of them, even my dad. I'm not sure why." She nudged me with her shoulder playfully.

"Because I'm damn charming," I said, absorbing in her beauty.

"Do you even know how to spell charming?"

"Of course—C-h-a-l-i-a."

Elanil groaned. "Obviously you were home-schooled." And then she nuzzled her head on my shoulder, and I wrapped an arm around her waist, and life was amazing.

I tried to think of something to say, something perfect for that moment. "So . . . you don't dance?" I settled on, cringing at how lame it was.

"I love it. All of us red-ears do."

"I didn't see you on the dance floor."

"I was waiting for the right person to ask me." She swiveled her head on my shoulder, and her eyes looked into mine. Her breath was tickling my lips, and it was a moment before I realized I'd stopped breathing.

"Want to dance?" I whispered.

"Love to."

My pulse quickened as I pulled her to her feet. I pressed my body against hers and ran my hands to the small of her back, fingers just grazing her bottom. Surely she must feel my heart pounding against her chest; she must know how I feel.

Elanil rested her head on my shoulder, and we rocked gently, back and forward, and nothing could have made it a more perfect dance.

"You smell nice," she whispered.

"I know." I squeezed her tighter to me.

Elanil's fingers ran through the hair on the back of my neck. "I don't want you to leave," she breathed in my ear.

I didn't answer immediately—I didn't trust what I would say.

"I have to," I said.

Elanil pulled her head from my shoulder and looked me deep in my eyes. "Is there no way I can convince you to stay?"

She was so close I could taste her words.

I wanted to close the distance between our lips—I hungered for it with all that I was. My breathing came is quick gasps.

Elanil moved her hand from my neck to my cheek and slowly, ever so slowly, moved her lips to mine.

CHAPTER 25

- CHALIA -

Our lips touched, sending a thrill racing down my chest to settle in the tips of my toes. It was perfect, powerful, more so than our first kiss. It was everything I never knew I wanted and more. I would have given every penny I earned to stay lost in that kiss. Instead, I did the hardest thing I'd ever done—I pulled away.

Elanil's eyes snapped open, and she gave me a searching look. Then her expression closed, and she took a quick step back. "I'm sorry . . . I—I thought you were interested . . ."

"I am, Ela, but I can't," I said as my throat burned. I reached for her hand.

She pulled away. "I thought you liked me. I thought—"

"I do!" I protested. "I like you more than I've liked anyone."

She crossed her arms. "You've been playing me a fool the whole time, haven't you? Was it fun? Is that what city lasses do for a laugh?"

"What? No! Ela, listen to me—"

"No, Chalia, you listen to me. You're no different from the other boys in Belbury. You play your games and don't care who you hurt." Her eyes shimmered in the moonlight.

"This isn't for me," I pleaded. She had to understand. "I have to do it for Pop—"

"Save your excuses," she said, then with a tremble in her shoulders, she turned and disappeared into the darkness.

I stood motionless for a long while, staring over the brook with a heavy heart. Why was it the one person I liked I couldn't have? Sure, Pop deserved to see Mom again, but didn't I deserve happiness too? The image of them reunited at last, of the smile on both their faces, flitted through my mind. I sighed. I couldn't be the monster who denied that, no matter how much it pained me. I turned back to Duke's cottage.

The party was no longer bright and bubbly; it was noisy and smoky, and the laughter grated my ears. I sat at the table and did my best to avoid talking to anyone. At around eight o'clock, the guests sat for supper. They set more tables and chairs to accommodate the drop-ins. Roast meats, baked veg, breads, pies, grilled foods, and stews filled the tables. It was a feast unlike any I'd seen before. I should have been in heaven, but I felt I was drowned in the bottom of the brook.

"Tuck in!" Stanthrop and Darna cried together at the head of the table, and like hounds out of the gate, the guests obliged. They snatched what they could, spilling food here and there in a feeding frenzy. Talgodge, sitting beside me, set his fork to spearing with such an impressive speed, it forced me to take my hand from the table, lest he mistook it for a bunch of carrots.

Elanil returned not long after dinner began. She wore a forced smile and ignored the empty seat opposite me, instead joining Mrs. Zinvyre at the other end of the table.

"How's your first Belbury party?" Pop asked from the seat to my left. His voice was slurred, and I assumed it had something to do with his pear cider.

"Good," I muttered, wishing I could sound happier for him.

"You should see the Christmas celebrations; makes this seem a Thursday tea party." He took a swig from his bottle and smacked his lips, savoring the taste. He caught me watching him and said, "I don't let myself enjoy these much anymore. The result of over-indulgence in my youth, if I'm being honest. It used to be the only thing which helped forget . . . well . . . no need for those stories. Suffice to say, I learned a thing or two about moderation."

"Mind if I try one?" I asked, wanting something, anything, to help forget the touch of Elanil's lips.

Pop frowned and lowered the bottle. He spun it on the table so the fiery glow of the burning torches morphed in the glass. After a while he looked to me. "It would be hypocritical to tell you not to drink, seeing as I began when I was younger than you. Yes, dear, you may have one. But only one, they are terribly strong, and it would be a sin to give you a pear cider hangover."

The cider was sweeter than London Pride and had more fizz than my stomach could handle. I burped after my first sip, and Pop laughed.

"Take your time with it, lass. I added too much sugar to this batch."

Despite Pop's warning, I finished the entire bottle before the main meal was done. A pleasant numbness took my mind, and the events of earlier that night didn't seem to jab at my chest with near as much force. Everyone at the table reclined in their chairs, more than a few with unbuckled belts. Groans of contentment and slaps of stomachs echoed over the crackle of coals in the barbecues. My eyes were drooping when a yell shocked me.

"Arthur!" Darna cried, jumping to her feet and looking to the cottage. "Glad you could make it!"

An old man dressed in a clean-pressed suit stepped onto the top terrace from the kitchen. His thin mustache twitched as he looked at the guests. An air of arrogance clung to him like a turtle's shell.

Arthur removed his bowler hat and gave a little bow to Darna. "Please excuse me for being late—work has been murder lately."

Stanthrop waved aside the apology. "We've finished our meat stuffs, but there's plenty of veg left, if you like."

"Thank you," Arthur said, and much to my displeasure, sat in the empty chair opposite me. He interlocked his fingers to his front, and his eyes caught mine. They narrowed as they spotted my nose ring.

Pop leaned forward. "Chalia, this is Arthur Princeton, the—"

"Mayor," I finished. I'd know the moment I saw him. He had the same self-aggrandizing air as the mayor of Barden.

"Indeed," Arthur said, cold eyes unblinking. "Observant girl. How are you fitting in? None of that nonsense you were doing in Barden, I hope?"

A wave of fury raced through my veins. Who was he to judge what I'd been through? I ground my jaw to stop from throwing the cider bottle at his stupid head. Before I could answer, Mrs. Zinvyre spoke.

"Chalia has been working the abattoir with me," she said,

sounding as annoyed as I felt. "And has been doing an outstanding job."

"Hmm," Arthur said, sounding underwhelmed. "Let us hope it stays that way."

"Or what?" I said. Before I knew it, I was on my feet. "You'll throw me out of Belbury like you did my mom?"

The table froze. Even the piglets, who were busy gnawing on bones, looked up.

"Sit down, dear," Pop said, placing a hand on my arm.

I couldn't sit. Everything that happened to me over the last few weeks boiled over; Kingsley's murder, the kiss in the abattoir, Elanil rejecting me, then me rejecting Elanil. It was too much to hold in anymore.

Arthur looked at me a moment, then loaded two potatoes onto his plate. He cut a small portion and placed it in his mouth. He chewed, swallowed, and then put his knife and fork down. "No," he said, "I do not have the option of sending you from Belbury like your mother, at least for the time being." He reached for the tray of honeyed carrots and found a small one to drop to his plate. "No one may leave or enter the village for the foreseeable future."

I opened my mouth to lash out, but then his words registered, and I faltered. "It's illegal to leave Belbury?"

"In a sense."

I sneered at him. "Good luck trying to stop me—"

"I'm the mayor!" he shouted suddenly, losing composure and slamming his fist on the table. "My word is law!"

I rocked back, then went at him twice as hard. "No—you're a nasty old git who gets off abusing power. You're a scumbag, nothing more."

Pop stood and placed both hands on my shoulders. "Chalia, please sit. Come on, lass—"

"It's okay, George," Arthur said, his eyes trembling. "You think I am a scumbag because you disagree with my laws? Well, I have news for you, girl, and the sooner you hear it the better. *That. Is. Life.* It isn't always sunshine and teacups—sometimes it's lightning and nails. Sometimes doing what is right means drinking vinegar instead of Twinings."

"Not you, though," I said, leaning over the table. "I see you, *Arthur.* You love power. You *crave* it. Well, you've none over me. I'll leave Belbury when I want, and there's not a thing you can do to stop it."

With a last look of disgust at the rotten bastard, I turned and stormed toward the brook, my muscles tensed. I'll leave the cursed village this very night, just to show him.

CHAPTER 26

- CHALIA -

I booted a stone into the flowing brook, though its splash was drowned out as I cursed into the night sky. I was marching toward the bridge, though I had half a mind to turn back and bury a fist right in Arrogant Arthur's annoying face. In fact, I'd doubled back twice already, but both times common sense prevailed. What would bloodying his nose achieve other than causing trouble for Pop? No, I knew what I had to do, and that was leave them all far behind.

I stumbled on some reeds in the darkness and only just caught my balance to stop from falling in the water. Cursing again, I found an oak tree to lean against. I needed to calm down and think. The gate was a long way off, Cheltenham even further. Should I go to Pop's for supplies before the journey? No, I decided, having no wish to return to his cottage. Supplies would not make the night-time walk any easier.

I pushed off the tree and made my way up the bank, and almost reached the bridge when a hand grabbed my arm. I swung around, fist cocked, ready to flatten whoever it was.

But it was Duke, doubled over and panting.

"Put that fist away before you break it on my head," Duke wheezed. "Why didn't you stop? We've been calling to you for ages!"

I lowered my hand and shook my head, too angry to talk. Elanil was with her, a few paces back. I'd been so lost in my thoughts I hadn't heard them at all. It didn't matter; my mind was made up, and I was leaving. I turned and stepped onto the bridge.

"Where are you going?" Duke asked, following.

"Away."

"Without saying goodbye?"

I snorted. "To who? Pop? He is better off without me."

"To us, you dolt," Duke said.

I slowed. "Sorry," I mumbled. "And goodbye." I placed my hands in my jacket pockets and carried on.

Duke's heavy footsteps pounded after me. "It's at least a full day's walk to Cheltenham—why don't you stay the night and leave in the morning?"

"Stay where?" I asked, eyes fixed on the road. "With Pop? With Mrs. Zinvyre? With the *mayor*? No—I'm done with this place."

The three of us walked in silence until we reached the church.

"The White Tree," Elanil said.

I rolled my eyes. "Your cubby house? I'd rather walk all night."

Elanil spun me to face her, her hands digging into my shoulders. "Are you going to be this bitter all your life? We are trying to *help* you, Chalia." She had a fierceness in her eyes that told me she hadn't forgiven me for earlier.

I ground my teeth. It *was* a long road to Cheltenham, and knowing my luck, I'd just as likely end up walking a full circle back to Belbury. "Fine."

"Good," Elanil said. She started walking again. "Let's go. It's a big climb, and I'm tired."

Duke linked her arm in mine and pulled me after her. We passed the Village Square, turned right at the intersection, and climbed the incline beside the Pointed Ear. A little way out of town, we turned left onto a deer track through the forest and climbed the hill overlooking the village. Trees blocked most of the moonlight, but Duke and Elanil walked surefooted.

We crested the hill twenty minutes later. Sweat stung my eyes, and I was panting heavily when we reached a viewpoint over Belbury. Cottage windows lit the cobbled streets with flickering firelight, some reflecting on the brook as it snaked its way through the center.

"See that light waaaaay out there?" Duke asked, pointing to a tiny dot of gold on the horizon to our left. "That's the gate. You can't even see Cheltenham."

"That's the gate?" I asked, more than a little surprised. It would have taken the rest of the night to reach.

"Yep."

I rubbed the back of my neck as I realized how stupid I had been. "Thanks. For everything."

"No probs," Duke said. "You city folk need all the help you can get. Anyway—" She turned her back on the village and swept her arms out wide. "Welcome to the White Tree."

A tree taller than most of Barden's buildings stood in a clearing atop the hill, dwarfing the surrounding pines. It looked a cedar, if I had to guess, but it was bone white and didn't grow any leaves. The trunk was large enough to fit a school bus inside, and if someone had to run around its base, they'd be out of breath by the time they circled it. Bark spiraled upward around it in great sweeps, looking like someone carved a staircase into the trunk.

I looked to each of the thick branches, expecting to see a treehouse. "Where's the cubby?"

Duke tapped a finger to her nose. "Follow me."

She led me to the trunk, grabbed a knot between the spiral bark, and pulled. A round door, small enough to make adults stoop, swung open, revealing a hollowed center in the tree, dark with shadow.

My skin crawled as I pictured spiders creeping over the floor. "In there?"

"Yep," Duke said, then she disappeared into the darkness. Elanil followed.

I looked around, hoping they were playing a joke. Where was the real cubby? I was about to call out to Duke and Elanil when something rustled in a bush to my left. My heart jumped to my throat, and I raced inside, crashing into Duke in the darkness.

"I thought city kids were tough?" Duke muttered as she regained her feet.

"Against blades and pistols," I said, standing as close to her as I could. "But not whatever the hell is out there at night."

The room had an earthy smell, not in an unpleasant way, but like Pop's garden after it rained. Shafts of moonlight filtered through porthole windows as Elanil opened curtains around the den.

Duke knelt in front of a stone hearth fireplace, and seconds later flames burst to life, roaring as though they'd been burning for hours. The effect was immediate and impressive. The trunk was no longer a haunted tree skeleton but had a cozy cottage vibe. It had all the comforts of a home—a dining table in the center, two beds pressed against the wall, their mattresses yellowing with age, a full bookshelf, photo frames nailed to the walls, a tub and sink beside the door, and copper pots and pans hanging from the hearth like baubles on a Christmas tree.

"Well, what do you think?" Duke asked.

"It's amazing," I breathed, spinning on the spot to take it all in. I'd never been interested in camping; I was a city lass and liked my concrete and fast food. The White Tree changed things.

"Did you hear that, Ela?" Duke asked. "Chalia gave a compliment. How unusual."

"Hmm," Elanil said. She unhooked a pot, carried it to the basin, and turned on the tap, which was screwed into the trunk. A stream of water poured out. "Do you mind picking some leaves for us?"

Instead of being confused by the tree's plumbing, it upset me at how cold Elanil was acting. I needed to explain things to her before I left in the morning, to set things right. She deserved to know how I felt, and I couldn't stomach the thought of her hating me forever.

"Come along, daftie," Duke said, grabbing my arm and leading me outside. "I'll show you the gardens." She stepped onto the thick bark that spiraled up the tree and climbed it like a stairwell.

"Aren't we going to the gardens?" I asked, not wanting to follow; heights had never been a strong point for me.

"Yes." She disappeared around the trunk.

I took a breath and climbed after her. We reached the first branch by the time we finished a full revolution. It was wider than a car.

"Not this one," Duke said and continued up. "That's our patch for starches: Potatoes, pumpkins, parsnips."

The next one was for broccoli, tomatoes, and beans. And the third—we were now so high my head swam—held herbs and "flavor plants," as Duke called them. We climbed off the spiral bark and onto the sturdy limb.

A garden grew right atop the branch in four neat rows. Plants, small trees, and shrubs sprouted as though they were in a well-tended nursery. Rosemary, basil, thyme—the garden had it all. I walked between the rows in amazement.

"Impressive, huh?" Duke asked as she plucked some leaves from a shoulder-high tree growing at the end of the patch.

"I've seen nothing like it, and I've watched David Attenborough."

"Why were you watching people?" Duke asked. "That's weird." Then she looked at me. "And more importantly, why are you blundering things up with Elanil? She's pretty upset."

I looked down to my hands. "I know," I said. "I wanted to kiss her, I really did—"

"But you're scared?"

"What? No." I flexed my fingers and then sighed. I might as well tell her everything. "Pop told me what happened to my parents. How they were kicked out of the village."

Duke froze, the leaves dropping from her hands, and a look of terror spread across her face. "How much did he tell you?"

CHAPTER 27

- CHALIA -

Duke's reaction caught me off guard. She reminded me of a kid who'd been caught stealing cigarettes from her dad and was at a loss of how to talk her way out of it.

"Pop told me that Mom fell in love with a red-ear," I said, watching her closely, "and was kicked out of Belbury for it."

Duke sighed, and her shoulders relaxed. "Oh, right. Well, yes, that's what happened." She picked up the tea leaves. "Anyway, tell Elanil why you didn't kiss her; she might understand. Better than her thinking she did something wrong. Come on—"

I grabbed her wrist to stop her from turning. "What aren't you telling me?"

"Plenty," she said, pulling out of my grip with ease. She started toward the trunk. "Such as my secret exfoliating regimen, but you ain't never getting that out of me. Now, do you want to stand here gossiping like school lasses, or do you want to tell Elanil how you feel?"

I narrowed my eyes. What was she hiding from me? Her tongue normally wagged more than a dog's tail, but she was reluctant to talk about my parents. I needed to figure out a way to get her to loosen up. In the end, I said, "I want to tell Elanil, just not tonight. It will be easier for both of us in the morning, before I leave."

Duke looked to me. "How is it you're a lass, yet you do not know how lasses work?" She clucked her tongue. "Your funeral; do what you will."

We made our way down the spiral bark and entered the trunk, which had grown toasty with the fire. Elanil was perched in front of the hearth watching a pot boil. She didn't look up when we approached. "Took your time."

Duke collected three mugs from the sink and placed a few leaves in each. *"Took your time,"* she mimicked in a whiny voice. "I wanted to show Chalia our gardens." She collected the pot and poured water into all three and handed one to me and one to Elanil. Elanil accepted it without saying a word.

We drank in silence. Not a nice silence, like the one we'd shared in the boat journey that afternoon. This one tore at the ears like a feral cat in a pet store. Elanil ignored any attempt I made at eye contact, and Duke was busy prodding the fire. I sat in the spare seat.

"Who else knows about this place?" I asked, desperate for the silence to end. "It's nicer than my old apartment in Barden."

Elanil sipped her tea. "No one."

And the silence doubled.

Duke put away the prodder and turned to me. "We found it yonkers ago, and it's been ours ever since. Most of our, um, *acquired*—" she mimed air quotes, "—vegetables go to stocking up our garden beds. It's not an easy place to find, and most villagers prefer walks in the forest by George's cottage than up this hill."

I thought back to our run-in with Thomas and his gang as they were heading into the forest. I couldn't believe it was only that morning when I met him.

I took a sip of tea, and my eyes grew heavy. I thought of my warm bed at Pop's cottage. As though reading my mind, Elanil stood and moved to one bed. She pulled the mattress off and dragged it in front of the fire. Duke grabbed the other one and butted them up, forming one enormous bed.

"We will have to share," Elanil said.

Despite it all—the overwhelming weariness, the residual bitterness from my fight with the mayor, and the sadness seeping into me from the knowledge I was leaving the village, a trickle of excitement spread from my stomach to set my chest on fire. I knew nothing was going to happen with Elanil and me, but as I thought of lying next to her, my breathing came in quick gasps.

Elanil took the left side of the mattress, I lay the middle, and Duke finished her mug before taking the right.

"G'night," Duke mumbled as she pulled her bonnet over her eyes. Two minutes hadn't passed before she was snoring loud enough to rattle the pots and pans. I rolled onto my side to face Elanil, who was staring at the ceiling.

"I'm sorry," I whispered.

Elanil closed her eyes. "Are you still leaving?"

"Ela . . . the adults here . . . I was wrong; they're just as bad as the rest of them."

"Then there is nothing to be sorry about." She rolled onto her side to face the wall, leaving me to look at the back of her head.

As tired as I was, it took some time to find sleep. My heart wouldn't stop telling me how stupid I was for leaving Belbury, but my mind was there, dressed for war, and beat it back with the hatred I felt for the mayor.

CHAPTER 28

- CHALIA -

Sleep finally took me sometime after midnight. It was fitful and uneasy, with crimson concrete and war drums beating frantically. My pulse raced in time to that rhythm, and a sheen of sweat coated my skin. I tossed on the old mattress and rested my head on my arm. That's when I heard it, an explosion, like a firework in the distance, reverberating through the tree.

Or was it thunder?

It must be thunder.

I rolled onto my stomach and tried to find sleep once more, not relishing the thought of walking to Cheltenham in the pelting rain.

Another boom, this time accompanied by something else. A bell, perhaps, tolling as though it were in a heavy metal song.

I opened my eyes. Why was a bell ringing in a thunderstorm? My skin prickled on the back of my neck. Something was wrong, out of place, though I couldn't put my finger on it. I climbed out of bed and crept to the window. Duke didn't miss a snore, but Elanil woke.

"What are you doing?" she asked through a yawn.

"A storm is coming," I said, pressing my face against the pane and using my hands to shield the reflection from the glowing coals.

And then I heard it again, this time clearer. The ringing of a bell, incessant, desperate almost. My first thought was someone had too much holy wine and was having a laugh in the church's bell tower.

"How much does your priest drink?" I asked.

"Father Richard?" Elanil asked, sitting up. "Only on weekends and weekdays. Why?"

I looked to the night sky for any signs of lightning. "I think he might be . . . I don't know . . ." I turned away from the window. "The church bell is ringing like crazy."

Elanil's eyes widened in the dim light, and she raised a hand to her heart. "The bell is ringing?"

"Won't shut up."

The fire popped, and the burning log fell to embers, spraying flecks of gold and orange heavenward.

In a flurry, Elanil jumped from bed and hurried to the window. She lifted the side of her earmuff and pressed her ear against the glass, eyes closed. Then—

"Duke!" she screamed and raced back to the bed. "Duke! Wake up!"

Gooseflesh prickled my skin. I'd never heard a voice shake with fear like Elanil's.

Duke groaned and rolled over. "I promise I won't paint your cow again."

"Wake up!" Elanil pleaded, shaking her as hard as she could.

I didn't know what had gotten into Elanil, but the dread in her voice froze my heart. I raced to the sink, filled a pot with water, and emptied it over Duke's face.

Duke sat up, spluttering. "I'll knock your ears off!"

"The bell," Elanil said, gripping Duke's hands and pulling her to her feet.

Duke fell straight back to the mattress like a plank of wood.

"The bell's ringing!" Elanil shouted, slapping Duke on the cheek. "They're here!"

Duke's eyes burst open. "No . . ." she whispered. They shared a wide-eyed look. Then, quicker than a viper, she jumped from bed and raced out of the trunk with Elanil hot on her heels.

"Who's here?" I asked as I followed them to the lookout.

They didn't respond, but I doubt I would have paid them any attention if they had. As soon as I reached the lookout, my mind collapsed in on itself from what I saw. Forks of electricity and tongues of fire lit the village as though a freak thunderstorm was erupting from the ground. Explosions of yellow and blue bloomed through the cobbled streets while clashing metal screamed into the night, with it muffled wails and shouts of anger.

There was a pause in the chaos just long enough for a buzzing to be heard. Fifty wasp swarms couldn't make such a racket. In many ways it was more terrifying than the screams.

"It's happening," Duke whispered.

I grabbed her by the shoulders and spun her around. "What is?"

The whites of Duke's eyes shone in the gloom. "They're here."

"Who?"

"Aurocans," Elanil said. "Visitors."

Duke suddenly shook her head like a dog shaking water from its coat, and when she stopped, her eyes were hard and clear. "We have to help," she said and then took off racing down the hill at breakneck speed, her tan dress flapping behind.

Elanil grabbed my hand. "Stay here," she said, giving it a squeeze before chasing after Duke.

I watched her disappear into the darkness for the second time that night. I did not know who those aurocans were, but they sounded like trouble, and if there was one thing Barden prepared me for, it was how to handle people who thought they were too big for their boots. I raced after Elanil and Duke.

Duke set a blazing pace, one I couldn't hope to match in the dark of night. I tripped on roots and rocks but didn't slow. I couldn't. By the time the hill leveled out, I was covered in scratches, and my breathing came is quick gasps. I looked for the others, but they were nowhere to be seen.

The commotion was much louder in the village; the shouts and screams, the explosions and roar of fire, and always, over the top of it all, the buzzing. Constant. Threatening.

I gulped and resisted the urge to run straight back up the hill. Instead, I followed the highway into town, hoping to catch the others.

After a few minutes, I spotted movement ahead. It was Elanil and Duke, creeping through a garden toward the Pointed Ear. I breathed a sigh of relief and hurried after them, realizing how stupid I'd been to waltz into town in the middle of the road where anyone could have seen me.

"What are you doing here?" Elanil whispered pulling me down beside her. "I told you to stay."

"I'm not your dog," I said, looking around wildly, unable to control the shaking in my hands. "And I couldn't let you run down here to fight the Acarans by yourself."

She smiled briefly. "Aurocans—"

An explosion rocketed just to our front, the blast of hot air rolling over us. We dropped to our stomachs behind the Pointed Ear's oak tree and covered our heads with our hands.

A moment of near silence, except for that terrifying drone, which echoed in my soul.

"It's coming from the Village Square," Elanil said, looking up.

Duke pushed herself to her knees. "The graveyard will give the best view." She looked to me. "This ain't no game, Chalia. You should go back to the White Tree before you see something you can't forget."

I wanted to do exactly that. Maybe to run all the way to Cheltenham, where a gangster war wasn't raging. But I couldn't leave Elanil and Duke, not like I left Kingsley. "I've grown up in Barden and have seen things that would scare the curls out of your hair." I sounded braver than I felt. "I will be fine."

Duke gave a small nod. "Your funeral." She peeled around the tree and sprinted behind the stables of the next cottage.

Elanil gripped my hand. "You're about to see things I can't explain just yet. Keep your questions behind your teeth until we're safe."

CHAPTER 29

- GEORGE -

George's stomach roiled as he lay on his bed watching his ceiling wave like a storm-tossed ocean. He had not intended to drink as much as he had at Stanthrop and Darna's party, however men in Belbury are a prideful folk, and nothing set fire to their competitive nature more than brewing. Refusing to sample other villagers' batches had often caused many a fight, and George no longer had the arms for such activity, so he drank what they offered, and that was that.

But nausea wasn't the only culprit keeping George awake. Repeatedly his muddled mind dragged him back to Chalia. She hadn't returned after she blew out of the party, and with the trouble looming in the village, wandering the streets alone could end in a terrible, terrible way.

George closed his eyes and turned onto his side with a groan, making a mental note to have a stern talk with Arthur in the morning. It was dangerous for Chalia to not know of the dangers of the village, and despite how she felt about him, George loved her like a daughter and would do anything to protect her. With that thought in mind, George finally drifted to sleep.

George's dream was troubled with the ghosts of time. He was back in France, a young buck with too much confidence and not enough brains. Knee-deep in mud, his nose stung with cold, and his heart ached for the safety of his mother's arms. Bullets shrieked above the trench, their whistle piercing, and explosions bucked him and his brothers like an unbroken stallion. Luck saved him, nothing else. Not his skill or courage or leadership. He should have died fifty times over.

He didn't.

His mates did.

And it was their screams that haunted him. Howls of pain and confusion and denial and anger.

But something was out of place in that dream. A bell. Tolling. Crooning on and on without breath. What was it calling?

A warning, perhaps.

Rations?

Withdrawal?

Charge?

And then his mind fell away from the battlefield and a water well appeared; beside it, a timber frame.

From that frame dangled a bell.

The village bell.

George sat bolt upright, heart pounding against his ribcage and a cold sweat on his forehead. His mind was still muddied with drink and the echo of his dream. He shuddered.

It was just a dream.

He was safe, home in Belbury-on-the-Brook, not in France—

But then he heard it; the screaming, the explosions, the dying all over again.

And that bell.

"Damn it!"

He threw his duvet aside and swung his legs out of bed. Using the bedside cabinet as support, he stood on shaking knees, lit his lamp, and hurried out of the room, stumbling from the alcohol still in his blood.

The aurocans had arrived, and he needed to loose his attack beasts before the invaders destroyed everything. He collected his ring of keys from a hook on the wall beside the back door and sped into the backyard.

Lives depended on his haste, and he could not let them down. Reaching the barn, he fumbled with the keys until he found the right one. Before he unlocked the door, an incessant buzz engulfed him, beating at him from every angle.

And then the ground shook, as though a boulder crashed behind him.

"Where are you going, human?" said a scratchy voice.

George froze, his lantern and keys falling from his hands. *He was too late.*

A scream sounded from Moira's cottage.

No! He would free the beasts, he had to!

George squared his shoulders. He needed to take care of the aurocan.

An odd calmness flushed through him, and he no longer suffered the fogginess of drink. Straightening his back, George turned to face the monster, grim determination furrowing his brow as he craned his neck to look the ugly creature in its icy eyes.

The aurocan glanced down as George clenched his hands into tight fists. It laughed. "Really?"

George didn't answer; talking would do no good. He lifted his fists in front of his face, elbows crackling as they bent.

The aurocan shook his head. "Let it be said humans do not lack courage. Don't worry, I will not kill you."

A grave smile spread across George's face. "I can't promise the same."

Then he launched at the foul creature, arm cocked and a fire lit within.

CHAPTER 30

- CHALIA -

The explosions of fire and bolts of electricity erupted less frequently as the seconds dragged to minutes. I scurried from shadow to shadow, bent double and on the edge of vomiting from fear. The closer we got to the village square, the stronger the stench of smoke grew and the louder the buzzing. Repeatedly that hum—as though of a mutant bee—passed directly overhead, sending me sprawling to the ground with arms covering my face.

I did not know what the noise was. Could it be a drone—or an army of drones—that the aurocan gang were using? But what could they hope to see at night? It made little sense. Nothing made sense. But my skin didn't need sense to crawl the way it did every time one flew by.

We ignored the left turn at the intersection leading to the bridge and continued straight until we found a part of road dark enough to cross undetected. Once on the other side, we doubled back until we crouched with our backs to the cemetery's stone fence. The shouting and buzzing were at its fiercest in the village square. Screams of pain and shouts of fury sliced through the ever-present humming. My muscles knotted. *What on earth is happening in Belbury?*

Duke wiped sweat from her eyes on the back of her hand. "We have to cut through the cemetery," she said, her voice stony.

"What?" I asked, looking at her as though she was a nutter. "No—they'll spot us for sure!"

"We've a chance of being caught anywhere we go," Elanil said, eyeing the sky.

But the cemetery? Hadn't these lasses read *any* horror novels? "What about the brook? It doesn't sound as bad down there—"

"We can't see nothing from the brook," Duke said and hurdled the fence without waiting for a reply. I peeked over the top and watched as she darted to the first crumbling tombstone.

"Come on," Elanil said, a little more gently, before following Duke.

I looked over my shoulder, suddenly alone. "Damn it," I muttered, then jumped over the fence before I could talk myself out of it.

We raced from tombstone to tombstone, crouching behind each for a moment before making the next bound. We reached the church, breathless. Before I had a chance to relax, Duke peeled around the corner and started toward the square.

I gripped Elanil's dress before she could follow. "Ela, please, it's dangerous out there—"

"There's no other way," she said. Her eyes met mine for a moment that was an eternity, then she disappeared around the corner too.

With a breath to calm my nerves, I gave chase. I hadn't taken two steps before I slammed into something in the darkness.

"Oof," Elanil said, stumbling into Duke.

"Shh," Duke whispered.

And then I spotted *them*, and I knew I was in a nightmare. Yes, that's what it was. A nightmare so vivid it set my lungs to ice and stole the marrow from my bones.

It's not a nightmare, a voice teased in the back of my mind. *Nightmares are too small for such monsters.*

Thirty paces to our front stood two hulking creatures in conversation. They hadn't noticed our arrival, but how long it would stay that way, I couldn't know. Their grating voices carried through the cemetery like nails on a blackboard. They weren't creatures from a child's story, like the Big Friendly Giant or the Gruffalo. No, these things looked like they'd eat them for an entrée and use their bones as toothpicks. They were taller than the tallest NBA player, eight feet or more, and had skin that shined like polished steel and could deflect bullets. Insectlike wings buzzed from their backs, humming.

Droning.

My chest cramped into a knot so tight it made breathing impossible. I was rooted to the spot, another statue among the graves.

Duke recovered first. She pulled Elanil and me back around the corner and out of sight.

"W-what the heck?" I stammered. "They . . . what? Damn it, what are those things?"

Elanil clamped a hand over my mouth. "Shh."

I shook free. "They're . . . they're *monsters*. Monsters, Ela. Didn't you see—"

"*We will explain later,*" Elanil whispered. "But there won't be a later if your questions get us caught." She turned to Duke. "What now?"

Duke chewed her lip. "We need to find out what they are doing with the villagers—"

A shout filled the air, coming from just around the corner. I clung to Elanil, my breathing frantic.

"Stay here," Elanil said, prying my fingers from her arm. "I have to see what is happening." She peeked around the corner. Duke did the same.

I stood there a moment, hyperventilating, until I realized the shout was human.

It could be Pop!

The thought forced air into my lungs and motion to my legs. I crept to the others and, crouching low, peered around the wall.

The first thing I saw was a red-ear sprinting at the two beasts, her hands glowing electric blue. She thrust her arms forward, and forks of lightning exploded from her palms like magic. The lightning crashed into one creature, tossing it through the air to smash into the church steps. The red-ear took aim at the second creature, but it moved quicker than its size should have allowed. Its powerful legs propelled it forward to slam into the red-ear, sending her spiraling toward us.

We pulled away as she crunched to the ground, where she slid just far enough for her head to poke around the church's wall. She wheezed as she tried to fill her lungs through blood-stained lips. Then her glazed eyes spotted us and widened. "Run!" she rasped.

Then she was yanked away by her foot.

I wanted to listen to her, but I didn't. I couldn't. I was transfixed.

I dropped to my knees and peered back around the corner. Pop needed me.

The creature held the red-ear by the back of the shirt, her legs dangling from the ground. It looked to the sky and bellowed, and four other creatures dropped from the heavens to land in front of it, their knees bending backward to absorb the shock. They were smaller than the monster with the red-ear.

"Tie her with the others," it said, tossing the woman to the nearest one.

"Yes, Ghultar," said the creature who caught the red-ear.

"Alive," Ghultar said, his voice a growl.

"Where's the fun in that?" a creature with deep-green skin dared ask. "I haven't killed one in seventy years!"

Ghultar turned to the speaker, his broken wing twitching. "How will we learn of this world if you kill the knowledge?"

The creature opened its mouth to argue, but Ghultar snatched him by the neck and lifted him from the ground in one movement. He pulled the creature close. "Something to say?"

The creature's legs kicked wildly as it tried to pry Ghultar's fingers from its throat, a pitiful squeal escaping its mouth.

"I can't hear you," Ghultar said, turning his head so the hole where his ear should have been was close to his captive's mouth.

And then he squeezed, and the creature's head jolted to one side with a crack like a breaking branch.

Ghultar dropped the convulsing body and glared at the others. "Anyone else have an opinion?" he asked. The remaining three lowered their eyes. "Good. Finish rounding up prisoners and store them in that building." He nodded to the church. "I'll question them once the town is secure. *Do not kill any!*"

Then all four of them disappeared into the night on horrible backward-bending legs.

All except the twitching creature on the ground.

It was dead. Just like that; dead. Its life snapped out of it, even if its convulsing body refused to listen.

Dead.

Like Kingsley.

The creature blurred as tears welled in my eyes. It was too much.

A hand rested on my shoulder. "We need to leave," Elanil whispered. She pulled me around the wall and carefully rested my back to the stone.

Numbness dulled my mind. Monsters didn't exist. I was dreaming. Yes. That crunching neck was a trick of sleep. I was in the white tree, snuggled next to Elanil.

I smiled.

"Chalia," Elanil whispered.

I looked to her, and all my worry disappeared. She was so beautiful.

Elanil cupped my cheek. "Chalia, we have to leave."

That neck. The crack. A convulsing body. A *dream*.

Strong hands lifted me from the ground, and the village moved around me.

I was later told Duke carried me from building to building as aurocans buzzed around us, and eventually all the way up the hill to the White Tree.

I do not remember the journey, but I remember sunrise.

It was blood red and cold.

I have snapshots of time. Of me shivering in front of the fire.

Of Duke and Elanil wrapping me in blankets and rubbing my limbs to warm them.

Then nothing. Sleep.

I woke sometime around five in the afternoon.

Elanil and Duke huddled at the table. When Elanil spotted me moving, she rushed over and placed a hand on my forehead. "How are you?" she asked.

"Okay," I croaked, though it felt as though every ounce of energy had been sucked from me. I rubbed sleep from my eyes. Surely I wasn't the only one who felt so rubbish. "How are you feeling—"

I stopped, mouth dropping open as I saw her clearly.

Then I recoiled as though she were a snake, pushing myself to the other end of the mattress. "Y-your earmuffs," I stammered, looking at them dangling around her neck. And then more loudly, "Your ears!"

Elanil's shoulders slumped. "Are you ready to know the full story of Belbury-on-the-Brook?" Her voice was quiet with apprehension. And then she pulled her hair behind her ears in a tight bun.

CHAPTER 31

- CHALIA -

The White Tree's glowing fire reflected orange in Elanil's shimmering hair. She fidgeted with the neck of her dress. She needn't have bothered tying her hair in a bun; her ears' peaks were so stretched they needed an afro to hide. Or at the very least, a fluffy pair of red earmuffs.

"Y-you're an elf!" I stammered, climbing out of bed and backing to the mantle.

"Yes," Elanil said, her voice faint.

My mind scrambled like twice-beaten eggs. Elves didn't exist. This wasn't a Tolkien novel.

But . . . there she was; she couldn't be anything else.

How could I not have known? We spent weeks together. She hid it the whole time? I thought of our moment in the abattoir on my first day. She kissed me when I tried removing her earmuffs. Did she do that just to distract me? Did that mean she never really liked me?

No. My heart wouldn't believe that.

"Aye, she's an elf," Duke said from the table, picking at her fingernails. "What of it? You've just seen *aurocans*, and you're scared of pointy ears?"

"And magic," I said, remembering the lightning erupting from the red-ear's hands in the cemetery.

Duke groaned and wiggled her fingers at me. "Magic and ears—run for your life!" Then she rolled her hand over and clicked her fingers and a ball of fire ignited in her palm. It danced on the spot like a candle flame.

I flinched and knocked a pan from a hook on the mantle. Duke rolled her eyes and closed her fist, extinguishing the fire.

"You're an elf too?" I asked, surprised my tongue was working at all.

Duke choked on a cough, her face turning red, and thumped the table until she could breathe again. "Elf?" she wheezed, tears welling in her eyes. Then she threw her head back and boomed a laugh that echoed in the small room. Elanil, who'd been silent, giggled then, and raised a hand to cover her mouth.

I folded my arms. The village was under attack by monsters, and the lasses I'd come to love were fantasy characters. What was so funny?

"Oh, drop that sour look from your face," Duke said as she wiped tears from her cheeks. "Enjoy the laughs as they come—I'm not sure how many are left to us." She rocked back on her chair and looked at me as though I was a toddler what needed learning. "No, I'm not a durned elf, you daftie. I'm a dwarf." She removed her bonnet and threw it at me. "Ta-daaa."

I dropped the bonnet, and my cheeks burned. "I don't understand . . . elves and dwarves aren't real."

"Says who?" Elanil said, standing. She reached out a timid hand. "Come, we have a lot to talk about."

Her fingers were delicate, not the claws of a monster. I'd felt them many times, and not once had they hurt me. But . . . an elf? I chewed my lip.

Elanil's eyes dropped to the floor. She pulled away. "I understand."

I watched her mouth fall into a frown, and my heart ached. Elf or not, she was my Elanil; nothing could change that. I pushed off the hearth and wrapped my fingers around hers, and a nervous smile spread across her beautiful lips.

"I should have told you," she said.

"Maybe," I said and led her to the table. "But I can't blame you for keeping it a secret."

"Oh?"

I nodded. "If I was friends with a dwarf, I'd want to hide that too."

Elanil snorted, and Duke threw a half-eaten carrot at me.

"You saw me click birth to fire, right?" Duke asked. "Be all too easy to make a candle from your hair." She clapped a heavy hand on my shoulder. "Glad to have you back. We weren't sure how you'd handle everything."

"It's a lot to take in," I admitted, Ghultar's terrible face flashing to mind. "I don't know, it hurts my head to think of it. I feel more drained than anything else."

Elanil stood. "You haven't eaten since the party. Here, we made stew. You'll need strength for tonight."

The hairs on my neck stood on end. "What's happening tonight?"

Elanil collected three bowls from above the sink. "We'll talk after you've eaten." She poured stew from a boiling pot into each and dropped them on the table.

The smell was too much to resist. I shoveled the stew into my mouth. It was creamy and tasted of rosemary and garlic. The others took their time with dinner, not as eager to discuss what was happening in Belbury.

"Well?" I asked, tired of waiting.

Duke burped. "Exactly."

I looked to Elanil. "Huh?"

Elanil placed her spoon down. "She means the water well in the village square. You know, the one we found you at on your first day?"

I nodded but didn't understand what that had to do with bone-crushing monsters.

"It's no ordinary well," Elanil continued. "At least, water is not the only thing which comes from it. There is a gateway to our home world inside. A door of sorts—"

"Portal," Duke said. "Heard some people call it a portal."

The corners of my mouth curled up as I waited for the punchline.

Only silence followed.

"Huh?" I asked again, leaning forward.

Duke picked up her bowl. "Tell her from the start." Then she licked it clean.

Elanil chewed the side of her mouth for a moment, and then, after a sigh, began. "Elves and dwarves are not from Earth, obviously. Our world is Hemoertha. Similar to Earth, so we've been told, only with magic and enemies humans cannot understand."

"Like Ghultar?" I asked, stomach knotting.

"Yep," Duke said, wiping her chin. "And worse."

"Much worse," Elanil said. She leaned forward on her elbows. "Hundreds of years ago, elves and dwarves lived together in Celebar, a relatively new village—"

"Then one day, a mighty dwarf explorer discovered the portal to Earth," Duke said, puffing out her chest.

Elanil smiled and shook her head. "Funny story, actually—"

"No, it isn't," Duke said.

"The dwarf wasn't so much mighty as she was drunk. She stumbled into a geyser outside town and fell out of a water well in a small village called Belbury-on-the-Brook."

"Well, she was mighty drunk, at least," Duke said.

Elanil nodded. "And it was still a significant discovery. The dwarf made friends with the townsfolk and stayed a while, then returned to Celebar with news of her exploration. But the Celebarians had no reason to visit Belbury, so they continued living in Celebar, and human memory of the dwarf's visit turned to myth."

A dark look crossed Duke's face. "Then the aurocans came. A swarm of them large enough to shadow Celebar. They attacked the village, what, maybe seventy years ago now?"

"You've already fought them?" I asked, wide-eyed.

Elanil nodded. "And lost. Ghultar led them back then too. He's the rottenest aurocan to escape the War of Trinnifain. He started the bloodiest battle in Celebar's history, and many elves and dwarves died. Some escaped, though, and fled into the geyser."

"Belbury took us in," Duke said. "Housed us and fed us. George was one of them—"

"Pop was *alive* back then?"

"Yes," Elanil said. "A war hero, by all accounts. He'd seen enough death and fighting and petitioned the mayor to offer refuge. It was his idea to close off the rest of the world and prevent anyone learning of us."

"And we were safe here for a while," Duke said. "But then we started getting sick. Just the dwarves and elves, and it took a while to learn why. Many died of the sickness."

"What was it?" I asked.

Elanil smiled grimly. "Remember that thing you were talking to Duke about when we were walking to the abattoir—that ectrickity thing?"

"Electricity?" I asked.

"Yes!" Elanil said. "Elves and dwarves had a reaction to it. The humans couldn't find a cure, so they shut down their electricity farms, or whatever they were called, and went without, all to keep us alive."

My mind muddled as I thought on everything that was told. It was too much to take in. I stood and walked to a window and peered into the afternoon sky. "So, what happens next?"

"We fight," Duke said.

I spun. "You're bonkers! There must be hundreds of them. Let's go to the prime minister. He can send armies to wipe them out."

Duke shook her head. "You're not the bluntest hammer in the forge, are you? Didn't you hear the mayor last night? No one can enter or leave Belbury. Magical barriers block the border."

"And besides," Elanil said, "Ghultar's gathering the villagers in the church. All we need to do is free them so they can help fight."

"Is that all?" I asked as I slumped back in the chair.

Duke squeezed my forearm. "First, we need weapons."

"And seeing as George's cottage is on the edge of town, that's the safest place to find them," Elanil added.

My gut twisted. They wanted to stroll back into the swarm? To risk being caught by those monsters? One crunch of Ghultar's hand would squeeze my head off my shoulders like toothpaste.

But Pop was in there, and they could hurt him. A fire lit in my stomach, burning away the fear. I had to help the old man, monsters or not.

"What's the plan?"

CHAPTER 32

- CHALIA -

The sun fell behind Belbury's western hills and set fire to clouds that hung like ripe fruit over the village. Elanil, Duke, and I lay beneath a low-hanging branch of a fir tree at the lookout and surveyed the village below. It was quiet; no explosions, no lightning, no villagers. Gone were children rushing home before last light, and in their place were aurocans buzzing above cottages and countryside in search of anyone left uncaught.

"There's three in each patrol," I said as I adjusted my position behind a mossy log, massaging the pain from my elbows.

Elanil scribbled in her notepad. "You're sure?"

I nodded, watching an elf struggle against the monster's hold as it dragged her into the church. "This patrol only caught one, though."

"Must have most of us rounded up by now," Duke said.

My stomach twisted. "You sure this is the best idea?" I asked for the third time. "All it takes is one of them to spot us, and they'll be on us like fleas on a dog."

A breeze whistled through the hilltop forest, sending branches clawing at the sky.

"Or lice on a dwarf," Elanil said.

Duke sighed. "It's dangerous, that's for sure, but there's not really much else for it."

I scanned the skies. Of all the people I could face this trouble with, I was glad it was Elanil and Duke. Not only because they knew magic that could blast the head off an aurocan—or so I hoped—but because even in the gloom, they held a brightness to them that lightened the shadows.

We tracked patrol movements until most of the light was leeched from the sky. A knife of pain was stabbing my lower back when Elanil pointed east of town, to the forest beyond the abattoir. I squinted in the dark.

"That's the best place to cross," she said. "The brook is wider but shallower, and not as many patrols fly that route."

Duke nodded. "And even if they do spot us, the forest on the far side is too thick for them to break the canopy. From there it's an easy stroll to George's."

"Nothing in this village is easy," I said.

Elanil closed her notepad. "You most of all." She regained her feet, dusted off her shirt, then froze.

"What's wrong?" I asked, then followed her shaking finger. A hundred or so aurocans filed out of the town hall to gather in the village square around the water well. I shifted in the dirt to get a better look. "What's happening?"

Elanil threw herself to the ground as the air thrummed to life. It grew to a roar and smashed through my chest, and then the sky filled with aurocans returning from their patrols. They circled the town hall and dropped to the cobbles as one. Most sauntered into the hall, though those with captives carried them to the church. The aurocans who previously vacated the hall took flight in patrols of three and starburst in all directions.

"They're nesting in the town hall!" Elanil said, scribbling furiously in her notepad.

I clutched at her arm. "And they change patrols at the same time! There could be periods where no aurocans are in the sky at all!"

Elanil nodded and smiled. "My little strategist."

I shrugged. "Life in Barden is a game of strategy—if you're not two moves ahead, your four moves behind."

We waited until the buzzing died down, then made our way inside the White Tree. Duke stir-fried some vegetables, and we ate our last supper in silence. It tasted of Belbury, fresh and wholesome, and sent me to thinking of my time in the village. If someone told me two weeks earlier, I'd be risking my neck to save a church full of adults—and a mayor, no less—I'd have called them a nutter. But back then, I hadn't known Mrs. Zinvyre or Stanthrop and Darna. I hadn't met Glenn and Torrock and Maisy and Moira.

My heart pickled. *I hadn't known Pop, not really.* I'd grown to love the old bugger, and felt I'd known him my whole life. I dropped my spoon into the empty bowl and stood, muscles tensed and ready for action. "Let's do this."

We reached the highway on the eastern side of the village in good time, but from there, we moved carefully. We used a leapfrog method to navigate our way to Banquet Road. It was painfully slow but meant that none of us was in the same place at the same time. If one was caught, at least two could escape.

Despite the cool night air, sweat dripped from my brow when

we arrived at the abattoir. It was more from terror than exhaustion. The entire journey I imagined aurocans dropping from the clouds to snap my neck to splinters, laughing in their ghoulish voices as they did so.

We rested in place for a few minutes, then with a wipe of my brow, continued into the forest beyond Banquet Road, the brook gurgling to our right. We were silent, tense, ready to run at a second's notice. Twice patrols buzzed overhead, obstructed from view by the forest canopy. Both times we froze, breaths held and praying for luck.

Both times the aurocans continued on their route.

Eventually the brook widened and swirled around smooth rocks.

"This is it," Elanil whispered, stepping out from cover just enough to scan the sky.

"I'll go first," I said, wanting to get it over with. I moved to the shore.

"The stones are slick with moss," Duke warned. "Be careful."

I nodded and stepped into the water. Coldness chewed at my calves, but the brook never climbed higher than mid-thigh. I slid a few times on the slippery rocks but made it across and hurried under the cover of branches.

Elanil and Duke followed without incident, then we trudged into the forest, shivering from the chill. Trees huddled together in gangs, their nasty roots tripping us while they grasped our clothes with clawed branches. Eventually we made our way through the thicket and stumbled across a narrow path wending west.

It was nearing ten o'clock when the pear tree in Pop's front garden came into view. I was covered in scratches, exhausted, and so overwhelmed with relief that I almost cried. The cottage was more than a creaky old home—it was a sanctuary, a place I could feel safe again.

We entered through the front door and were thrilled to find embers burning beneath a layer of ash in the hearth. With numb fingers, I placed a few small pieces of morning pine onto them and waited until they crackled to life. The warmth sent prickles up my icy limbs but eventually dried the cold from my bones, giving me a dose of energy.

I changed into a fresh pair of jeans and gave a pair to Elanil, but Duke refused.

"Pants? Me? Not ruddy likely!"

"Freeze then," I said, dropping the jeans onto the armchair. "I'm going to get the axe. There's cured meats and cheese in the pantry if you're hungry."

I paused at the back door. What if there was an aurocan on the other side, waiting with fingers outstretched? It took a moment to find courage again. I had to be strong, for Pop's sake. I pushed open the door and stepped outside.

A rustle at the back fence made me jump. Then clucking sounded, and I berated myself for being a chicken.

"Hoo-loo, my girls," I said when I reached the chicken cage. They walked to the fence to greet me. I filled a scoop of feed and tossed it to them. Then as an afterthought, I tossed two more. Who knew when I'd be back? "Keep laying breakfast," I said before walking to the chopping block. The axe was heavy and reassuring, and I was glad I had some practice with it. I also picked up the smaller hatchet and made my way back inside, wishing Pop owned a gun or two.

I found Duke chewing the end of a salami stick by the fire, while Elanil browsed Pop's bookcase.

"We found these," Duke said through a mouthful of food. She dropped the salami and held up four of the largest kitchen knives and cleavers Pop owned. Her eyes widened when she saw the axes, and a bit of salami fell from her mouth. "Ohhh! Give me one of those!"

"Take your pick," I said. With her broad shoulders, she would put them to better use than me. I looked to Elanil. "Going to paper-cut your way into church?"

"Hmm," she said as she returned a book. "Unless you have a better idea?"

I sat in front of the fire. "I do, actually." I'd been thinking on it the whole journey from the White Tree. I accepted the cheese Duke offered. "The villagers are being held in the church, right? But how many aurocans are there? Most are on patrol or sleeping. What if the church aurocans weren't there at all? We could sneak in and free everyone."

Duke shoved cheese into her mouth. "But they *are* there."

"For the time being. We can lure them away."

The fire popped, and sparks floated up the chimney on hot air. Duke looked to Elanil.

Elanil chewed her bottom lip. "Who will do that?"

"The lucky one," I said. "It's the safest part of the plan. The two who sneak *into* the church are in the most danger."

Duke waved her salami stick at me. "For a lass, you've got the biggest bollocks I've ever seen."

CHAPTER 33

- CHALIA -

I placed another log on the dying coals and sat with my back to the wall beside the hearth, massaging my temples. The fire's glow removed shadow and fear from the room, letting us feel safer while we went over our plan. Again. We'd gone over it so many times my mind was deader than a stray cat on Second Street in peak-hour traffic.

We were to step off after midnight when the aurocan patrols were most tired. Duke and her booming voice would be decoy while Elanil and I slipped into the church to free the villagers. I'd rather have high tea with Pickering and Newlin than tiptoe into that death-trap, but for once, it wasn't about what I wanted; it was what others needed. Adults, no less. I had purpose, and that fire burned hot.

"Not much of a plan," Elanil sighed, collapsing in the chair. "We should flesh it out more."

"Takes the fun out of winging it," Duke said. She yawned, loud enough for the neighbors to hear.

I glanced at my watch. "We have a while before we leave. Get some rest, Duke. We can't have you falling asleep out there."

"Don't need nothing but a chance of knocking in an aurocan head," Duke said, but she curled on the armchair and pulled my duvet up to her chin. She closed her eyes.

Elanil sat on the floor beside me, and I followed her gaze into the flames. The fire had a chaotic rhythm. It was beautiful, despite destroying the log it danced on. It might have been how tired I was, but I found it profound that the fire had to kill to survive.

"You did well today," Elanil said, startling me from my trance. "After, well, you know . . ." She mimed buzzing wings and then pointed to her stretched ears. "Everything."

I shook my head. "I fainted and had to be lugged up the hill by someone half my height," I said, rubbing the back of my neck.

"At least you didn't piss your boots."

"How do you know?" I winked and almost fell asleep. I shook off the exhaustion. "I need to pack before I rest."

"I can help—"

"No, get some sleep. I'll be fine."

I took my bag to the kitchen and stuffed it with anything that may prove useful. A cleaver, meat tenderizer, tin of Walkers shortbread biscuits, and some dried fruit and nuts. I pursed my lips. Was it enough? How long would we be on the run for? It wouldn't be easy to return to the cottage a second time. *If we survived.* I added some cured meats and a loaf of bread and zipped the bag closed.

That's when I spotted it—the envelope Mom asked me to give to Pop. It was open on the table, the letter unfolded beside it. My throat tightened. What I would give to hug Mom one more time. To apologize for everything I'd done, all the fights, all the trouble. I needed to hear her voice, even through a letter, to feel her strength.

I sat in the chair and lit a candle on the table with the cigarette lighter from my bag.

Dear Poppy,

The only way to begin is by saying how my love for you grows stronger every day we're kept apart. It aches me to think it's been so long since I've seen your smiling face or heard your loving voice. For that, I shall never forgive Arthur his laws, and when I see him, I will deliver him some lip service.

I've read your last letter a hundred times, and every time brings more tears to my eyes. I haven't cried like this since Alastair left, though those were a different type of tears altogether. I'm amazed—and more than a tad suspicious—that you convinced the Founders to change their minds about my eviction. I've little doubt swaying Arthur's stubbornness required a great deal of persistence and even more magic. However you did it, thank you. I cannot wait to come home!

You're going to love Chalia—she has grown so much since you saw her. She has your strength, Alastair's compassion, and my rebellious attitude. You'll have your hands full, mark me, but I'm positive you'll enjoy every moment. Please be patient with her, as she has been dealt a rough hand lately and may take a while before she opens up. She has trust issues, especially with anyone she deems an adult, and that fault is my own. I never told her why Alastair left—she wouldn't understand—and I fear she blames me for his departure. Her grief is on my mind before I sleep and after I wake, and hurts more than I care to write, because I believe she may be correct. I hope by escaping this toxic city I'll be able to show Chalia how much I love her. How much she means to me. How special she is.

Please, take good care of her until I arrive—she is my everything. And be careful—she will surprise you in more ways than one!

I love you always,
Valerie

P.S.: Don't let Chalia taste Mrs. Moira's pies and puddings. You'll have a lot to answer for if I arrive to find a daughter bloated from dessert.

I finished reading and stared at the page. Many words were blotched, the ink having run as though it was left in the rain. I wiped my eyes on the back of my hand and gently folded the letter and fitted it into the envelope.

How could Mom think I blamed her for Dad leaving, when the entire time I thought she blamed me? I'd been a terrible kid growing up, and she deserved better. She deserved Pop. I pressed the envelope to my lips. I would make things right, no matter what it took. All we needed was to survive the next few hours, and then Mom would have the life she earned.

I placed the envelope in my bag, blew out the candle, and breathed in deeply to stop my hands from shaking. Forcing a smile, I walked back into the snug, where Duke snored on the chair and Elanil lay curled by the fire. I sat beside her.

"What's happening?" she murmured as she opened bleary eyes and stretched. Then, seeing my face, she sat and placed a hand on my knee. "Chalia, is everything okay?"

"Yeah," I said. "Just thinking of Mom."

She squeezed me leg. "Want to talk about it—"

"No," I cut her off. Then, gentler, "Not yet."

The fire crackled.

"I'm here when you're ready."

We watched the flames in silence. Elanil's hand was still on my knee, its touch causing tingles to roll up my thigh and settle in my stomach. After a moment I found it was hotter than usual by the hearth, and breathing became difficult. Eventually, Elanil turned back to me, her eyes somber. "Duke said George told you about your parents. That's why you didn't kiss me, right? Because I'm a red-ear and you didn't want to ruin the chance of your mom coming home?"

I nodded and tried to answer, but my throat burned.

"I'm sorry for acting so rubbish about it. I . . . I've been hurt before. Lads, right? Who needs them?"

"It's okay," I said, fidgeting with my jacket hem. "I'd be upset too if I'd been rejected by someone as stunning as me." I gave my short hair a flick, and Elanil giggled.

"You wear modesty well."

"Where does modesty get you?" I said with a shrug. I looked into her eyes. "I thought you were going to throttle me. You know, back by the brook."

"Thought about it," Elanil admitted. Then she threw a couple jabs at my arm. "You would have been a sorry mess then."

I caught her hands. "I've seen flea turds bigger than your fists. Wouldn't have taken two seconds to lay you low."

She struggled, but I was stronger. I clamped her arms to her side and forced her onto her back, pinning her beneath my weight.

I froze, suddenly aware of how close we were.

Of the press of her chest against mine.

Of her gentle breath on my lips.

Her back arched, and I trembled.

I couldn't fight my feelings for her any longer. I *had* to kiss her. But . . . what if she no longer felt the same? What if this ended as it had in the abattoir?

Her legs snaked around mine and pulled me into her, trapping me. I grew weak.

"I'm an elf," she whispered, her lips brushing mine. "Can you handle that?"

I breathed in, tasting her words. Her heart pounded against my breast in time with my own.

"I'm sure I'll manage," I said, and kissed her.

She parted her lips just enough to wrap them around mine, her tongue finding its way into my mouth. Tremors raced through me, making my body shake. I grabbed the nape of her neck and pulled her into me, desperate to be one. She untangled her legs, and her knees fell away, and passion took me on a flight of sensation I'd never experienced.

Elves and dwarves were a foggy memory.

Aurocans a myth.

Magic an illusion.

For the first time in years, anger did not control me, but by something far stronger: love.

Time stopped long before we did, though when we finally collapsed in sweaty heaps, the fire was embers once more.

I brushed my fringe from my face and rolled to face Elanil, wrapping my leg in hers. Her perfect amber eyes found mine, flecks of gold blazing. How could someone be so perfect?

"What are you thinking?" she asked softly, tracing my bullring with a finger.

I closed my eyes, enjoying the feeling. "Why we didn't do this in the beginning."

Elanil's fingers stopped. "Who says we aren't?"

And I fell for her even more.

CHAPTER 34

- CHALIA -

I turned my wrist to see my watch again, eyes stinging with fatigue. One fifteen in the morning, and I hadn't slept a wink.

Elanil nuzzled deeper into my arms, and I stroked her hair. How could I sleep when I finally had her? When my mind wouldn't shove off with stupid ideas for the future, like me staying in Belbury just to be with her? I watched her sleep a while longer before I kissed her forehead and untangled myself.

I stumbled into the kitchen and spooned tea leaves into the kettle before returning to the snug and setting it over the coals. Within minutes it simmered, and I couldn't put off waking the others any longer. They groaned as I shook them and opened bloodshot eyes. They hadn't slept all day like I had, and it showed. They accepted the tea and drank in grim silence.

Duke finished first and placed the mug down. "Needed that," she said, stretching.

"I added some peppermint," I said, thinking of all the times she'd farted in her sleep. "It's good for upset stomachs."

Duke looked to Elanil. "Butt-burping again?"

"*Me?*" Elanil said, spilling tea. "You almost set the couch on fire!"

Duke leaned forward. "Really?" she asked. "Rating—"

"Ten," Elanil answered without hesitation.

Duke fell back into the chair and beamed. "You've never given me a ten before; tonight ain't so bad after all."

I squeezed Elanil's thigh. It had been, without a doubt, the best night of my life. "It's perfect."

Elanil blushed.

Duke rolled her eyes. "Way to ruin a special moment." She climbed out of the chair and slung the axe over her shoulder. She looked ridiculous in her tan dress, like a lumberjack in drag. "Come on, these aurocans aren't going to chop their own heads off."

My hand froze on Elanil's leg. "Right," I said, my lungs icing over. Ghultar's nasty face burned its way into my mind, and my breath caught in my throat, almost like he was already squeezing it. I grabbed my bag and the hatchet and walked to the door.

"Ready?" I asked, gripping the frigid handle.

The others gathered behind me and nodded, Duke with a smile, and Elanil biting her bottom lip.

I braced myself and opened the door. The buzzing was still there, though off in the distance. I waited a few heartbeats to make sure there were no lingering patrols and then stepped outside. The first step was the hardest, my body battling every move, begging to just run back into the snug. But I needed to do this. For Pop and Mom.

I passed the pear tree, and walking grew easier. I couldn't give in to fear, not when so much was at stake. I squared my shoulders.

"Silly humans finally come out to play," a scratching voice sneered from behind.

My stomach dropped.

I whirled, hoisting the hatchet, and caught sight of shadows moving on the roof.

"Get back inside!" Elanil screamed, grabbing my hand and yanking me toward the cottage.

An ear-piercing hum filled the air; filled my mind. Two of the creatures struck from the sky like black lightning, snatching Duke and Elanil in a rear hug, lifting them from the ground, pulling Elanil's hand from mine.

Duke thrashed and snorted like a bull in a teahouse but was no match for the monster. The aurocan threw back its head and laughed, sounding like a screeching axle. "Oh, you want to play?" It shook her like a rag doll, her legs flapping back and forth.

Someone screamed.

Elanil!

Blood streamed down her face from a nose bending to one side. She beat at the aurocan's arms, but it held her tight. "Run!" she screamed, then the aurocan yanked her head to the side.

I growled as a vein pulsed in my neck. I would chop its rotten head off! I lifted the hatchet over my head and sprinted at the foul beast. I wanted its blood.

A force crashed into me from the side, blasting the breath from my lungs and knocking the hatchet from my grip. Agony tore through my ribs, and I yelped as the aurocan carried me into the air as though I were a pack of crisps.

"*Elanil!*" I screamed as I battered the beast holding me.

I needed to save her.

I failed Kingsley. I failed Mom. Please don't let me fail Elanil.

The aurocan tightened its grip, squeezing me like a stress ball.

"Look at this one flopping like a fish," it shouted to the others. "Wonder if it tastes as good."

"Wouldn't be eating it if I were you," the aurocan holding Duke said as it leapt into the air beside us. "Their stupid could be contagious. Lighting a fire—really?"

I froze. The fire—that's how they found us. I lit it. Elanil and Duke would be killed because I was too thick to think about the chimney's smoke.

No. I *wouldn't* let any harm come to them. All the anger I'd stored over my life exploded in a violent force. I kicked and elbowed, screamed and scratched. I threw my head back, and it connected with the monster's nose. It crumpled with a satisfying crack, and the beast's grip weakened.

I began to slip.

If I could get to the ground, I could reach the hatchet—

A stonelike fist crunched into my temple. Bright lights burst into existence. Then, numbness. The night grew dark. The last thing I saw was Elanil screaming from the ground.

Then I was lost.

CHAPTER 35

- CHALIA -

Agony.

A white-hot knife of it sliced at my brain with the skill of an alcoholic surgeon on payday. I ground my teeth, stifling a scream, and squeezed my eyes tighter together.

It would go away if I ignored it.

Please let it go away.

Focus on something else. The bed. It was hard and unfamiliar. A coffin? No, that was ridiculous. I was too young to curl up my toes. What then?

A voice boomed above me, echoing, each syllable feeding the surgeon another shot of tequila.

That voice! I knew it. But from where?

My breathing quickened. I couldn't take it anymore. I opened my eyes and found a blurry reality. I was on my back, staring at a high, vaulted ceiling. The candles in the candelabrum did little to combat the shadows of night.

Where *was* I?

Willing life to my limbs, I sat with a grunt, head swooning.

Slowly, like fog blowing away from a window, my vision cleared, and then all at once everything came rushing back.

I gasped and shuffled back on the altar table until one of my hands slipped off. I was in the church! The pews were crammed with villagers, each row so full that many were forced to sit on the floor. Coils of rope bound the strongest villagers and the red-ears. Most, if not all, were caked with enough blood to make a black pudding baker excited.

Aurocans were stationed around the walls. They fidgeted and muttered and looked like they would rather be anywhere else. More than one was battle haggard.

"'Bout time," a voice said from beside the altar. I leaned over and found Duke grinning up at me through a fattened lip. Elanil, slumped on her shoulder, looked like they had thrown her in a dryer filled with bricks. Her nose was bent to one side, pointing to a black and swollen eye. Her hair was matted with blood and her clothing torn. She winced as she looked up at me.

"Ela," I gasped, voice shaking. *It was all happening again.* Kingsley's bloodstained footpath crashed into my mind. Why couldn't I save anyone I loved? I reached for Elanil, but a shadow fell over me, and I froze.

"Don't worry about them," Ghultar said, his left eye quivering as though it had been soaked in a double espresso and couldn't decide which way to look. "They aren't nearly as bad as the soldiers who caught them. One of them suffered frostbite, of all things."

Duke shimmied forward on her backside. "Give me another crack, and I'll freeze his balls to snowflakes."

A grin twisted to life on Ghultar's hard lips. He crouched in front of Duke so his face was close to hers. "I wonder how loud you will be with no teeth in that enormous mouth of yours." He yanked her head to the side.

I leapt at the beast without thinking twice. *"Leave her alone!"*

Ghultar caught me in midair by the throat and slammed me back onto the stone altar. A thousand candles exploded in my vision. He pressed down, hand crushing my windpipe. "Or what?"

I gasped for breath, clawing at his steel-like fingers. He was going to snap my neck like he did the aurocan in the cemetery.

The church dimmed.

Ghultar snorted, and his head twitched to one side, where it shuddered. He released me and stepped back, forcing a smile, fangs gleaming in the candlelight. He opened his arms. "Let's not resort to violence if we can help it. Agree? My name is Ghultar. I'm the leader of this swarm of ruffians. Unlike them, I hold a civil tongue, and can see the big picture. How about you, girl? Can you see the big picture?"

I raised a hand to my neck and tried to swallow. A lump was lodged halfway down. "Yes," I gasped. I would do anything to stop him from hurting my friends.

"Good," he said, and with a bounce, leapt onto his backside on the altar beside me. "You are in a fortunate situation, girl, as you alone have the power to save them." He nodded to Elanil and Duke. "It is quite easy, I assure you. All I need is information—"

"Don't tell him anything, Chalia!" someone shouted from the crowd. Pop stood in the front row, hands tied together, and blood staining his shirt. Despite this, his back was straight, and he held a glare in his eyes that spoke of trouble. "Give them hell, lassie, for all of us."

My heart leapt. He was alive!

"Hear, hear!" the villagers chorused, their chant echoing though the hall.

"Silence!" Ghultar roared. He motioned to the closest aurocan. The beast leapt forward and backhanded Pop, sending him crashing onto the laps of the people behind him.

I jumped from the table "Pop!"

Ghultar grabbed the collar of my bomber jacket and spun me to face him. He raised his other hand to his temple and massaged it, closing his eyes. "Why won't you people stop whining?" he said in a low voice that carried in the church. "We didn't kill you all—you should be grateful! Instead, you cry like babies and give me a headache." He breathed deeply, held, and after a moment, exhaled. He opened his eyes. "Chalia, is it?" he asked, dropping his hands. "I have tried the friendly way. I find I am running out of options, and you are running out of time. You have answers to give, or they—" he nodded to the villagers, "will give their arms. If they survive, and your tongue hasn't waggled, then they will give their legs too. And so on and so forth until they are nothing but teeth and bones. The old fool will be first."

The villagers gasped, but Pop jutted his jaw, blood streaming from his nose, and glared at Ghultar as though he would like nothing else but for the monster to try to rip his limbs off.

"What answers?" I asked.

"Where are the others hiding?" Ghultar said, crossing his legs and leaning toward me.

I raised my eyebrows. "What others?"

A growl rumbled in Ghultar's throat. "Don't. Play. Dumb.

Where are your little friends with their little bows, little hammers, and little magic?"

At a loss for what he was on about, I looked to Duke, who shrugged. The monster had lost the plot. "Everyone I know is here," I said. Ghultar's growl deepened. "But we don't have hammers or bows."

Ghultar slammed a fist onto the altar, making it vibrate beneath me. "No more games! No more! Your friends have slaughtered many of my swarm, and I want to know where they are hiding!"

"My friends are here—"

"I'm warning you," Ghultar snarled, poking a cruel finger into my chest. "I'll tear your tongue out if you use it to tell one more lie!"

Instead of shaking with fear, which any smart person would do, I clenched my fists and glared at him. He was just another one of *them*. Another Pickering. Another Newlin. Another Arthur. Another *bully*. I'd put up with them my whole life. No more! I was done with his games. "I. Don't. Have. Any. Friends—"

"Wrong answer!" Ghultar leaned forward, grabbed Duke by her hair, and hoisted her from the ground. She tried to wriggle free, but he clamped his monstrous hand around her jaw and squeezed. Duke's eyes widened, and she fell limp. "Tell me the truth or tell her goodbye."

"No, wait!" I needed more time. "Please, let her go. Take me."

"Wrong answer!" With a snap of his arm, he pelted Duke from the altar like she was a rugby ball. She sailed through the air and crashed to the floor in the aisle with a sickening thud. She slid along the stones some distance before coming to a stop in a tangle.

"Duke!" I cried, struggling to reach her, but Ghultar had me in his grasp again. No one could survive that beating. Not even Duke.

Elanil scrambled around Ghultar's feet and hurried to Duke in a lopsided crawl.

Ghultar shook his head and sighed. "This isn't going anywhere. What we need is to shed some light on your situation." He looked to a guard and nodded to the candelabrum above the lectern. The guard fetched it. Ghultar, head twitching again, brought it between us. "Last chance, Chalia—tell me where the others are hiding, or I'll burn the sight from your eyes."

My heart froze. He wouldn't do it. Surely he wouldn't. The flames moved closer until they filled my vision. Dancing. Burning. Eating.

One touched my cheek, and I flinched. I tried to answer, but my throat was ash. I pulled away, but Ghultar yanked me back.

And then an idea grew in my mind. *The candles!*

"Okay, okay—" I said, my mind racing. "I'll tell you! But please don't hurt us!"

Ghultar lowered the candelabrum and leaned in, his eyes flashing. "That, my dear, is up to you. Do not poke a sleeping snarzi and expect not to get bit."

"Don't . . . tell him nothing," a voice growled from the aisle. Duke was standing there, arm wrapped around Elanil for support. She winced but still looked a powerful figure of defiance.

She was okay! The two of them, they could do it. *They could win.* Once I caused the distraction, they could flee and make a new plan. A plan to exterminate the whole damned swarm!

I looked to Ghultar, my chest swelling with hope. He didn't know what kind of hell Elanil and Duke would unleash on him.

His beady eyes narrowed, but they no longer chilled me. I knew my role to play, and it would likely see me killed. *Hold tight, Kingsley. We'll be causing a ruckus up there in no time.*

"I need my bag," I said. "That's where the map is."

"We searched your bag," Ghultar snapped, raising the candles closer. "There is no map."

"There is, but it's hidden. We couldn't risk it falling into the wrong hands."

Ghultar scowled. There was silence for a few heartbeats, then he spoke, "For your friends' sake, there had better be." He clicked his fingers, and an aurocan rushed forward with my bag. Ghultar held it to me but didn't let go. "We removed those knives, if that's what you're hoping for."

"No," I said, forcing my voice to tremble. If the plan was to work, he needed to buy into the idea that I was terrified. I took the bag and set it between us. Using both hands, I dug through the contents, moving clothing and food aside. *Please*, let them still be in there. Please! What would I do if they had been removed?

My fingers knocked against hard cylinders. I gripped them, and they were cold in my hands. Reassuring. This was it, my time to light up the world with my brilliance. I looked one last time to Elanil. So beautiful. So perfect. In an ideal world, we would have more time together, but my life had never exactly been ideal. Until a week ago.

I moved my head closer to the bag and peered in. "I need light."

Ghultar raised the candelabrum above the bag, leaning in as well. The flames danced between us, longing to be set free.

I snatched two cans of black spray-paint from the bag and squeezed the nozzles. Mist rushed out, catching the candles' flames and erupting into two blistering tongues of fire. I turned them on Ghultar's face.

Ghultar howled, dropped the candelabrum, and tried to escape, but I wrapped my legs around his waist, forcing him to carry me with him. The stink of burnt flesh filled the air. I clung tighter, a barnacle to a keel. It was game over if I let go.

"Run!" I screamed to Duke and Elanil. My legs ached—I couldn't hold on for long.

Ghultar's howl turned rabid, and he lashed out. His elbow caught me in the chest, knocking me to the altar. He loomed over me, clawing at his face, which came away in charred strips.

It'd worked! I was a hero!

No, I realized. I was trapped in a church full of monsters who wanted to kill me. I was screwed.

CHAPTER 36

- CHALIA -

Ghultar howled in rage and pain and lashed out with his clawed foot, smashing the altar beside me to send debris firing through the church.

I rolled from the table, bag in hand, and leaped down the stairs to the nave. Duke and Elanil raced ahead, aiming for the double doors.

The church erupted into shouts and cries. The aurocans lining the church walls sprang into action, racing between the pews on their backward-bending legs to cut off our escape.

We would not make it! I looked around, desperate for another exit, but my heart sank. There were too many monsters.

"For Belbury!" Pop yelled, loud and defiant. I turned just as he tackled an aurocan rushing past him to take me down. The pair fell in a tangle, and nearby villagers leapt on top.

The church descended into chaos as the villagers sprang to our aid, tripping and kicking and punching the passing monsters. Skirmishes sprang up left and right, but our path was clear. We had seconds at most.

The door was just there.

I dared to hope.

Bowing my head, I strained my legs, urging my body to greater speeds. The church was a blur. Screams of pain followed my every step, but I couldn't stop—I'd be no good to anyone if I was dead.

We were so close.

A humming shadow fell from the ceiling and swooped toward Duke and Elanil from behind.

They were going to be caught.

Not on my watch!

I launched at the aurocan, colliding with it in midair. We crashed to the ground, bowling over Elanil and Duke.

I punched the aurocan's rock-hard face with everything I had. Pain shot up my arm, but I couldn't stop—I needed to buy Elanil and Duke time.

The aurocan didn't retaliate. I punched again, but it lay dead still. For an absurd moment, I thought I knocked it unconscious. Then I noticed an arrow shaft sticking from its head. I stared at it, confused, before the chaos of the church brought me back to my senses. I leapt to my feet and tailed Duke out of the church into fresh air.

We threw the doors closed, and I leaned my back against them. I strained with all my might as something collided into them from inside.

"Hold it!" Duke cried, dropping to her knees. She thrust her hands forward, and a blizzard whistled from her palms. The doors fused together as ice filled the seam. She built layer upon layer until the doors looked like they'd grown from an iceberg.

"Quick!" I said, helping her to her feet. "The aurocans in the town hall would've heard." I was halfway down the steps when my stomach twisted and I stopped.

Something was wrong.

"Where's Ela?" I asked, turning back to the door with wide eyes.

Duke's face fell. "I thought she was with you."

I gasped. "She's still inside!" I turned and sprinted back up the stairs, taking them three at a time. I rushed past Duke and kicked at the thick layer of ice, trying to break it free. "Elanil!"

The doors shuddered as a force slammed into them from inside. Shards of ice broke free.

Duke grabbed my arm. "There ain't no time—"

"I'm not leaving her!" I pushed Duke off and clawed at the door, tearing a fingernail free.

More ice shattered under impact.

"We can't be saving her if we're caught!" Duke said.

I pounded the bottom of the doors with my foot and fists. The ice was thinning.

"Damned fool," Duke cursed.

Something hard slammed into my chin and I crumpled to the ground as though someone had removed my bones.

Duke stood over me, fist clenched.

Then, once again, the darkness consumed me.

* * *

A crack of thunder split the pitter-patter of rain. I groaned, the movement sending a spasm of pain jabbing at my jaw.

My eyes flicked open. How did I get back to the White Tree?

The stained mattress was soft beneath me, which I was grateful for, because my body was living agony. Had I gone five rounds with Conor McGregor?

I sat, mind swooning, and rested my head on my knees, wrapping my arms around my legs. The party, I remembered that. The argument with the mayor. Then Pop's cottage. And . . . and that kiss. I would never forget that kiss.

The image of an altar flashed through my mind. *The church!*

Like a freight train on greased tracks, everything came racing back in stark clarity. The smell of Ghultar's sizzling face. The aurocan snatching at Elanil and Duke as we tried to flee. The arrow that killed it.

And the door. Latched beneath a lock of ice, sealing the aurocans inside. And—

"Elanil," I moaned, pulling chunks of my hair. I abandoned her, sacrificed her to the monsters, just as I had Kingsley. I rocked back and forth.

Cancer. That's all I was. Once people let me in, I killed them.

My jaw spasmed again; I thought of Duke, and my veins lit with anger. I hadn't left Elanil. *Duke* had knocked me out!

I turned from the hearth and spotted the dwarf sitting in front of a window, looking into the stormy sky.

"You," I croaked, standing on shaky feet. Duke flinched but didn't reply—didn't look at me. "You abandoned her!" I stumbled and bumped into the table. "Left her with those things."

Still, Duke was silent.

I ground my jaw, ignoring the pain. She *would* answer me. She needed to tell me why. I grabbed her shoulder and forced her around. "You . . ."

Duke's face was hidden beneath a bloated layer of black

bruising. A tar-coated marshmallow. Blood crusted her skin, and the white of her right eye was a sickly red around the iris. Rivers of tears flowed over the mountains of her cheeks.

"I know," she whispered, shuddering. She turned back to the window. "I can't help but know. They were all there, Chalia. Me mom and dad, me family and friends." She thumped her legs with her fists. "Everyone I know is stuck in that church w-w-with them termites. Don't talk to me about what I have done like I don't already know it." She broke down, burying her face in her arms, her shoulders heaving.

My anger fell away and was replaced with shame. Duke, the sturdy icon of our group, had broken. She sobbed and spluttered, and my heart went to her. It hadn't occurred to me she locked more than Elanil in the church.

I wrapped an arm around her shoulder and pulled her head to my chest. "Hush. I'm sorry, I didn't mean that. I'm so sorry."

"I-it's my fault if they die," she sobbed. "I'll never forgive myself."

"It's not, and don't you dare believe it," I said, stroking her curly hair. "I'm the one to blame. If I didn't light the fire, they never would've found us."

Cancer. That was my calling card. Everyone I loved grew ill from me and left, one way or another.

Dad.

Kingsley.

Pop.

Elanil.

I couldn't take it anymore. No one would ever leave me again. *I would make sure of it.*

How long we stayed like that, Duke's head to my chest, lost in mourning, I didn't know. I needed her as much as she needed me. The storm raged outside, wind and rain pelting the tree, and though it was only midday, the brooding clouds made it seem night was approaching.

Long after my legs grew numb, I broke apart from Duke and left her by the window. We needed food, and I needed to be doing something, anything, to distract myself from the terrible thoughts boiling in my head. I climbed the branches, fighting for footing through the gale, and scampered through the gardens until I had an armful of vegetables. By the time I returned, I was wet and muddy, but my mind was the clearest it had been in a long time. I knew what I had to do, and that brought with it a calm resignation.

I cut the vegetables into chunks—carrots, broccoli, and beans—then divided them into two bowls. We didn't speak as we ate the raw food, both prisoners of our own minds, but the whistling wind sang us a haunting melody. Once finished, I collected the scraps and threw them in the hearth, washed the bowls and stacked them. Duke watched without saying a word. I looked around the trunk to ensure I had forgotten nothing and shouldered my bag.

"Look after yourself," I said, my voice out of place in the silence.

Duke blinked. "Huh?" She stood, favoring one leg. "Where are you going?"

"To set things right."

"I'm coming with you—"

"You're not." My throat stung.

Duke's lip trembled. "Chalia . . . if this is about the door—"

"Elanil is caught because of me, not you. I have to save her."

"You'll die!"

"Yes."

CHAPTER 37

- CHALIA -

Duke placed her hands on her hips. "Your brains are mashed to boar crap if you think I'll let you go out there by yourself!"

I walked to the door. "Look after yourself, Duke."

"Like hell!" She hobbled to block my path. "You're a daftie if you think I'll sit here while you kill yourself."

I stepped around her, but Duke caught my jacket and threw me against the wall. "What's wrong with you?" Her nostrils flared. She pulled me away and slammed me back again. "You'll die for nothing!"

"It's not for nothing!" I screamed, shoving her off. "Elanil is down there! Pop! Moira! Mrs. Zinvyre! And it's my fault. It's always my fault. I—I'm toxic, and the sooner you realize it, the safer you'll be."

"How is getting your melon squeezed from your shoulders going to save them?" She shook her head and pursed her lips. "No. I don't believe it—you'll not go down there."

"Why?"

"Because you're not a fool."

I laughed. "No, I'm not a fool, I'm just fed up." I turned and rested my forehead against the door. "I'm tired, Duke. Tired of it all—of everyone leaving me. Dad left. Kingsley left. Pop and Elanil. Do you know what it's like to have no one?" My voice cracked. "If I die saving them, well, it's all for the best. They'll likely live long and happy lives without me in the picture." Bitterness burst on my tongue as tears streamed into my mouth.

Thunder cracked overhead and echoed through the forest. A moment later, the door rocked on its hinges as gusts of wind buffeted it.

Duke stepped to my side and wrapped her arms around my waist. "Bah, you're a thick one, aren't you?" she said gently. "We're not going anywhere. Not me, not Elanil, not Pop. You're stuck with us, whether you like it or lump it."

I tried to swallow but choked instead and made a sound like a frog. I fell into Duke's touch, my defenses crumbling. I was paralyzed, mentally and physically.

Duke led me to the dining table and lowered me into a chair. "We'll get through this; you have me word. But let's do it together. None of this Terry Tough-arm business, okay?"

I sniffled and nodded. "But we need to act—"

"There're things what need saying before we do anything," Duke said, sitting in a chair and clasping my hands. "Especially before we march into church and sing Ghultar a hymn he ain't like to forget. It's gonna be a hard listen, so I'll make some tea to soften me words."

She filled the pot from the fire, grabbed two mugs from the sink and some tea leaves and returned to the table. She held the pot by its handle and placed her other hand under it. With a click of her fingers, she ignited a flame in her palm and had the water boiling in seconds.

"Could've done that at lunch," I muttered, rubbing my neck. Had I really broken down like that? What was happening to me? It was like Belbury had sapped the grit from my bones and replaced it with . . . with tissues and tears.

"And ruin a good carrot with a heat?" Duke asked, crushing leaves and adding water and sugar to the mugs. She slid one along the table to me and sipped her own. After a moment, she placed it down and fixed me with a hard stare. "Want to know what I think?"

I tensed. No. I'd felt enough for one day. I just wanted to be moving, to be doing anything.

"You're a victim of your own making," Duke said, not waiting for an answer. "You create reasons to avoid people. You think they don't love you. You think you'll hurt them. You think they'll pick on you because of your age. Who did you say he was? The police officer in Barden? You said he was always up your ass—"

"He was!"

"You destroyed the mayor's wagon! If that doesn't deserve a hard time, I don't know what does. And I can only imagine what other hell you've given him. And Belbury's mayor—"

"Is a pencil-lipped pillock—"

"He locked the borders to stop aurocans from destroying the rest of the country. He didn't do it to inconvenience you, he did it to save lives."

I ground my jaw so tightly I was on the cusp of crumbling teeth. It was fine and dandy when she said it like that, but after meeting

Arthur, I knew he was a bell end of the highest degree. I leaned forward. "And my dad? What justification have you for him?"

Duke sighed and stared at her hands with a sad shake of her head. "Shouldn't be me what tells you this, Chalia. Should be your mom or George."

I fixed her with a stare. "Mom is locked out, and George is locked in. What is it?"

Duke hesitated, then placed her palms on the table. "Alastair was sick—he didn't leave because he didn't love you. He left because he was dying."

A flash of lightning lit the dark room. I didn't look away from Duke; I couldn't. She was lying, making it up to make me feel better. Dad was a jerk; I'd known it since I was seven. He abandoned Mom and me, that was that.

"No," I said, rejecting Duke's story.

Duke frowned. "Remember the etricity illness?"

It took me a moment to understand what she was trying to say. "Electricity?"

Duke nodded. "When your parents were evicted from Belbury, they moved to the city where there was no shortage of it. Alastair battled as long as he could, but in the end the sickness had him, and he knew it. He was allowed back in Belbury for his death."

I watched her lips move, but it made little sense. The illness only affected elves and dwarves. She must be mistaken—

Then, with a slashing guilt, I remembered. On our way to Darna and Stanthrop's party, Pop told me Mom fell for the charm of a red-ear.

An elf.

I raised my hands to my ears and ran fingers across their tops.

No—I would have known. I fell back in time to when I was seven. Dad suggested we move to the country, that fresh air would do us good. I threw a tantrum and refused to go—I didn't want to leave Kingsley. I stormed out, and Dad died. Would he be alive if we had left? Had I killed Dad? I dropped my hands and kneaded my legs.

Duke grabbed my hands and brought them to the table, squeezing the movement from them. "They buried him in front of the church. I will show you after this is over."

I nodded and fought back tears. I'd cried enough for one day. If I got through the next, then perhaps I would allow myself to feel again. I nodded. "Thanks."

"That's what I'm here for."

I took a sip of tea and listened to the rain. "Guess we should come up with a plan—"

The door shuddered as someone—or something—hammered on it, the sound resounding around the small room.

I whirled to face it, gooseflesh prickling my skin. For one dim moment I allowed myself to hope it was Elanil. "Expecting company?"

"No one knows about this tree," Duke said, though she need not have spoken. Her wide, panicked eyes spoke more than words ever could.

I lowered my mug and picked up the pot of boiling water. "Reckon you can do that fire trick again?"

CHAPTER 38

- CHALIA -

Boom boom boom!

The door shuddered, pounded with a force that sent it rattling in the jamb. The cadence was too rhythmic, too purposeful to be the wind. Someone wanted to get in, and Duke and I weren't exactly prime candidates for a tea party. Whoever it was, they weren't expecting a scone and conversation.

I stood, the chair's legs scraping the floor, and looked to Duke. "Well, we wanted a fight, right?"

Duke closed her mouth and smiled grimly. "Here's to hoping it's Ghultar what's come a'knocking."

The stench of Ghultar's burning flesh returned to me as his howl of pain echoed in my mind. I needed to finish it, to finish him. The sooner, the better.

I nodded to Duke, and we crept to the door. The handle vibrated under my fingers as I gripped it, ready to accept my fate.

"Ready?" I whispered.

Duke smiled and flicked her hands, creating two balls of fire in her palms.

I raised the pot of boiling water and swung the door open, then brought the pot bearing down—

Thomas Princeton saw the pot coming and dodged, barely getting out of the way.

"Not the worst welcome I've had," he muttered. He straightened, glared at Duke and me, then barged past. Water streamed from his clothes, leaving puddles where he stepped.

"Thomas!" Duke cried, extinguishing her hands. "Of all the creatures who could've knocked on my door, you're damned near the ugliest."

"Good to see you too," Thomas said, not looking at her as he unstrung his bow and removed his quiver. He winced as he wiped water from his heavily scratched face, opening up some unhealed wounds.

The rest of his gang followed in a tight file, all of them looking half-drowned and exhausted.

"What happened to you?" I asked, noting his gang were just as bloody.

Thomas grunted but did not respond. Instead, he turned to Duke and raised his eyes at her bruised face. "Head-butting rams again?" he asked, collapsing into a chair.

"Not since last week," Duke said, collecting the pot. "This time it was an aurocan's fist." She squeezed into the kitchen, where she filled the pot with water again.

Thomas's gang shook out of their coats by the hearth. There weren't enough seats for them, so they lingered awkwardly. Two elves, one dwarf, and four humans. They looked as though they just completed an obstacle course buried in a swamp. Their faces were caked with grime, spots of blood seeping through, and their clothes were more tatters than cloth. After a moment they collapsed to the ground, where those with bows redistributed the remaining arrows in silence.

The quiet was too loud for comfort. Why hadn't they been captured? Why were they so bloody? I needed to say something. My eyes rested on the elves. "You don't need those," I said, indicating their earmuffs. "I know what you are."

A gasp rose from the group, sounding like steam from a kettle. Arrows from a quiver clattered to the ground, and everyone looked to each other, shocked. For a moment, no one spoke. Then—

"You *told* her?" Thomas said, jumping to his feet and jabbing a finger at Duke. He wore a look of someone who learned someone had farted on his scone.

Duke placed the pot on the table. "Yep," she said, unfazed. She crumpled tea leaves into mugs.

"Once my great-grandfather finds out—"

"Let's hope he finds out," I said, stepping toward Thomas and squaring up. He'd only been there a minute, and already I was disappointed it wasn't Ghultar at the door. "Because that means we have saved them . . . that—that Pop and Elanil are free."

Thomas clenched his fists. It was apparent he was not used to being spoken to that way. For a moment, I thought he was thick enough to have a crack at me.

Then, to my surprise, his face lost its edge. "I'm sorry about Elanil. I thought we saved her too."

Duke looked up. "Huh?"

Thomas closed his eyes, looking like someone had fed him a syringe of instant exhaustion. "At the church before, when you were escaping. I thought we got her free too."

"You were in the church?" I asked. I hadn't spotted him anywhere.

Thomas shook his head. "No. Well, not exactly. I guess I should start at the beginning. We were camped in the forest when *they* came. Miles of trees and streams and hills did nothing to dull the bell, or the chill that came with it. We had, of course, prepared for such a moment—the woodland is littered with our food and weapon caches. But that first night . . . when the forest turned still, and the air iced over . . . I—I . . ." He interlaced his fingers, stopping them from tapping on the table.

"That night, we crept into town," Thomas continued after a moment. "And what we saw . . . Bekka, it was terrible. We knew charging into the fight wouldn't help anyone; They would swarm us in seconds. But we are not cowards. We do not sit and hide, not while our families are prisoners, do we, squad?"

"Wey aye!" the gang chorused, thumping the floor with palms and fists. Though they were beaten and battered, their eyes were sharp and hungry.

"We turned to guerrilla tactics, taking down a patrol at a time. We fill them with arrows and burn them with magic and then disappear into the forest. The trees shielded us from aerial attacks, and the aurocans quickly learned not to follow on foot. Not in our domain.

"Anyway, last night, Mary was on lookout piquet at the edge of the forest, near George's cottage." He nodded to a human lass on the floor. "She saw what happened to you and raced back to tell me. I knew it was going to be a risk, but we had to try to save you if we could. The more people we have in our gang, the stronger we will be."

"Wait a minute!" Duke said, slapping the table. "You're who Ghultar was talking about! He wanted us to snitch on you."

Thomas raised his eyebrows and looked to his gang. "Hear that, squad? We're getting to him!" His friends sat straighter.

"Gave me this shiner for not ratting you out," Duke said, pointing to the whole of her head. "Told him to get nicked, I did. He wasn't much a fan of that."

Thomas chuckled. "No doubt you did more damage to his fist than he did to your skull. All that head-butting animals came in handy, I guess."

I narrowed my eyes at Thomas, remembering the aurocan with an arrow in its head. "That aurocan in the church, that was you?"

Thomas nodded. "I am quite the shot."

"You could've killed me."

"But did I?"

I crossed my arms. "Well, no—"

Thomas leaned back in the chair. "You can thank me later."

That smug, crap-eating grin; I wanted to knock it off his face. I was about to say something undoubtedly scathing and witty, when Duke pushed a mug of tea in front of me.

"Sorry, but we're going to have to share," she said as she dished out the other mugs. "We don't normally have guests."

Everyone thanked her and sipped the tea.

Thomas gave his mug to one elf. "So, this is where you and Elanil escape to every weekend?" he asked Duke. "Decent job. If I hadn't followed you when you carried *her* up here, I wouldn't have found it."

Duke pointed a finger at him. "Keep your mitts off; this is our tree."

Thomas placed a hand on his heart. "I'd never dream of taking this from you. Well, at least not while we're at war. Speaking of which—" he raised his voice and looked to his gang, "How about it? Should we add Bekka to the squad as an honorary member?"

The group cheered and thumped their hands on their thighs in applause.

"Excellent," Thomas said. "Consider yourself—"

"And Chalia," Duke said.

Thomas raised an eyebrow. "You can't be serious."

"If Chalia isn't good enough, then neither am I—"

Thomas opened his mouth to argue, but I got in first.

"Never mind," I said, gripping Duke's arm. "I don't need no gang." Though I sounded convincing, my chest prickled with a twitch I'd developed from growing up in a city where appearance counted for more than personality, and the clothes you wore said more about you than your actions ever could. Me, in my too-small Metallica shirt, earned little in the way of inclusion, and it was a truth I'd lived with my whole life.

My face must have betrayed my pain, because when Thomas spoke again, it was in a consoling tone. "It's nothing to do with you personally. You might even be all right, if you're anything like George. It's just . . . you look like you don't know to sharp end of an arrow from the nock—"

"Thomas!" one of the human girls chastised from the floor. "Leave her be! How can it hurt if she joins?"

"How can it hurt?" Thomas scoffed. "We can't beat *them* if we are too busy babysitting. She doesn't know magic or weapons, so is only a liability."

Duke's lips pulled into a faint grin. "Two things—" she said, raising two fingers. "First, Chalia knows weapons. It was her who burned the smirk off Ghultar's face, not Thomas Princeton." She lowered one finger. "Second—"

"Hold on," Thomas interrupted, leaning toward me. "You burnt Ghultar?"

I picked at one of my nails. "A little—"

"A lot," Duke corrected. "She had canned fire."

Thomas laughed. Then seeing we weren't joining him, stopped. "Really? You're not having me on? Canned fire . . . I've never heard of such a thing."

"Well, you were never exactly top of the class, were you?" Duke asked, and Thomas reddened. "Anyway, second thing: Chalia *is* magic, she just doesn't know how to use it."

It was my turn to smile. I loved Duke for lying; it was something Kingsley would've done, but I couldn't pull off that ruse.

"Her dad's an elf," Duke continued. "So, she has magic fighting to escape her pores, mark me."

I blinked. "Huh?" There must be a mistake. I certainly wasn't magic.

But . . . Dad *was* an elf, Pop said so himself. And if Dad had magic, did that mean . . . could that mean . . . ?

Thomas cleared his throat. "Well, what use is she if she doesn't know how to use it? Might as well have none, for all it counts."

Duke dropped her mug to the table. "You're a stubborn git, Princeton." She stood and addressed the others. "Let's put it to a vote, then. Those who want to see Chalia burn aurocan flesh to ash, raise your hand."

There was a moment of stillness where even the pounding rain let up. Then, the dwarf raised his hand straight in the air, eyes fixed on Thomas. The elf beside him did likewise, then one by one, the squad—excluding Thomas—lifted their arms.

Duke clapped me on the back, a broad smile in place. "Welcome to the squad."

Warmth filled my chest and overflowed into my stomach. I'd never been accepted into a crew—not like that. I stared at my palms, not sure what to say. When I looked up, the entire gang were smiling, their eyes crinkling. I smiled back. "Thank you."

It was time to fight. Time to kill. Time to free the village I'd come to love. Deep down, I knew Ghultar and I would not both be alive at the end. One would fall, and odds were in his favor. I needed a strategy, to think four steps ahead. Without it, I may as well write my eulogy now.

I was never much of a writer.

CHAPTER 39

- GEORGE -

Ghultar roved between the church pews with the sobriety of a widow walking among graves. Slow. Somber. His burnt face was reddened with angry, seeping blisters that stank of decay, and a bloodied cloth covered one of his eyes.

"I wanted things to be different," Ghultar said as he clasped his hands behind his back. "I truly did. I don't enjoy killing. I'm not a monster, but I will do everything in my power to save my swarm, my family. They will *always* come first, but that doesn't mean others have to die. We can work together. Why can't you see that?"

George watched the beast pass from the corner of his swollen eye. When Ghultar was beyond sight, he twisted his arms in the ropes binding him, trying to loosen them enough to break free. The fibers carved into his wrists and turned red as blood seeped into the rope.

"Hush, George," Maria, the elderly woman to his right, whispered. "They will see you again."

George did not stop. "All I need is one more chance," he said through gritted teeth. "I'll get him. *I must.*" He'd seen men like

Ghultar in the war. Twisted men who lived for blood and were competent enough to draw it. The monster would not hesitate to kill them all once he was done playing.

George couldn't allow that.

He did not fear death; he had lived longer than most. He had loved, had children, grandchildren, and great-grandchildren. He called many people friends and seen many sunrises.

No, he was not scared for his own death, but the safety of the women and children beside him lit a fire in his lungs. He feared for Chalia, the lass who stormed into his life like a tornado. For Valerie, stranded in the dangers of Barden, alone.

Maria shook her head. "I doubt you have any chances left."

"Don't place your tips yet, Maria dear. I'm far from through . . ." George's voice trailed off as Ghultar's footfalls stopped halfway down the aisle.

"My captains argued I had lost my mind when I told them you would cooperate," Ghultar said. "That your tongues would not be so rusty. They challenged my authority, but *I* won out. For the time being." He took three steps. "They grow restless, and soon my orders will fall on ears deaf from discontent. In their eyes, gratitude dictates you help us with knowledge of this world and the magic at the border—"

"Gratitude?" someone shouted from the back of the church. "For what, destroying our homes?"

Ghultar's footsteps stopped once more, and he chuckled. "Gallant dwarf, we have fed and watered you, allowed you to keep your life and limb—for the most part—and beat you little more than you deserved. Yes, gratitude is the correct word, yet you reward *me* with *silence!*" He spun and strode toward the altar. He reached the first pew and looked down on George, his one eye quivering in its socket.

George glared at the beast, his heart thumping, pulsing blood boiled with hatred through his veins. *If only the ropes weren't so tight!*

Maria placed her hands on George's thigh. "Do not run your race early," she whispered.

Ghultar knelt in front of George but still towered over him. "You are old—that is a compliment. Aurocans only live until our bodies cannot defend us. You can see clearly? Milk hasn't colored your sight?"

"I see just fine," George said, trying not to breathe the stench of rot.

"Words I'll never say again, not when one of my eyes was boiled from my skull." His voice softened to a deadly whisper. "You helped save the girl who did this to me. You led the attack, allowing that half-pint to escape. You betrayed the trust I placed in you. You will die first."

George narrowed his eyes and smiled. "We will see."

Ghultar's face twisted in fury. "*We will see?*" he snorted, then straightened, his hands forming fists. He cocked his arm, glowering at George like an enraged bull. His eye twitched in its socket. Left, right, up, down. Maria shook beside George.

Then Ghultar's breathing calmed, and he stepped back. A soft chuckle escaped his lips. "Oh, you're good," Ghultar said. "Yes, you are good. I am better. Your death will not come easy." He spun and walked up the steps to the altar and faced the prisoners. "Dawn tomorrow will be the beginning of this man's death. Do not mourn him yet, for we will draw it out for several days. Perhaps in a week you can start your tears."

A gasp rose from the villagers, and for the first time in many years, George's stomach churned from fear for his own life. His hands were clammy when Maria grabbed them in hers. They shook together.

"When he eventually accepts death, a new villager will take his place. Perhaps a dwarf, just to distribute the fun. This will continue until we capture the cretin who dared to burn a king. If she has any compassion, your screams will draw her out of hiding and the killing will stop. If not, we will paint your village red with blood."

CHAPTER 40

- CHALIA -

Wind and rain cut through the fourth branch garden in biting sheets as Duke and I cowered in the mud beneath tomato trusses, looking over Belbury.

"This is rubbish!" I shouted over the howl. Mud squelched up my backside as rain lashed my face like pellets from an air gun. "We should be attacking the church, not waiting here to be caught like fish in a puddle!"

A fork of lightning raced over Belbury skies, illuminating the entire branch. I didn't truly think we would get caught, not in that weather, but damn it—we'd been on piquet for hours already, and I needed to get started.

Duke looked to me over her shoulder. She was lying in the mud, using the rosemary bush as cover, taking her role of sentry seriously. "You saw how knackered the gang is. Unless you plan to march sleepwalkers into town, you best let them rest."

I pulled my jacket tighter around me. "We could at least wait inside."

Duke shook her head and turned back to Belbury. "Nah,

Thomas is right. We need lookouts. If the aurocans catch us off guard, then we're done in like last year's mutton."

I hugged myself and rubbed my arms. "If you're gagging for Thomas so much, why don't you just go shag him. Might get us out of this damn rain."

Duke snorted, and with a wet sucking sound, pulled free of the mud and sat. "Thomas?" she said, scooping mud from her tan dress. "You're a nutter. I'd rather take Arthur."

For a moment I forgot the cold and giggled. "You'd probably kill him."

"A piglet humping his leg would probably kill him. I'd kill him *and* his ghost."

We both laughed and huddled closer.

Duke scanned Belbury one more time. "I don't know, maybe you're right. Ain't seen much action tonight and don't think we're like to see any soon. Reckon you might be up to learn a bit of magic?"

I choked. "Hell yes I am!" Magic? That was some heavy Harry Potter stuff, and it was happening to me? I leaned forward. "How do I make fire?"

Duke chuckled and shook her head. "Jumping straight in the deep end? It's no simple task, you might not be able to—"

"Please," I begged. "I need this." Burning Ghultar with fire had . . . I don't know, it had made me powerful, like we were fighting on a leveled playing field. He had his size and strength; I had my charm and flame fingers. "And when we're done, you can call me Hot-Hands Chalia."

"Not convincing me with that."

"The Ember-Emitting Emissary?"

"Nope," Duke said. Then she sighed. "But I guess we'd better start somewhere. We can work on your name later."

And so began my first lesson in what Duke called elemental affinity. It was slow and complicated—nowhere near as simple as Duke made it look. By the end of the hour, my brain was a knot in the middle of a tug-of-war rope. All I had accomplished was mildly steaming hands and a raging headache.

I'd bet my bottom dollar I was a Hufflepuff. Too dim to even spell *magic*, let alone use it.

Or worse . . . what if I wasn't magic at all? What if I was a squib?

No, I couldn't let it beat me. I needed this, for everyone's sake.

"Show me one more time," I pressed.

"I'm not a bucket of pitch—I can't burn all night," Duke panted, her shoulders drooping.

"Bugger it," I said, slapping the muddy water around me. "It doesn't make sense. I'm doing exactly what you said."

"It sort of worked before," Duke said in a placating tone. She closed her eyes for a moment.

"Sort of worked? It was a wisp, Duke. A wisp thinner than a fart."

"You need to feel the energy—"

"Don't feed me that. I've been feeling the energy the whole damn time, and it feels very similar to exhaustion and a migraine."

"That's because you're not listening with your body!"

And so it went. Time and again I'd raise a hand, close my eyes, and try to *feel* the world around me. I'd suck in all the sounds and smells and absorb them with everything I had, but in the end, all I had to show for it was a mouth full of rain and a hyper-oxygenated body.

"It's useless," I said, hunching over, more steam rising from my head than my hands. "I'm done with this magic BS—"

"Good to see you are taking our lives seriously with your piquet responsibilities," someone said behind us.

I jolted and turned to find Thomas looking down his nose at us, wind whipping his hair around his face.

"Might as well have put a sack of potatoes up here to keep watch," he said.

Duke shrugged. "Waste of potatoes; everyone knows pumpkins are the real observers. Anyway, there's nothing going on. Figured teaching Chalia elemental affinity would serve us better."

"Whatever. I actually thought you would be asleep," Thomas said, and I resisted the urge to shove him from the branch. "Come on, we have a plan and want to tell you your parts."

The gang were seated in a circle in front of the cold fireplace, sketches of Belbury strewn before them in a mess.

I shrugged off my wet jacket and joined them, savoring their body heat.

"We've been monitoring the aurocans' movements since they arrived," Thomas said, showing a piece of paper that had different colored lines star-bursting from the center of the village. "And the good news is they don't deviate from their routes. This means we can strategically lay ambush to patrols as we please, with our withdrawals already plotted out." He laid a finger on the map, east of the abattoir, where a red and yellow line crossed. "These two patrols are our targets. The plan is simple—hit them both as they intersect, and withdraw into the Southern Forest. Taking out two patrols at once is a risk, but if we plan the ground right—and you follow my orders—then it will be a glorious victory."

I pulled the map closer and inspected it. "That's a bad idea."

The room fell silent.

"Oh?" Thomas said, glaring at me. "Do go on."

"You want to take down six aurocans tonight?"

He rolled his eyes. "Yes. How are you confused already? City education must not be worth its salt after all."

"I *am* confused," I admitted. "I'm confused that this rubbish plan is the best you could come up with."

Duke snorted, but everyone else gasped.

Thomas flushed. "If you don't like it, don't come—"

"There are *hundreds* of aurocans in Belbury," I continued, speaking to the rest of the gang. "We will never win by taking them out at patrol level. It would take years, and Ghultar won't tolerate that."

There was a mutter of agreement, but Thomas silenced everyone with a look. "And what would Chalia do? Attack the entire swarm? You're welcome to it. For the rest of us who don't mind living, let's get back to the plan—"

"Let her speak," the dwarf said, nodding to me. "Better to weigh up all options so we don't have any second thoughts later."

"Damn it, Wyn!" Thomas said. "I never have second thoughts— that's the luxury of having great first ones!"

The lass beside me spoke. "I'm with Wyn and Chalia. If we continue with this ambush pattern, soon they will catch on, and we will be the ones getting ambushed."

Thomas's jaw clamped so tight it would take several cans of WD-40 to loosen it. He looked around the circle. Each member of the gang nodded their agreement.

"Fine," Thomas said, throwing his hands in the air. "Let's entertain this fantasy. What do you propose, Chalia?"

All eyes turned to me, and my mouth dried under their gaze. Wyn smiled comfortingly, and the lass beside me gave my knee a squeeze. I nodded my thanks. "We need a decisive strike, one large enough to finish them. One last attack to win the war."

Everyone continued to stare at me for a moment, but when it became clear I'd said everything I meant to say, they shifted uncomfortably.

"I think you have the right of it," Wyn said. "We need to finish them once and for all. But . . . what's your plan?"

My mind raced. That was as all the plan I had. My shirt tightened around my throat. I looked down to the map to avoid watching Thomas's growing sneer.

Then I spotted it. A dot on the map. *Everyone had a dot that belonged to them.* Aurocans were no different. I jabbed a finger to the paper. "Here."

And then everything fell into place. I formed a strategy based on what I'd learned over the last week in the village. It was wild, chaotic, and relied on no short amount of chance. But—and it was a big but—if we could pull it off, there was a likelihood the aurocans would be destroyed with little to no loss of our own lives.

So I hoped.

By midnight we had a three-phase operation to be conducted in two groups—Thomas and his gang in one, Duke and I in the other. After one last cup of tea to warm our bones and toast to our good fortune, we stepped into the torrential rain and began our slippery descent into Belbury-on-the-Brook.

Into the hornets' hive.

CHAPTER 41

- CHALIA -

"Grab that one!" Duke shouted over the rumble of the storm as she pointed to a wheelbarrow in a cottage garden. Her dress hugged her like cling wrap, and her hair whipped about her face in a frenzied dance. "I'll get me another and meet you at the mill."

I gave her a thumbs-up, and she scurried down the dark lane in the elf district, lost to the downpour before I finished my breath. Squinting, I searched the sky for movement, any shadows with claws. It was hopeless. Aurocans could've been right above me and I wouldn't be able to spot them.

I darted from under the juniper tree and leaped over the fence to the garden, where I found the wheelbarrow being used as a planter box. I emptied it and pushed it toward the gate. The wheel screeched like a tortured dolphin. I froze. The storm was loud. The wheel was louder. How good was aurocan hearing? I glanced back to the sky, more a nervous tic than from any hope of seeing anything.

Dark and stormy; no change.

Our plan didn't have spare minutes for me to stand still, gazing about like a numpty. I had to risk it. I pushed the barrow in a jog, out the gate and into the lane, pretending the squeal was in my head. Every hundred feet I paused beneath a tree, waiting with hairs on end for a beast to swoop in and carry me back to Ghultar. Back to my death.

Defying all odds, I made it to the mill without so much as a raspy *hoo-loo* from an aurocan. I hid the barrow and collapsed in the shadow of the great spinning wheel. That was the first part done, the easiest. I wedged my hands between my legs to stop them from shaking. There was still so much to go.

My mind wandered to Thomas and his crew. They turned east at the base of the hill while we turned west. Were they having similar luck as Duke and I? Or were they already being tortured as I sat in hiding? Our entire plan relied on them. If they failed, we failed. I shook my head—I couldn't think like that. They were fine. If anyone could get through the night, it was Thomas. The lad was a complete nob, but he was fearless, and that made all the difference.

Time wore on, and water pooled around my bottom. Where was Duke? She should have arrived not long after me. My stomach tossed like I'd swallowed a blender. I rubbed my eyes and searched the darkness.

Was that a shadow falling from the sky?

I froze, tense—

No. It was just a tree, branches whipping in the wind.

The harder I looked, the more movement I saw. Hulking silhouettes flitted between cottages and road. Giant beasts flew across the brook and charged from the water's edge. Twice I stood

to flee, certain they caught me. Both times a flash of lightning re-
vealed the truth; my mind was playing tricks on me, creating something out of nothing as though it was a sick joke. I wrapped my
arms around my knees and pulled them to my chest.

"Chalia?" a voice called from the side of the mill.

Duke!

I jumped to my feet and raced around the building. She
stood behind her wheelbarrow, wiping rain from her eyes on her
wet sleeve.

"Take longer next time!" I said, resisting the urge to hug her. I
was safe again.

"Damned patrol near got me," Duke said, smiling as though
someone had offered her a bowl of carrots.

I looked over her shoulder. "How did you escape?"

She chuckled. "Froze on the lawn. Them dolts must've thought
I was a garden gnome. Flew on by, they did."

How was she laughing? I was sick to my stomach. We still had
so much to do and so little time.

"Lighten up," she said, picking up the barrow handles. "We
ain't got time to take things seriously." She pushed her barrow
next to mine and walked to the edge of the brook. "Anyway,
you're going to need all that steam rising from your ears for the
next part." With that, she held her nose and leaped into the brook.

I stared after her for a moment. The water, disturbed by the
downpour, looked cold and miserable, and a cloak for all kinds of
nasty, biting things. I shivered. No, it's just a warm bath. That's
all. Relaxing. Soothing. And the worst thing to find in there was a
goldfish. I took a breath and stepped off the bank.

My breath froze in my lungs. If it was a bath, it was one on top

an iceberg. I trudged forward on cramped legs, wishing the stinging needles poking my shins would jog on.

At its deepest, the brook rose to my waist, but it neared Duke's
neck. She kicked into freestyle and reached the other side and
climbed out. I clambered after her, hugging myself, and stumbled
under an awning attached to a cottage. I massaged my arms, trying to get blood flowing again, but my cardiovascular system held
a grudge and refused to forgive me for the shock I put it through.

"Come on," Duke said, teeth chattering. "Not far to go."

Darna's resin store was two streets back from the brook on
the edge of a square. It was more a workshop than anything, with
small skiffs and timber boxes strewn across benches. I followed
Duke into the storeroom, where large tins of pine resin were piled
high against the far wall.

I grabbed two tins, and Duke grabbed four. They were heavier
than they looked, and my forearms burned by the time I dropped
them into a skiff attached to a jetty. Duke added hers and untied
the skiff.

I grabbed her arm. "This isn't enough."

"Bah, it'll do. Ain't no time for a second run—we're late already." She continued with the knot.

I didn't let go. "There's no second chance with this, Duke. We
need more."

"I know my resin, it'll work—"

"Please," I said. I couldn't risk everyone's life over a few tins.
"It won't take long."

Duke harrumphed and dropped the rope. "You're difficult
sometimes. Anyone told you that?" She charged back into the darkness, splashing in the streams cascading down the cobbled street.

I tried to keep pace, but she was already sprinting out of the shop with four more tins by the time I entered. She dropped her tins in the skiff and doubled back to help with my load.

"That's it," Duke said, untying the skiff, which was sitting dangerously low under the weight of twelve tins.

We climbed back into the water and pushed the skiff to the mill, careful not to capsize it, where we loaded the tins into our barrows, panting with effort.

"Just a few seconds," I wheezed. Duke, who was also breathing heavily, nodded.

What we were about to do was so incredibly stupid, so outrageously insane, that it made rolling in dog crap while singing "Rock 'n' Roll Star" seem the height of sophistication. If an aurocan saw us, our lives were done. Over. Squished. And seeing as we were about to prod the bees' hive, the chance of getting stung was almost guaranteed.

With a heavy breath, I gripped the barrow handles. "For Belbury," I said. For Pop and Mum and Elanil. For everyone.

"For Belbury," Duke echoed, no longer smiling. She had a hard look about her, staunch in the rain with shoulders back and chin up. I was glad to have her on my side.

We stepped off.

It was slow going. The rusty barrows were unwieldy, and we stopped every few cottages to make sure no patrols were about. My shoulders and back screamed for a break, but not once did I give in. There was no time.

We were almost at the highway when I heard it. At first, I thought it was a roll of thunder. But the roll didn't stop. It grew, louder and louder, until it reverberated through my chests, stopping my heart.

Then I saw.

A hundred shadows flooded into the heavens above the village square, spiraling upward like a torpedo. At its top, aurocans shot off in all directions.

"Hide!" I dropped my barrow, grabbed Duke, and pulled her beneath a chestnut tree just as three aurocans raced overhead. They were so low their ugly faces were visible. They were searching, hunting, and I held no illusions who their prey was. They continued to the west, having missed our wheelbarrows.

"That was close," I breathed a moment later, hand on heart.

Duke raced back to her barrow, ignoring me. "They've changed patrols—we're hell late!" She stepped off again, her short legs striding out.

I collected my barrow and followed. She was right. It was already three in the morning, and we hadn't even started painting. Sunrise was just around the corner.

Everything finished at sunrise.

Duke stopped at the intersection to see if the coast was clear, but I ran straight past her, tins bouncing in the tray. There was a time for caution and a time for stupidity. Caution had just packed it in for the night.

It was three fifteen by the time we wheeled our barrows into the front yard of a cottage overlooking the town hall. The square was silent; all the aurocans who had returned from their patrol were inside and hopefully asleep.

I parted the hedge we were hiding behind and looked to the hall. Two aurocans stood on the deck, stretching and chatting.

I gasped. "Thomas never said anything about sentries."

Duke looked through the hedge for a moment, then fell back. "Doesn't change our plan."

"Course it does! You need to get to the front doors—"

"Worry about that later. Right now, we need to waterproof the floor." She picked up her first tins and darted to the back of the building.

I shook my head and followed. Chihuahua with a lion's shadow. That shadow got people killed.

We stockpiled the tins under the hall and crawled in. The air, heavy, clogged my lungs and stank of rot and mold, like a decaying cat in a Barden park bathroom. There was just enough height for us to move on our hands and knees but not enough to stoop.

"Don't paint too close to the sentries," Duke whispered, leading the way, pushing two tins in front of her. "They might smell it."

Floorboards creaked above as hundreds of aurocans tossed in their sleep. My skin crawled as sheets of cobwebs stuck to my face like a woolen jumper. I tightened my lips. *Ignore it. Think of Mom, of her smile and smell and terrible macaroni and cheese.*

Think of making her happy again.

We reached the far side, and Duke popped my tin lid with a screwdriver. The pitch inside was black and rock hard.

"Need to be quick after I heat it," she said, giving the tin handle back to me and placing both hands on the base. "It sets quicker than a Sunday sun." She closed her eyes. "Hold still—if even a bit of flame touches the resin, we'll both go up in enough spark to put Talgodge's fireworks to shame."

And then her hands were on fire.

CHAPTER 42

- THOMAS -

A flash of lightning illuminated Charles Longston's vegetable garden. Corn stalks grew there. There were also bean sprouts, pumpkins, strawberries, and at that moment, Thomas's motley crew, not that any passers-by would have noticed, such was the gang's skill in camouflage.

Thomas scanned the sky again, his ears sharp. *Curse the atrocious weather*, he thought. It made spotting aurocans a near-impossible pursuit. After a moment, he sighed and gave Enyathil the hand signal to push across the road. She was the group scout, and none was better. Already she had saved the gang from two aurocan patrols with her prompt warnings, giving everyone just enough time to vanish like sleet on a warm day.

A small smile played across Thomas's face as he watched Enyathil slink across the road. *She would go far*, he thought. She obeyed orders, was competent, and was an all-round decent lass. And, if he was being honest with himself, quite something to look at. He had known her his whole life, but recently his feelings had grown to a new level. Often he thought about her, even when she wasn't about.

Even when he knew it was wrong.

He shook his head and refocused on the mission. The village needed him, and he would not fail them, even if it cost him his life.

A flame flickered in the darkness ahead. The path was safe. Thomas stood, gave the signal for everyone to move, and scampered across the road in a crouch.

The gang continued the stop-start fashion, wending east and south, until they emerged on Banquet Road, where they set a blistering pace and reached the abattoir before their allotted time.

Thomas circled a finger in the air, telling everyone to look out. He half drew his bowstring and climbed the stairs to the abattoir, his feet almost as silent as an elf's. A prickle raced down his neck, and his breathing quickened. *Please let there be an aurocan in there*, he thought. Just one he could take out. One he could fire his anger into. He pushed the door open.

The structure was dark and motionless.

Thomas hung his head and dropped his bow to his side. He would get his opportunity before dawn, he consoled himself. They all would. He leaned out the door and waved everyone up. They huddled around him in the middle of the floor.

"Chalia said the cart was beneath the back chutes," Thomas whispered, his voice just audible over the pounding rain on the tin roof. "Kate and Mary, I need you to run hoses from it to the blood vats and begin churning. Enyathil, find a capable beast in the pens and harness it. Wyn, Merain, Will, and I will search for the tarp and rope. Understood?" He looked to each of them, and they nodded. "Good. Let's be quick with this."

The gang dispersed without query, and Thomas followed in

the rear. They found some tarp and rope in a small shed outside. Between them, they secured it to the cart, making the tray waterproof. By the time they were done, Kate and Mary had finished running the hoses and were busy cranking the vats, mixing the blood and water together to dissolve the solids.

Thomas held two of the fat hoses in the tray, while Wyn grabbed the other. "Send it!" Thomas shouted. A moment later, the hoses writhed in his hands, and thick, crimson gravy gushed out. Thomas wrinkled his nose and turned his head to the side, the smell too sweet to handle. The hoses coughed on clumps of congealed blood, spluttering and spitting. The cart filled after a few minutes and began to overflow. "Cut it!" Thomas ordered as he tossed the hoses aside. "Where's the spare tarp?"

Will rushed forward, a coil of rope around his shoulder and tarp in his hands. They made a makeshift lid with the tarp and tied it down. It wasn't pretty, and they would lose a lot of blood by the time they arrived, but it had to do.

"We step off in two minutes," Thomas said. "Prepare your kit and form up around the cart in open file. Weapons ready, eyes sharp. Let's not get complacent."

After two minutes, Enyathil coaxed the harnessed steer forward, whispering in its ear with a hand placed on its shoulder. The steer, now timid as a mouse, followed her without complaint. The cart jumped along, sloshing its load from side to side.

Half a mile beyond the abattoir, the brook grew wide and shallow. Slick rocks breached the surface and churned the water into pools.

Thomas held his fist in the air, and the gang stopped beneath the cover of trees. Thirty yards, he judged, to the other side. Not

far, but with the cart they would be sitting ducks for an aurocan patrol. If they lost the blood, they lost the battle. They lost
the village. They lost their lives. He chewed his lip. He wanted
to hurry to the safety of the Southern Forest. It was right there.
But he needed to wait and watch to see if any enemy was about.
He sighed and gave the signal for everyone to face out for a short
break. He found a spot on the edge of the brook, concealed by
shrub, and drew his eyes to the sky again.

For a long while, the only sound was the rushing brook, pounding rain, and occasional clap of thunder. The steer, under Enyathil's
elf charm, was silent and calm.

Deeming enough time had passed and the route was as safe as
it was going to get, Thomas gave the order to bring it in.

"Enyathil and I will guide the cart across," he whispered.
"The rest of you stay undercover with arrows and spells ready.
Once we reach the other side and give the signal, join us one at a
time as quickly as you can. This is our choke point, team. Move
with purpose."

The gang nodded their understanding then spread out along
the water's edge.

Enyathil stepped in first, guiding the steer. Thomas followed,
slipping on rocks slick with moss. He grabbed the cart for stability,
his feet numb from cold. The cart bounced, sloshing more than a
few pints of blood over the sides.

They were halfway across when an uneasiness settled in
Thomas's stomach. He tightened his hold on his bow and looked
skyward. Goosebumps spread down his neck. What was it? Had
he seen something? He spun on the spot slowly.

"Enyathil," he said, "be ready—"

Black streaks dived at Thomas from above. He raised his bow, but there wasn't time to aim.

A golden missile crunched into the first aurocan's face, knocking it off course to crash into the brook at Thomas's feet.

Thomas dived to the side as the second aurocan landed in the stream right where he was standing. The beast drew back its fist, aiming at Thomas, but several arrows skewered its chest, sending it spinning to the water to float face down.

Thomas waved his bow left and right, frantically scanning for the third. *They always travel in threes.*

An aurocan crashed behind him and plucked him from the brook, using him as a shield against the gang's attacks.

"Drop your weapons or I'll chew his neck out!" the aurocan yelled, backing away to keep Enyathil in sight. His breath was rancid and his body rock hard.

The forest was silent.

"*Do it!*" the aurocan shouted, shaking Thomas like a doll.

Thomas grimaced, his ribs caving beneath the strength of the monster. "Drop your weapons," he wheezed, preferring to keep his neck. He couldn't see the gang from their hiding spots, but he knew they would listen.

The aurocan growled. Or was it a chuckle? "Not so dumb, are you?"

Thomas glanced at the two dead aurocans in the stream, one with its face caved in, the other with three arrows poking holes in him. "Compared to you?"

CHAPTER 43

- THOMAS -

The aurocan yanked Thomas's head to the side, exposing his neck. "You've a busy tongue for someone who just got caught," it said, its foul breath hot in Thomas's ear.

"It is a trademark of mine," Thomas said. He writhed in the beast's crushing grip and ended in a skewered position, like a boomerang, his head twisted one way, his shoulders the other, his left hand near his foot.

The aurocan snorted. "Want to know what else is a trademark of you squishy creatures?"

"No."

"Blood," the beast said, digging its claws into Thomas's skull. "Vines of it and ripe for the squeezing—"

Thomas kicked his leg up to bring the knife in his boot to hand. He yanked it free and plunged it into the aurocan's side. It scraped along the armorlike skin until it found a weakness in the groin. The aurocan howled and slackened its grip on Thomas.

Thomas fell free. Quicker than a coffee-infused fox, he jumped right back, twisting to face the aurocan, blade angled upward. It plunged into the beast's bottom jaw, snapping its head back with a sound of grinding cogs.

When Thomas landed in the brook once more, the aurocan remained standing, staring at him with inflated eyes. Then, like a tree felled, it crashed forward. Thomas dodged and watched as it twitched face down in the water.

"Quick," Thomas shouted, bending to wash his blade. "Get the cart moving!" He sheathed his knife and spotted his bow floating away downstream. He raced to retrieve it before helping the others.

They pushed forward into the dense forest, the canopy above so thick it blotted out the rain. Thomas didn't call for a halt until they were a few hundred yards in and concealed from eyes in the sky. He lifted the tarp on the cart and grimaced. They had lost almost half the blood. There might still be enough, but he didn't dare lose any more.

"Bring it in," Thomas called to the gang, who had assumed a circle of all-round defense. "The time for care and prudence is beyond us now," he said, speaking quickly. He turned to Kate. "I need you to get the blood to the Hermit's Fork and follow the southbound road for a few hundred yards. Allow us thirty minutes before dumping the package, then hide the cart well off track." Kate nodded, and Thomas looked to the others. "Enyathil and Merain, once we collect the parcel, make sure they behave. Drowse them with your elf voodoo, but not too much that they refuse to work when we need them. Wait for my fire orders before releasing. Got it?"

Enyathil and Merain nodded.

"This is it, team," Thomas said, his lips curling up. "Let's do it right and do it with a smile on our faces."

Wyn placed his hand in the center of the group. "Aye, seems like a right bit of fun."

"I don't think you understand what fun is," Enyathil said but placed her hand on top.

One by one, the group added their hands, leaving Thomas until last.

"Let's give them hell," Thomas said, and the group threw their hands in the air and cheered.

Then, ghosts in the night, they whispered through the woods to begin the most dangerous hours of their lives.

There was no movement in George's gardens, no life inside the dark windows. Thomas glanced over the cottage from forest's edge, then motioned Will forward.

"Scout the rear. We don't want to be walking into a trap."

Will nodded and faded into the brush to the left.

Thomas squinted against the rain. Duke, Elanil, and Chalia were caught in the front garden. If the aurocans' prehistoric brains had any spark in them, they would have a squad observing the cottage in case Duke and Chalia returned. He scanned the pear tree, the hedge and busy garden, then moved to the windows and ivy-covered walls, before finally searching the thatched roof—

There! Three spots of darkness against the gleaming straw. They were as rigid as frozen rocks and would have been easy to miss if he hadn't been careful. *Got you*, Thomas thought with a smile as he ran a finger over his nocked arrow.

Will returned a few minutes later. "Clear."

"Good." Thomas waved Mary in and nodded to the three shadows on the roof. "Will, you take left, Mary, right, I'll have center."

A few heartbeats later, three arrows whistled through the air.

Another two beats and three satisfying splats sounded as the aurocans hit the ground.

Thomas led the gang out of the forest and over the hedge to the barn in the back, a new arrow nocked.

"It's locked," Wyn said, pulling at the thick padlock connecting the two doors.

Thomas kicked at the base in frustration. "Obviously." He looked around for a bar to pry it open and caught sight of something glistening at his feet. He stooped to pick it up. A key.

Will chuckled. "If that isn't the luck of it all."

Thomas crammed the key into the lock. "Hold out on what you call luck until you see what the key reveals." He turned, and the lock clicked open. Wyn threw the doors wide.

An a capella group of whipped howler monkeys couldn't match the cacophony that erupted from the barn. Hisses and snorts, screams, yips, yaps, and flaps echoed from the darkness.

The gang raised their weapons, eyeing the barn with trepidation.

"Bloody hell," Wyn whispered, lifting his golden hammer higher. "What kind of twisted beasts has old Georgie-boy been playing with?"

"You—you sure Duke isn't having a laugh with us?" Mary stammered. "Probably thinks it funny to get us a little maimed. She grapples with boars, Thomas. Boars!"

Thomas shook his head. "If Duke wanted to hurt us, she'd do it herself. She said she heard the founders discussing this, and I believe her." He took a breath to calm his nerves and stepped into the chaos, praying he was right.

It took a few moments for his eyes to adjust to the gloom. Forms took shape, stables on both side walls and cages at the rear.

A growl came from his left, low and threatening, and Thomas knew he had found what he had come for.

"Enya, Merain, get the snarzis first," Thomas said, motioning to a large, steel-barred pen. He took a step closer to get a better look at the beasts. They loosely resembled black panthers, if you had been born with short sight, been spun around by your feet for half a day, and fed a gallon of Torrocks home-brewed ale. Snarzis stood on six muscled legs, each ending in claws capable of shaving metal easier than a potato peeler on custard. The crown of their heads reached Thomas's shoulders, and their fangs were longer than his hands. Perfect killing machines, if they knew who to kill.

Enyathil unlatched the gate and stepped in without hesitation. The seven beasts howled and strained against their chains, their collars digging into their thick necks. They pushed onto their rear legs, front claws whistling through the air as they swiped at Enyathil.

"Hoo-loo, lovelies," Enyathil cooed as she edged in, hands raised before her, palms forward. "Aren't you beautiful! Hungry though, right? Poor darlings haven't eaten in days." The snarzis strained harder, their chains taut to breaking point. Enyathil stopped just beyond reach. "We have dinner for you. All you have to do is come for a walk. Is that okay?" Her voice was gentle, but not a whisper. It was layered with more than tone; it had a magical weave in it, a calming presence, a suggestion of good will.

The beasts stopped growling, cocked their heads, and dropped to the ground. They sniffed the air. Their muzzles were no longer pulled back, but their hackles remained on end. Enyathil held her hand to the largest beast's nose, right above its razor-sharp fangs, and the snarzi's nostrils flared.

Thomas took several paces to the right to put himself in a position to loose an arrow at the creature if it made a move on Enya. He hadn't imagined the beasts would be anywhere near as big. A sneeze from one of them would be enough to take off Enyathil's arm. He opened his mouth to order her to pull out. The words were on his tongue, but he didn't release them. He had to trust Enya. For the entire village, he had to trust.

Enyathil held her hand there, waiting, until her arm shook and a bead of sweat found her neck. "Come on, girl. Let's do this together."

The rain pitter-pattered on the tin roof, an eerie tattoo in the barn. All animals grew quiet, and the smell of mold intensified.

The snarzi snorted and shook its head, sending cords of saliva flying through the pen. It thrust its nose forward and nuzzled Enyathil's hand, tail wagging.

Thomas released his breath and wiped sweat from his eyes. That was closer than he hoped.

"You had me worried for a while," Enyathil said. The snarzi licked her like a pup at play. She ran her fingers through the bristle-like fur on its back and moved to untie its chain from the beam. The other snarzis rubbed against her like domestic cats. Merain stepped into the pen to help free the rest.

"Well, this is us," Enyathil said a moment later once she joined the others, four chains in her hands. "Good luck and stay safe."

Thomas nodded. "Make sure you steer clear of the blood once you reach the fork. Take a long detour upwind."

Enyathil nodded, and then she and Merain departed, leaving Thomas, Mary, Wyn, and Will behind.

"Let's not dally, team," Thomas said, shoving his arrow in his quiver and shouldering the bow. "If we miss our marked patrols, we miss our opportunity." He opened the gworth pens on the right. Unlike the snarzis, gworths were beasts everyone in the village was familiar with. Their jaws ground slowly as they chewed cud with their eyes closed. He turned to Mary and Wyn. "Take the first two and wait until the opportune moment. Get their attention and get the hell out of there. Don't play hero and don't push your luck."

Mary and Wyn leaped onto their gworths, eliciting a groan from the sleepy beasts. "See you soon," Wyn said before nudging his gworth into motion and leading the race out of the barn, Mary hot on his heels.

Thomas clasped Will's shoulder. "Take two gworths and off-load one to Kate when you reach her."

Will nodded, then guided his gworths out of the barn, one tethered to a rope. He mounted and looked back to Thomas. "Same goes for you, Tom. No heroics. We need you in the forest."

"I'll see what I can do," Thomas said, shooing him away. He turned to the last gworth. "Just you and me, old girl. It's the farthest for us, so I hope you have some stamina." The gworth snorted, and Thomas smiled. "I will take that as a yes." He mounted and dug his heels in. The gworth flew out of her pen, skidded on the loose hay on the floor, and raced out of the barn into the drizzle. Thomas nudged her again and was almost thrown off by the speed. It was a smooth, bounding gait though, and Thomas soon found his seat as he galloped toward the bridge.

Toward the horde.

Minutes later, Thomas skidded to a halt in the cobbled square of the dwarven quarters. He craned his neck and scanned the weeping sky.

There was no movement.

He nocked an arrow, pulse racing. Where were they? It was that time of night they should be everywhere.

And then he heard a wasp.

He turned and spotted two patrols flying above the brook. He stretched his bow, thirsty for blood, but stayed his shot. He needed more than six. The more he killed now, the fewer there were to hurt the gang later. His eyes danced across the sky, seeking more . . .

And then he found them.

A swarm of aurocans rose from the Village Square, spiraling outward in great numbers. Fifty or so flew in his direction, dressed perfectly in a box formation. Thomas tried to swallow, but his mouth turned to dust.

"Bit more than we bargained for," Thomas muttered to the gworth. He glanced around the square. There was a forge shelter he could hide under and wait for a smaller group. He turned to the sky again. No, it was now or never. "So be it," he said, drawing his bow. He would not die wondering.

He waited until the swarm had mostly passed, then fired into their midst. He nocked another arrow before the first hit its target and fired again. A shout of surprise echoed, and Thomas released once more. He'd fired five arrows before the aurocans spotted him, and then they bore down on him like steaming bullets. Their hum had purpose, an insistence, like a wasp protecting its hive.

A fierce smile arced across Thomas's lips. He fired a volley into the ranks, no longer taking aim, as there were too many of them to miss. He waited in spot until he could make out the aurocans' enraged faces, and then, at the very last minute, kicked the gworth in the flanks. The creature raced out of the square like its tail was on fire.

The road to the forest stretched forever, and Thomas was deaf to all but the roar of wings behind him. He glanced over his shoulder to find a wall of aurocans, the closest of which had their hands outstretched, grasping for his soul.

He would not make it, not at that speed. Not with them in spitting distance. He reversed his seat and unslung his bow. He fired an arrow into the face of the closest aurocan, the missile barely leaving the weapon before it connected. The creature tumbled from the sky, collecting some of its companions on the way down.

Thomas fired again and again, dropping as many of the beasts as he could. By the time he passed the bridge, the swarm had grown cautious and backed off a little. Thomas spun in his seat, knowing he was drawing closer to the George's cottage, and what he saw stole his breath away.

Dozens of aurocans dropped from the sky to peer into the forest depths, their backs to Thomas and ignorant of his approach. They must have followed the others but were wary to enter. Thomas smiled. He couldn't blame them, not with the number of aurocans they had lost flying over those trees. Thomas slung his bow and pulled free the knife from his boot.

He had to make them angry enough to forget their fear and chase him.

Things were about to get bloody.

CHAPTER 44

- THOMAS -

Thomas clenched the stampeding gworth's woolen coat with one hand and swung himself low as he charged into the swarm of surprised aurocans. His knife flashed left and right as he hacked ribbons through the monsters, eliciting screams of pain and shock. The gworth, no tame piglet, used its middle legs to snatch, scratch, and rake the beasts to shreds, cleaving a path of destruction through the horde as easy as a heated blade through buttermilk.

The aurocans were so surprised, they didn't have time to turn, let alone mount an offensive. Eight aurocans fell by the time Thomas breached the swarm and galloped into the dark, empty forest.

Thomas didn't slow for several heartbeats. He bent over the gworth's neck and urged her away from the deadly claws of the remaining swarm. After a hundred yards, Thomas chanced a look over his shoulder, and bile rose in his throat; the stupid gits hadn't followed.

"Cowards," Thomas muttered, then reined the gworth to a stop and turned her around. He thrust his bloodied knife into the air and waved it back and forward. "What are you waiting for?" he shouted to the aurocans teetering at the tree line, who looked on with a mix of fear and anger. "It's just little old me!"

There were easily a hundred of them pressed into a line, each wanting to tear Thomas to shreds, but all too apprehensive to give chase into the forest which had bit and stung them so many times.

Thomas looked around for something, anything, to entice them to follow. If his gang didn't kill them before Duke and Chalia began the next phase, the lasses would be slaughtered in seconds. He reached over his shoulder and felt the arrows in his quiver; only a handful left, and he would need those for the battle.

"I'm terribly sorry you have to witness this, old girl," Thomas said once he decided what he needed to do. He turned the gworth around so her rump faced the aurocans. "But there really isn't anything else for it." He planted his feet on the gworth's wide flanks and unzipped his jeans. After a moment, he began pissing toward the aurocans.

"Come on, you willyless wankers!" Thomas shouted, waving his stream about.

The aurocans froze, staring at Thomas in disbelief, and their shouts faded to nothing. The trees muffled the outside world, so all that was heard was the tinkling of Thomas's piss against the compacted dirt path.

Then, like pine needles to a fire, the aurocans' anger flared to a white-hot climax. Their wings thundered as they beat their anvil-like chests with clenched fists. They shouted and screamed, wavering on the edge of the forest.

"Come on," Thomas breathed. "Come at me."

One creature, the largest and most ferocious, took a step into the Southern Forest, and the hoard fell to hushed whispers.

The aurocan crouched, ready to jump back to safety as it scanned the trees to its left and right, up and down. After a moment, it took another step. Then another. It was soon a handful of paces into the gloom and still breathing.

Thomas smiled. "Welcome to your funeral." He zipped up his jeans. "I'm glad you made a reservation—we are busy this morning."

The aurocan turned back to the horde and roared, punching its fist into the air. The swarm screamed, whipped into a frenzy, and scrambled into the forest. They jostled for point position, fighting for a chance to lay claws on Thomas.

Thomas threw himself onto the gworth's back and dug his heels in. The gworth took off in a canter.

"Easy does it, girl," Thomas said, looking over his shoulder to make sure he wasn't putting too much distance between him and the pursuers. "Let's not remove the thrill of the chase."

Bit by bit, Thomas teased the stampeding swarm toward the fork, adjusting his speed to always remain in sight. Branches scratched at his arms, and he was grateful. The dense forest gave the aurocans no room to fly. No room to escape.

Thomas looked ahead and spotted Wyn on the back of his gworth, trotting onto the fork's right path. His eyes were full moons as they watched the approaching horde. Thomas pulled up beside him.

"Is that all you found?" Wyn asked, a slight shake to his voice.

Thomas clapped his shoulder. "Don't worry, there's plenty more in the village when we are done."

"Lucky us," Wyn muttered, resting a hand on the hilt of his golden hammer.

Thomas looked back to the swarm. They were so close he could drop one with an arrow. "Wait in the forest north of the road. Use ranged weapons until there is no other option. Pass it on to the others."

Wyn nodded and looked Thomas in the eyes. "Don't be a hero." He turned to the horde a moment longer, then steered his gworth into the shrubs to the left.

Thomas set off at a trot and hadn't gone a hundred yards before he smelled it. Blood, rich and sickly sweet. The path before him had been turned into a mud pit of abattoir juice. It spanned thirty feet and looked greasy enough for a shadow to slip on. Thomas steered around it, careful not to make contact with any, and continued down the path.

Enyathil jumped out from behind a tree and waved to Thomas. Her hair was frazzled and her movements twitchy. "We can't hold them," she said. "They smell the blood and are crazy for it. They will pull down the damned trees they're chained to unless we release them soon—"

Thomas looked over his shoulder. "Give me a minute."

Enyathil opened her mouth to argue, but Thomas cut her off. "Wait for my signal. Go."

Enyathil's eyes darted down the path, and then she gave a quick nod and rushed away.

Thomas moved to the center of the road and faced the oncoming troops. He raised his bloodied knife high in the air and waited.

The lead aurocans saw he had stopped and howled with renewed energy. On they charged, splashing through the blood pit without a care, kicking claret on beasts around them, covering them in the rich muck.

The distance to Thomas halved in seconds.

Thomas's breath quickened. It was his time to shine. His time to show his worth.

His time for revenge.

He gripped his knife tighter, palm sweaty. The aurocans' arms were outstretched before them like chiseled stone. Their backward-bending knees propelled them forward with unnatural speed.

Thomas's arm twitched, begging to give the signal. He didn't dare do it too soon. Most of them needed to cross the pit.

The closest aurocan launched, claw cocked and ready to separate Thomas's head from his neck. Its eyes were narrowed, mouth open mid-roar.

Thomas threw down his hand, and shouts echoed behind him.

Then chaos.

Thomas's gworth reared and plucked the aurocan from the air with its middle claws and tore it in two before landing again. Four more aurocans filled its spot.

Seven black nightmares crashed into them, scattering them like a bowling ball through cricket stumps.

The snarzis had joined the fray.

The beasts tore through the aurocan files, furry messengers of death, feral from hunger. The blood-covered aurocans were too much a delicacy to resist.

A shrieking opera of dying aurocans filled the forest. Thomas's stomach swirled as he watched the carnage. The aurocans were getting butchered, and he was the one who gave the order. The one who signed their death contract. All the screams and limbs and crimson were his doing, even though he hadn't yet joined the fray.

Did that make him a monster?

He ground his jaw. No. He couldn't think of that. Not yet. He squeezed his left hand into a fist to stop it shaking.

A group of aurocans clumped together and swarmed a snarzi, pinning it to the ground. They raked and beat at it, overwhelming it with their combined weight. The snarzi yelped and tried to leap free, but the aurocans smothered it with numbers.

"Bollocks!" Thomas said, sheathing his knife and unshouldering his bow. He nocked an arrow and fired. The shot flew high. He missed.

He never missed.

He looked down at his hands, both shaking uncontrollably. What was happening to him? He nocked and fired again; this one, too, was off, but it collected an aurocan further behind.

"Come on," Thomas begged his body. He couldn't fail now, not when winning mattered most. He nocked once more, but when he took aim, he knew it was a lost cause. The snarzi was dead.

Missiles streaked into the battle from the right. Arrows and a flying golden hammer, spinning end over end. Arcs of lightning zapped, and balls of fire exploded, lighting the forest. Aurocans died in the dozens.

Thomas emptied his arrows into the thinning aurocan ranks, missing just as often as he hit.

The bombardment from the right slowed. *The gang must be running low*, Thomas thought. He slung his bow and unsheathed his blade. "Time to get dirty, old girl," he said, petting the neck of the gworth, trying not to vomit. "For Belbury," he whispered.

Then charged.

The assault lasted over ten minutes, though Thomas couldn't remember a thing from the moment he swung at the first aurocan. The path was littered with corpses, the dirt stained red. Some aurocans had fled, though the ever-hungry snarzis bounded after them in a game of cat and mouse, and they heard screams from all directions.

When at last the fighting was done, Thomas collapsed forward on his gworth, panting heavily. His heavy eyes lingered on the shredded bodies. How could there be so much blood?

"Thomas?" Mary asked, squeezing his leg. She bit her lower lip, looking at his blank face. "Are you all right?"

Thomas blinked, having not noticed her approach. His knife fell from his sticky hand. "Oh . . . Mary. Hello. Yes, yes, fine. Just exhausted." He slid from the gworth's back, and his legs buckled. Why was he still hearing the battle when it was over? He shook his head, then looked to Mary. She had a gash on her shoulder. "Are you okay?"

Mary picked up Thomas's knife and wiped it clean on her shirt. "I'll live." She hesitated. "Thomas, maybe you should sit—"

"I'm fine," Thomas said, straightening. "Assemble the rest of the gang."

With a final worrying look, Mary darted away.

Thomas closed his eyes. *Get it together, old boy. The gang needs you. The village needs you. You can have a meltdown after it's done.*

Once everyone gathered, Thomas inspected each of them for wounds and tended them with his own hands. There were several cuts and a broken hand, but everyone would live.

Thomas didn't like the way the gang watched him like he was

a bomb about to explode. He was fine, just tired. Exhausted. He shook his head. That screaming needed to stop.

"You fought bravely tonight," Thomas said, leaning against a tree and forcing a smile. "Keep hold of that rage—you will need it again before noon. I have asked you to do things no one should have to do, and I must ask more. The sun will rise, and we need to be ready with it. Fill your quivers and drink your water. We step off in fifteen."

The gang nodded, some giving Thomas a timid smile, and left him to his own. They walked among the dead, pulling free arrows.

As Thomas watched, he felt inside his pocket and pulled out a shard of glass. That simple bit of broken mirror was his second signal for butchery.

He remembered the battle and trembled.

CHAPTER 45

- CHALIA -

I held the resin tin aloft as Duke fired the bottom with flames from her hands. Tongues of fire bounced up the tin, reaching for the black surface but falling just short. Heatwaves assaulted my fingers as I held the handle until they felt like bangers in an oiled pan.

I gritted my teeth and focused on the black resin as a bubble formed. It inflated like a balloon and popped with a gulp. The floorboards above my head creaked, and dust sprinkled in my hair. Someone was moving.

I pulled the tin away. "I've got this one—"

"Not yet," Duke hissed, her blazing hands following the resin. "It's still too thick."

"We've a fire up our ass and a gut full of gasoline—"

"Then let's do it right the first time."

"Can't you burn hotter?"

I could hear Duke's eyes roll.

"Just a moment longer," she said. She poked her tongue between her teeth and focused on the tin.

I waited.

A day. A year. An age. My hair grew gray and toes wrinkled. Storms of dust fell from above, and creepy-crawlies made homes of my clothes. They gave birth to children, who birthed children of their own.

And then, after seconds, the resin bubbled like a pot of water.

"Go," Duke said. She picked up her own tin and placed the handle between her teeth, hands flaming at the bottom.

I didn't need telling twice. I scuttled to my side of the floor, ignoring all the webs, and tipped the tin against a timber beam supporting the floorboards. Thick resin oozed and clung to the wood like toffee.

It took longer than I'd expected, but I eventually finished with the tin and wiped sweat from my eyes on hands shaking with exhaustion. By the time I finished my second lot of resin, my shoulders were unset jelly on a thrift-store washing machine.

Duke completed her tins first and helped with mine. A hundred scald marks pocked my hands when at last I collapsed onto my stomach, the job done.

"All right?" Duke asked after piling the tins in the center of the building.

"Meh," I muttered, struggling onto my elbows. "You?"

"Could use a carrot or two," she said. "Ready for the next phase?"

I wasn't. I was ready for a warm bath and a comfy bed. A hot meal and a sunny day. A hug and plenty of Mello Yello. "Does it matter?"

"Afraid not."

I sighed and got to my knees. "Then what are we waiting for?"

We crawled to the side of the hall closest to the wheelbarrows.

"I'll go first," Duke said, poking her head out from under the building and surveying the area. "Hang here a while before following, just in case they spot me." She waited a few heartbeats, then rolled to her feet and sprinted to the hedge hiding the barrows.

I took her spot, ready for the dash to safety. I would have given my bomber jacket for a Red Bull at that moment. I slapped my legs, trying to shock energy into them, and failed miserably. So be it. I would use my teeth to drag me out of there if I had to. I sucked in a breath of moist air and rolled out. I planted a hand to push me to my feet—

Something moved to my right.

I froze, a stunned rabbit.

A sentry rounded the corner of the town hall. It was looking over its shoulder, muttering something to its out-of-sight companion.

Crap!

The damned thing was in spitting distance! If I moved, it would notice. If I stayed, it would trip over me. I was a rabbit in the jaws of a fox. The crunch of an aurocan's neck splintering played in my mind.

I would never hold Mom again. Never apologize for everything I'd put her through. Never tell her I loved her.

My end had come. At least I would be with Kingsley again—

Something whizzed through the darkness and smashed into the aurocan's face, snapping its head back.

A rock?

"Over here, ya filthy termite!" Duke shouted, jumping out from behind the hedge and waving her hands in the air.

The aurocan roared and leaped after her, its backward-bending legs propelling it in huge strides.

Duke spun and disappeared behind the cottage like a block of cheese on legs. She was no match for the aurocan's speed; already it was halfway to her.

"Stupid girl!" I hissed, my voice bubbling like boiled pitch. Why would she sacrifice herself for me? She was so much stronger, had so much more to offer. Without her, the villagers didn't stand a chance.

And now she was going to be murdered.

I balled my fists. "No."

I wouldn't allow it. I jumped to my feet and chased after the aurocan. I had to stop it from getting to her—

I dug my heels in and skidded across the wet cobblestones.

The villagers. They needed one of us alive.

I looked past the hedge to where I'd last seen Duke. "Oh, Duke," I spluttered. "I'm s-so sorry." I wiped my nose on my hand, and with a crumbling heart, turned my back on one of the best friends I'd ever known.

I stepped toward the brook, my footfalls shouting at me of betrayal. Each step tore at me until I was nothing but a shell of guilt.

I don't know how I reached Pop's cottage. I was a wreck, a grief-shattered corpse. The barn doors were open; that was a bit of luck, at least.

It was dark inside and smelled of hay and mold. A racket came from the far wall; a thousand pigeons singing thrash metal. I walked deeper, and the noise stopped. Silence. My skin prickled. I was being watched.

I bumped into something at the end of the barn, and a flurry of wings exploded. I stepped back and fumbled with my lighter.

The flame flickered to life.

Thousands of dead, milky eyes glared at me from inside large cages. Bats, of a kind, if bats were bred with sharks. I fought the urge to vomit. The creatures were near the length of my forearm and covered in a skin of black leather. Rows of razor-sharp teeth gnashed from an enormous underbite, each tooth an inch long. Their featherless wings ended in grasping, five-inch-long claws.

Vraps, Duke called them. Animals from her home world.

The vraps jostled each other, reaching through the bars with their spindly wings, jaws snapping like piranhas suffering a vegetarian diet.

I stepped forward. The ugly creatures had nothing on Pickering's disgusting face.

There were six cages, each crammed with vraps. I didn't dare get too close, so I searched the barn and found a metal bar against the wall. I threaded it through the top of a coop, and with a grunt, lifted it like a lantern. I staggered out of the barn with the swinging cage.

I reached the pear tree when I saw it, and my heart fell.

The sky was lightening in the east.

CHAPTER 46

- CHALIA -

My skin tightened on my muscles as though each pore held its breath. The sun was coming, and I was late! I ran as fast as I dared with the cage rocking like a pendulum.

"Feck, feck, feck," I muttered, glancing above the forest to the right. The rain had stopped, leaving the picture of a torn sky; midnight's shadow on one side, blueberries the other. Crimson lay beyond that, just out of view, and so did my deadline.

I loaded the cage into Pop's skiff and sprinted back into the barn for the next. By the time I loaded the last cage, my knees shook and arms hung limp. The skiff teetered from side to side as the vraps whizzed about.

"Can't you just act a pigeon for a while?" I begged, crouching down to look at them. They would capsize the skiff if I sent them down the brook like that. Unless . . .

I raced into the cottage, pulled a sheet from my bed, and grabbed cooking twine from the kitchen. I threw the sheet over the cages, covering them completely, and the effect was immediate. The skiff steadied, and the screeching stopped. I tied it with the twine and glanced back to the east. Strawberries and melon. Sunrise was near.

"Just a small jaunt," I whispered, untying the skiff. "Then you'll have your wings." I shoved the boat to the middle of the brook and watched as the current took it.

Then I ran for all I was worth.

I reached the bridge and slid down the bank to the concrete footing. Gooseflesh pocked my skin as I stripped to my underwear. The skiff approached. I grabbed my clothes and plunged into the frigid water. My breathing was more a convulsion than anything, but I caught the skiff and guided it to the church side of the bridge and tethered it to a rock.

I dressed quickly and turned to leave for my next location but stopped when an idea struck me. An idea that might save me from a nasty death. I untied the twine securing the sheet over the cages and lifted the linen just enough to show the door locks. I looped the twine through each door—getting more than a few gashes on my knuckles in the process—and placed the end under a rock on the concrete slab.

"Play nice," I said before scrambling up the bank to the park in front of Tilly's Teahouse, the park where I'd eaten with Elanil and Duke on my first full day in Belbury. I climbed the elm tree, my stiff limbs making it difficult, and balanced along the thick branch overhanging the teashop. I dropped onto the thatched roof and crawled to the ridge.

The church had two sentries reclining on the steps, motionless, either asleep or dead. My luck made it impossible for them to be dead. The town hall, however, was devoid of sentries. I looked beyond it to the cottage where Duke and I stored our wheelbarrows, and I grimaced. The hedges, just visible, were motionless. Duke should have been there at that moment. Duke should have been alive, chewing a carrot and making jokes. But she wasn't. She was dead, and she'd died to save me—

No! She was alive until I saw a body.

Or a footpath stained with fresh blood.

"Come on, Duke," I whispered, forcing myself to believe. She was the strongest lass I'd ever known. If anyone could survive the aurocan, it was her.

A ray of sunlight broke the horizon and caught my eye. The new day had arrived. With a last search of the hedge, I looked to the forest shouldering Pop's cottage. It was cloaked in shadow, but the agreed time had come. I pulled a broken shard of mirror from my pocket, eyes never leaving the forest, never blinking, and rolled it between my fingers. A tornado of emotion twisted my insides. Guilt. Dread. Misery. Everyone's lives depended on my success, depended on if I could do what needed to be done. If I failed, they died.

A sharp pain shot up my finger.

"Damn it," I muttered, placing my finger in my mouth and sucking the blood. It was no small thing, holding the lives of an entire village in the palm of my hand, when I couldn't even hold a mirror without cutting myself.

A glint of light flashed from Pop's jetty. I straightened, chest thudding, and searched the area for movement. It was dark again. Had I imagined it?

Another flash. *Thomas is ready!*

I lifted the mirror, angled it toward the rising sun, then twisted until it faced the town hall. I rocked it, side to side, heart beating in my ears, hopeful eyes hunting for the silhouette of a dwarf by the hedge. "Come on, Duke. For me. For everyone."

The hedge refused to move.

I rocked the mirror, quicker and quicker. *Please*, Duke. Stop playing—I need you. I trembled, fighting to see through the blurry world to the hedge. *Oh, Duke.*

The mirror slipped from my grasp, and I buried my head in my hands.

CHAPTER 47

- CHALIA -

Duke was gone.

She was dead, and it was all my fault.

Duke was gone, and I was the cancer what killed her.

The aurocan had been *right* in front of me—I should have attacked. I should have scratched and kicked, slapped, bashed and chewed. Done *anything*. Instead, I knelt and watched, calm as a pot of chamomile tea, as it toddled off to snuff out my friend.

And now she was gone, same as Kingsley, and I was alive and least deserving.

I wiped my running nose on the wool collar of my bomber jacket. I warned her. I told her I was cancer. And those . . . those filthy bastards—they were radiation therapy, and Duke got caught in the crossfire.

I ground my jaw. I *would* even then score. Hell, I'd make it a thousand to one in my favor. I could mourn for Duke later. First, there was a pyre what needed lighting, and it was now up to me to be the spark.

I pushed the tears from my eyes and looked to the town hall.

How was I going to get there without the aurocans on the church steps seeing me? It was too light for shadows, and if I went the long way around, I would be too late. I just had to make a bolt for it and hope for the best. The easiest place to light the resin would be on the side facing the wheelbarrows—

I gasped.

A figure charged from the hedge.

A block of a figure, a Rubik's cube with a mane of curly hair . . . and—and a carrot in its mouth!

My heart soared. *Duke.*

I climbed higher on the roof, not trusting my broken eyes, and a silly grin spread, like I'd just found a winning lottery ticket. I wanted to scream, to dance, to make a playlist, to paint a picture. She was alive, thank God, she was alive!

Duke hurdled the stairs to the town hall and crouched in front of the door. A few inches of wood separated her from an army of death. Her back faced me, but I knew what she was doing—I was the one who came up with the idea and helped collect the flat river rocks she was using to wedge closed the door. This was the Achilles' heel of our plan—if it failed, everything we'd been through was for less than nothing.

I shook the worry from my head. If Duke was good at one thing, it was mischief. I doubted this was the first time she'd wedged closed a door with rocks. Despite myself, I laughed.

And then the devil laughed with me.

Something moved to the left. One of the aurocan church guards had stirred and was walking toward the water well.

My insides turned to concrete. The monster was going to spot Duke!

No, I wouldn't fail her twice! I stood and cupped my hands to my mouth to shout a warning—

But the aurocan's head jerked as it caught sight of Duke. "Dwaaaaaarrrrfffff!"

Duke turned and stiffened.

"Run," I begged. "Get out of there."

Duke ignored me and continued her work in a flurry.

Why wasn't she running? Had all the carrots gone to her head?

The aurocan unfurled its wings and sprang into the air. It shot at the hall, a humming missile.

I couldn't watch, I couldn't bear it anymore.

Just as the aurocan neared the steps, Duke jumped to her feet and vaulted over the far rail.

The aurocan landed with a crack on the deck and gave chase. They both disappeared around the building.

I pulled handfuls of hair. How many times would Duke be killed in one day? I collapsed to my knees but refused to cry. It was up to me to save the village again.

I removed my backpack and half unzipped it, then stopped.

Something purred. A cat? No, it was deeper. It was coming from the town hall. I looked up, and the sound intensified.

Then I saw it.

A puff of gray smoke coughed from under the building, twirling into the golden dawn, a carefree ribbon on the breeze.

Seconds later the smoke was blacker than the ace of spades.

The smoke thickened to a brick wall as the hall puffed on all sides, a rocket about to launch. It rolled in a noxious veil across the square. Soon only the hall roof was visible, a beautiful orange halo dancing around it. That once-quiet purr reached the roar of a gale tearing through an underpass. Fire came next, towering flames trying to burn the clouds. The aurocan screams weren't far behind. They mocked the fire's trumpet with their sheer power.

The screams could have been human in that moment. I dug my fingernails into my palms as images of melting bodies came unbidden to my mind. My stomach churned.

I stuck out my jaw. "They did this," I said. "They deserved it." Did they, though? Did I really believe anyone deserved such a thing?

Aurocans poured out of the church and stood on the steps, watching the inferno. Some held their head in their hands, some turned away, and some fell to their knees. They were doing a good job at looking upset, but I knew they couldn't feel such emotion.

For the sake of my sanity, they were nothing more than ants, and their minds held no real estate for feelings.

I shouldered my bag, ready for what I had to do next, and was about to climb down from the roof when smoke in the village square twirled. Duke emerged from the darkness in a sprint, her hair streaming behind her as she set a bearing for the bridge.

Shouts echoed from the church stairs. The aurocans, listless only moments before, were animated once more, pointing sharp jabs at Duke. They took to the air in a hum.

"Damn it!" I slid down the thatched roof, dropped to the ground in a roll and sprinted to the bridge. Duke needed more than my help; she needed the help of shark-bats. I unlatched the vrap cages, picked up the end of the twine, and plunged into the brook, pulling open the doors as I submerged myself.

Terror blazed inside me. Or was that the brook boiling from the heat of the town hall? The vraps would save Duke. They had to. Duke was adamant they were territorial and would only attack airborne creatures. For her sake, I hoped she was right.

I held my breath until my lungs threatened to burst and then held it longer. If I surfaced to find vraps actually enjoyed the taste of sopping-wet humans, then I was in a pile of it.

Bright dots appeared in my vision, and I couldn't hold any longer. I kicked off the bottom and broke the surface, gasping and waving my hands over my head like a madman in case the vraps were still there.

Not a single one remained.

I clambered out of the brook and scurried up the bank, hoping to find Duke's smiling face. The only movement I saw was an aurocan bursting through the smoke shroud, flying erratically with vraps attached to it like leeches.

I stood there, eyes stinging with smoke, and waited. Minutes came and went, but Duke refused to come at all. My heart fluttered. If I didn't start the last phase while the aurocans were in disarray, I might not get a chance at all.

I pulled a can of spray paint from my bag and took my first step toward the church.

CHAPTER 48

- CHALIA -

I climbed over the cemetery's wrought-iron fence and stepped into the greedy cloud of smoke that ate the sun. An eerie silence followed, squeezing my ears until they crackled and popped. It was night in the graveyard, and while I was grateful for the cover, the smoke scrubbed at my throat with a steel-wire brush and drove needles into my eyes. Mustard gas would be a kinder host than that smoke. I tripped in craters of mud and trenched through slurries of churned earth. I passed broken teeth of tombstones and watched as ghosts swirled the surrounding air.

The door at the rear of the church was there, exactly where it should be, handle and all. I narrowed my eyes. After everything that had happened in the last few days, I half expected it to have disappeared or at least grown machete-wielding tentacles.

It was an unremarkable door. All I had to do was twist the handle and push. Simple enough. Walking through, however, would be like cage diving with great whites, only without the cage.

I pulled my hand away from the handle and rested my forehead on the wood. Ghultar. Was he an eye-for-an-eye type of Muppet? Would he melt my cheeks like candle wax, like I had his? Or would he simply crush my neck to dust?

How many villagers had he done that to already? I balled my fists. They needed me, all of them, autocratic bell ends and all. I shook my head in disgust. Risking my life to save adults; my world really had curdled.

I gripped the handle again. It was cool to touch, and the waving ridge pattern pressed into my palm. I turned it, pushed, and crossed the threshold to what would likely be a baptism by Lucifer himself. The small chamber on the other side was empty and free of the cloying smoke, yet somehow the silence doubled until all I could hear was my racing heart.

I crossed the chamber in a few strides and peeked through the stone archway. It opened into the apse, with the altar in the center and not a monster in sight. I craned my neck but couldn't see into the nave. My grip tightened on the spray paint, and I dashed from the chamber and ducked behind the altar.

I half expected Ghultar's claw to reach over and pluck me up like a fiver, or at least an aurocan to shout out a warning. But silence ensued, eerie and full of threat. I placed my spray paint and cigarette lighter down, wiped the sweat from my hands onto my jeans, and then peeked over the top of the altar.

Smoke wafted through the opened double doors, clouding the building in a thick haze. The villagers were even more haggard than when I left. Many had gags in their mouths, blood on their faces, and ropes binding them. But they were still alive, and that was more than I hoped for. They twisted in their seats to see what was happening outside, but their restraints limited them to that movement alone.

There were no aurocans among the villagers. A flicker of hope burned in my stomach. The smoke has drawn them out. So far my plan was working, but I had to act quick, or it would be all for nothing.

Then I saw her. A light in the darkness, the smoke too shy to touch her beauty. Elanil was in the first row, face covered in blood, and was struggling against her bonds, her wrists rubbed raw from the effort.

My arms fell by my side, and I forgot about monsters. I forgot about Ghultar and death and running out of time and all of it. For one blissful moment, it was only me and her, and I found it hard to breathe.

Someone coughed, choking on smoke, and my trance broke. I shook my head. I had one last task before I could fall into hopes and dreams. Scanning the church, I pocketed my lighter and can of spray paint, then darted down the stairs to kneel in front of Elanil.

Elanil's mouth dropped open. She moved her lips soundlessly, a fish out of water. Then she furrowed her brow and shoved me with her tied hands.

"You idiot!" she whispered. "You stupid, daft idiot! Run, while you still can—"

I grabbed her by the side of the face and kissed her. It was short and hard and tasted of blood, and the only thing I'd ever needed. "I'll never leave you again."

Elanil's face softened, and she melted into me. "Oh, Chalia, he'll be back soon. He's never gone long—"

"Then help me free everyone before he returns." I slid my

pocketknife between her wrists and cut her bonds. "First save those able to fight." I handed her a spare knife from my backpack and turned to go, but she grabbed me by the wrist.

"Run if you see him," she whispered. "If he captures you . . ." She bit her lip and left the thought unsaid.

A shiver ran down my spine. I knew what I was in for if he caught me, and it would not be a friendly chat over a beer and salted nuts. I nodded.

The church whispered with excitement as I trotted among the villagers, assessing each on the size of their muscles, their age, and how conscious they were. Many were dazed from beatings, many feeble from age, and many too weak to swing a pillow. Judging who was worth freeing was the harshest graft I'd done, and it tugged at my gut every time I had to walk past someone.

I'd released two dwarves and an elf by the time I reached a man tied to the end of the pew. Time had blotted his skin, his wrists weren't much more than pencils, and it looked like he'd done breaststroke through in a bath filled with the blood of a sacrificed ram. Despite this, he wore a grin wide enough to turn the lines on his face into canyons.

Pop beamed at me, eyes sparkling in the candlelight. "Your mom warned me you would surprise me in more ways than one."

I threw my arms around his neck and squeezed, my shoulders heaving. I never wanted to let go. "I'm so sorry," I whispered, tears streaming down my cheeks. In that hug, I found a comfort I'd long forgotten. I was back, a young girl in my dad's arms. I was safe.

"There's nothing to be sorry for, sweetheart," Pop said, his voice cracking. "I'm the one who made a mess of the whole thing. I guess time is not a cure for foolishness, after all."

I pulled away and looked into his gray eyes. Extra shimmers had blossomed, and some trickled down his cheek. "I'll make everything right," I said, my chest stuttering. "I'll save Belbury, and you will see Mom again, and everyone will be happy."

Pop's bottom lip trembled. "I can't imagine a finer gift."

I had to look away. Rope held his arms tight, turning his hands blue. It took some maneuvering to hack them free, but I made quick work of the bonds around his ankles.

"Save the red-ears first," Pop said, rubbing his wrists. "They have special skills which might help defeat the aurocans."

"You mean magic?"

Pop's bushy eyebrows arched. "Surprise me, indeed!"

I gave him one last hug. "There is a chamber off the apse; stay there until I collect you. Let's put these elves to work."

I raced across the aisle to the next pew, my footfalls made light by a delicate belief of victory. We could do it; we could actually *save everyone*. I knelt in front of Mrs. Moira, not wanting to pass the chance to uncage her quick temper, and slid my knife into her ropes.

Mrs. Moira's eyes were an inferno. "Get me my pitchfork, and I'll be making sieves of those termite bastards—"

A scream filled the church, high pitched and brimming with agony.

I whirled, and then my life fell apart.

First, I saw a blade with serrations large enough to fell a frozen tree.

Then I saw the exposed neck, fragile, bleeding where the knife was pressed.

And then I saw *him.*

Ghultar held Elanil before him like a shield, one arm bending her head backward to breaking point, the other holding the blade. His one eye was zoned on me, a sneer twisting his cruel face as he backed slowly toward the altar.

"Hello, my dearest *Chalia*," he said, his voice quivering in rapture. "Welcome home. I have missed you ever so much." He barked a laugh as he moved up the stairs.

"Drop the lass!" the dwarf I'd freed earlier said as she strode toward the beast.

"Oh, I wouldn't come any closer," Ghultar said, swinging his gaze on her. "Any of you. I twitch when I get excited, and, well—" He looked at his knife. "I'm afraid one twitch would be all it takes for this wisp of a neck."

"Wait!" I cried, dropping my knife and throwing my hands up. "Please—"

"Wait on what?" Ghultar asked, smile growing. "What can you offer to stop me making her neck smile—" His eyes snapped to my right. "Drop your hands, *elf,* or I will drop her corpse."

Elanil's father, Alamril, stood with blue fire racing up his arms. He glared at Ghultar, and the flames intensified. "You will not escape this church with your life. Leave the girl, and we will make it quick."

Ghultar laughed. "Well, if I'm going to die, I may as well have some fun. Wouldn't you agree?" He pressed the knife into Elanil's throat, and she screamed as blood cascaded down her neck.

I rushed forward. "Me," I shouted. "Take me instead. I prettied your face, not her."

Ghultar froze. "Oh, bravo! Such bravery! Such compassion." He looked into Elanil's face. "But why don't I take you both?"

"You don't have time," I said. "But you have a choice. Kill a girl who means nothing to you, or kill me, the lass who made you a laughingstock." I stopped at the steps to the apse and looked up at him, waiting. No fear touched me. If sacrificing myself would save the girl who taught me to feel again, then I would die without regret.

Ghultar didn't speak for some time. "I'd be lying if I said torturing you was not an enticing offer. It would be slow, girl. Your voice would fade from screaming before your blood would drain." He sat on the altar and stared at me for a long while. "Throw your bag up here."

"No!" A voice cried from the wall. "What pride is there in the death of a girl?" It was Pop, stepping out of a shadow on the wall. "Take me instead, I was a soldier—"

Ghultar's eye snapped to him. *"Shut it or this one's head will be on your shoulders!"*

Pop glared at him. He balled his fists but did not take another step.

Ghultar turned back to me. "Move."

"Don't do it, Chalia," Elanil screamed. "Get to Italy! I'm not worth it!"

Ghultar yanked her head back even further. "Don't test me, girl!"

"Wait, I'm here!" I said, removing my bag and throwing it at his feet.

Ghultar's wild eye crinkled. He looked at me the same way Pickering would a bucket of fries. "Come."

Three steps joined the apse to the nave. Carpet of deep red

cushioned them, three blood waterfalls seeping from the church's heart. As my feet touched each one, surges of fatigue flowed through my heels to flood my body. I savored each one roll of the tide, knowing my end was near and wanting to ride the wave as long as possible. It did not take long to reach the altar, but in those steps, I sailed the world.

Ghultar tossed Elanil aside and snatched me by the neck in the same motion, his icy fingers squeezing my throat as he pulled me in front of him, a new shield to protect him from the villagers.

I clung to his forearm, trying to lessen the strangle by pulling myself up. "Do it," I choked, my face swelling. "Show us the coward we know you are."

Ghultar's eye was an inferno of the purest rage. He pulled me close to his face, and the rancid smell of infection stole my breath. "Let's not be so hasty—"

A commotion sounded behind me. Shouts of surprise and an explosion.

Ghultar looked up, and a terrible grin crept across his face. His bared, crooked teeth gleamed in the candlelight, and a piercing arrow of dread stung my heart.

"Oh, you do not want to miss this," Ghultar said, his raspy voice bouncing. He spun me to face the rest of the church.

I drowned, a sinking boat in a sea of despair. "No," I breathed. We were so close. We almost won, we had them . . .

But now our rebellion was ended.

Belbury was lost.

We were lost.

Lord save our souls.

CHAPTER 49

- CHALIA -

Aurocans swarmed through the double doors and launched at the prisoners I'd freed, all flailing claws and gnashing fangs. The villagers fought back with lightning, fire, and fists but were devastated by the number of beasts. Within seconds, the aurocans herded them into a bunched circle in the middle of the aisle, where they fought with everything they had to defend the onslaught.

I wanted to scream at the world for its failure of justice. If I had more time, I could have freed more. There could have been a chance . . .

"How does it feel?" Ghultar whispered, his acid breath snapping at my ear. "To know that everyone you love is about to have their pretty little jaws torn off their pretty little heads?"

The villagers . . . so many were going to die. If I had released none, the aurocans would have no one to attack but me. I could live with that.

"You really should use your tongue while you still have the

chance," Ghultar growled. He lifted me high into the air and slammed me onto the altar.

My head crashed against stone, and the world exploded in whites and reds and confusion. Ghultar jumped atop me, his clawed feet pinning my shoulders while his backward-bending legs squished my thighs. His weight crushed my bones to their breaking point, sending spasms of pain slashing through my body. I screamed and writhed, a hare in a trap.

Ghultar leaned forward so his head was just above mine. "Yes, dear, that is what tongues are for—screaming."

I fought through the soup of my mind and focused on Ghultar's smiling eye. "Screw you!"

Ghultar chuckled and slowly brushed my hair from my face with one long, cruel finger. "Darling, you're not really my type. But—" His finger raced down my forehead and pushed my left eyelid wide open. "I am quite enamored with these beautiful eyes. Do you have a preference which I take first?"

And then I felt it. Dread. It stole my breath and spun my insides like a fork in spaghetti. Never in the deadly maze of Barden's lawless streets had I felt such terror. He was going to pluck my eyes out. One by one. Going to snatch my vision with those crowbar fingers. My chest quivered as I hyperventilated, and my hands fell to the altar, no longer having the strength to struggle.

Ghultar clamped a hand around my jaw and squeezed, popping my mouth open. "I want the last thing you see to be the death of your family. That way, even with no eyes, you can watch it time and again in your memory." He turned my head so my cheek pressed the stone and I was facing the battle.

The villagers were dwindling. Those who remained were fighting with everything they had, and more than a few aurocans lay scattered around them. Alamril was one of them, his blue flames scorching the church floor before him, holding some beasts at bay. But even as I watched, his flames dimmed as though he was a burnt log with nothing left to give. The aurocans closed in.

I couldn't watch anymore.

I tried to turn away, but Ghultar held me firm. Instead, I rolled my eyes up and focused on a statue on a stone pillar—

My breath caught in my chest. I'd seen that exact statue a thousand times! It was Mother Mary in her red and blue, hands raised before her, palms facing the heavens as though she were offering her soul to anyone in need. She was frowning, and her eyes were blank from fatigue. Mom had that statue in the kitchen. Many times I'd caught her leaning on the kitchen bench, just looking at it as though in silent conversation.

The church grew quiet, and a shadow fell over everything but Mary. All I could hear was my mother's muffled cries after Dad left, and all I could see was Mary's sad face.

No, not sad, I realized. *Hopeful.* She knew the strength of people and understood the worthy would always win.

Mary's confidence ignited a fire in me until my stomach, which only moments ago was twisted like knotted rope, was roaring with white flames of belief. I would not give up. I would not let those bastards destroy everything I'd come to love.

With a strength I'd never had, I wrenched my right arm from under Ghultar's knee and shot my fist into the bloodied cloth covering his melted eye.

Ghultar shrieked and rocked back, releasing my jaw to press

his hand to his face. His head twitched like the dying legs of a cockroach.

I bucked beneath him, a cornered lion, a caged bear. The only way to live was to fight with everything I had. I landed a punch on his face again and cocked my arm once more.

Ghultar slapped me with the back of his hand. My head snapped sideways, but I felt no pain. I turned back to him and lifted my head to spit in his face, but his hand found my throat and shoved me back down. His fingers squeezed until I couldn't breathe.

"Oh yes," Ghultar said, panting heavily. "You know how to play this game." Fresh blood streamed from beneath his bandage. "Scream for me, Chalia. I want to hear what you sound like when I tear your throat out—*arghhh!*"

Something crunched into Ghultar's head, knocking him off me to crash to the floor. Someone rushed past me.

I wheezed in breath, rubbing my throat, and peered over the side of the altar. I gasped. Pop stood hunched above Ghultar, smashing a candelabrum into his face like he was splitting firewood in the backyard.

Ghultar roared and lashed out wildly with a fist, collecting Pop in the chest and sending him flying to crash into the first pew.

"Nooo!" I screamed. I tried to run to him but was yanked back to the altar by my jacket. Ghultar stood over me.

Pop had to be okay. He was tough; he could handle a punch. He had to, for Mom's sake.

"You little bitch!" Ghultar spat as his hands found my neck again. Blood streamed down his face to cascade from his chin, and his pupil was a quivering pinprick in a sea of fury.

I tried to breathe, my mouth opening and closing, but no air entered my lungs. I gripped Ghultar's fingers to pry them open, but they were welded closed. Ghultar's face blurred until I could no longer see his eye. After a moment, my chest stopped convulsing, and my fear blew away on the breeze.

That was what it was to die? It wasn't so bad. I felt no pain. I was just tired, in a warm bath with lavender sprigs caressing my skin, twirling about me with a life and energy of their own.

Energy.

Whose voice was that? It was rough, carefree. Duke? Yes. We were on the branch in the White Tree; she was teaching me magic, and I was failing.

Feel the energy!

Yes, that's right. Is that what magic felt like? A bath of lavender? It would be a laugh to find out. My world was black, but I was holding on to something. I should try on that. I breathed in the tingling lavender, a vacuum in a room of fine dust, and I grew full. Not my lungs or stomach, of course, but my body. It bloated the pores until I thought I would simply peel apart—

Brightness exploded, tearing through the darkness cloaking me.

A scream and my chest inflated. The air was sweet and full of life. I breathed again, and like a sunrise, light and color filled my world.

Interesting.

Great tongues of fire crackled out of my palms to bite at the thing over me. Yes, Ghultar was his name, and he was bad.

Ghultar held his hands before him, trying to fend off the fire, but there was no hiding from me. My flames billowed around his hands and fed on his head and body. His screams were loud but short-lived. They died in a charcoal rasp, and he collapsed backward, black and smoking.

I released the energy stored in my body and lay still, chest heaving as though I'd sprinted a mile uphill. The air weighed me down, and the stench of burning flesh clogged my throat.

I shook.

I'd . . . I'd killed someone. I'd boiled the life from their veins. I struggled to a sitting position and stared at the remains of Ghultar. His face and body were midnight, his arms were splayed wide. I pressed a fist to my mouth and looked away. The arms ended in points, his hands burned to ash. The hands he used to choke me. The fist he had used to punch Pop—

"Pop!" I cried. I spun to find the church was still a battleground; however, the villagers had gained the upper hand. A gworth charged among the remaining termites, ripping them apart. Thomas had joined the fight.

I searched the chaos until I spotted Pop. He was crumpled face down at an odd angle in front of a pew.

"No," I stammered. I rushed to him on shaking legs and collapsed by his side. I cradled his head as I rolled him onto his back. "Pop, can you hear me?"

Blood bubbled from his mouth, and his eyes were glassy. I stroked his gray hair, and he eventually focused on me.

"Chalia," he whispered, making red raspberries from his lips. "We won?"

I spluttered and bobbled my head and tried to say something but only choked. His voice was weak, and that red . . . it was so overpowering. I wanted to tell him a hundred things. I wanted to tell him sorry. Thank you. I love you. Instead, a wail escaped me. I rocked back and forward and squeezed his hand. "Yes," I finally said. "You were brilliant. You saved us all."

Pop smiled, and bubbles burst. "Oh no, lassie . . . you saved me the moment I picked you up from Cheltenham." He coughed, spluttering blood. "You're the most magical thing to happen to me in a long time."

My chin quivered as I pushed tears from my eyes. He would be okay. It was just a little blood. A few days in hospital was what he needed, and some time to relax. I brought his hand to my lips and kissed the intricate pattern of his winkles. His grip weakened.

"Save your energy," I said. "I'll tell you about everything tomorrow."

Pop's smile shook, and he closed his eyes for a long moment. When he opened them again, the fog had cleared, if only for an instant. "Make sure you feed the ch-chickens, Chalia. There is great . . . shame . . . for a family without eggs for breakfast." His chest spluttered, and he coughed again. "Say hello to my dear Valerie for me." He closed his eyes, and he drifted off to sleep.

"I'll find a doctor," I whispered, not wanting to wake him. But I couldn't move. I sat there, stroking his hand, fixed to the spot like an axe wedged in wood.

The church vanished, and I didn't hear or see the dying battle. I didn't feel Elanil squeezing my shoulders or hear her sobbing. I was lost for a long time, and it was even longer before I was found.

My knees weren't working properly when I allowed Alamril to lift me to my feet. He half carried me into the sunshine, whispering in my ear, telling me everything would be all right. The town hall was a smoldering ruin, and people tending one another's wounds packed the village square. Aurocans littered the cobblestones, torn and dead, rubbish in the street. They weren't the only bodies. Several villagers lay still, their eyes no longer open to the beauty of Belbury-on-the-Brook. Elves collected these and placed them gently into several boar-drawn carts beside the water well.

They carried Pop to his own cart and placed him on his back with his trilby hat resting on his chest. The mayor stood by the cart, shoulders slumped. He glanced up as we approached.

"He was the greatest man I ever knew," Arthur said, voice cracking as tears streamed from his eyes. "My oldest friend." He paused for a moment. "I'm sorry, Chalia."

I wiped blood from Pop's stiff lips. He looked peaceful, happy almost. Arthur was right: Pop was the greatest man I ever knew too. "You did all you could."

We stood there in silence until the square emptied and the sun began its arc down the sky.

CHAPTER 50

- CHALIA -

The sun was a bell end that day. It hovered overhead, cocksure and smug, and broiled with the compassion of a starved fox in a chicken coop. Beads of perspiration trickled down my neck like shredded mozzarella sweating in an oven. I fanned myself with a hand, cursing the tree above, which mocked me with its waving limbs, sometimes moving into a position to donate shade, more often not.

It was a beautiful day, despite the heat. Birds chattered with unmatched enthusiasm, the occasional breeze carried wafts of fresh-mowed grass and basil, and people gossiped and laughed and went about their afternoon on bouncing feet. It was almost enough to make me forget the devastation of the week before.

Seven villagers died in battle for Belbury-on-the-Brook, including Pop. Seven villagers and hundreds of aurocans. Anyone who called that a victory had never known the tragedy of loss. Those seven deaths sent shockwaves through that village, and it would be a long time before the brook calmed enough for the people to rebuild their lives.

I was a bedridden mess for days after Pop died, inconsolable and irrational. Sometimes I thought it all a nightmare. Sometimes I knew it to be true. Worst of all, sometimes I blamed myself and crawled deeper into my unending well of darkness.

It wasn't until I woke shivering several mornings later on an unusually bitter day that it forced me to move from bed. First, I collected firewood and sparked the hearth. Then, while I was already up, I fed and watered the chickens and slipped into the barn to feed Pop's other animals. It was the first time I'd entered the barn during the day, and I was taken aback by how many critters Pop owned, all of which challenged the imagination. I played with a snuggly creature whose ears flopped over its eyes, and after a while I accidentally felt less lousy than normal. The pieces of my mind aligned and slotted into their right spots and left me with a clarity I'd not known in some time. Pop sacrificed his life so I could live. I owed it to him to make the most of every second, not hide away under a blanket like a kid in a storm. I owed it to myself to get on with it and let go of my past.

I owed it to Kingsley, whose dot on the map was robbed when they cut his life short.

A cool breeze tousled my hair, and it was heaven on that warm day. I sighed and pushed the images of the battle from my mind. I was a new me in a new life, and I needed to learn to enjoy the small wins. A chill in the heat was a small win, and I was grateful.

I sniffed, catching scent of a wood-fired pizza, and turned as the server approached with a large margherita on a wooden board. I smiled, and he smiled back.

The small wins.

The pizza looked exactly like the pizzas I'd seen in the travel Italy magazine. Crispy crust, bubbled and slightly blackened on the edges, creamy mozzarella melted in white clouds, and fresh basil to tie it all together. It was basil what made a pizza for me. Pizza without basil was not pizza at all. My stomach grumbled as I picked up my first slice.

Kingsley would love that place, my dot on the map.

"Going to share, or what?" Duke asked from across the table, wiping sweat from her brow with the arm that was not in a sling. "I have eaten nothing since lunch."

Elanil snorted. "That was an hour ago, and you ate a carrot on the way here." Her voice was clipped, as though she spoke through a bout of pneumonia. Like Duke, she wore battle scars, the worst of which being her shattered nose. The doc realigned it after they tended the more serious patients, but it would no longer be the cute button nose she once owned. I squeezed her thigh under the table, certain I couldn't love the girl any more than I already did, and her hand rested on top of mine.

Duke huffed. "A carrot? I've swallowed spiders bigger than carrots! Don't be counting that as food. Besides," she puffed out her chest, "I don't want to end up all scrawny like you. I'm a dwarf, and need to eat as such—"

"Scrawny, huh?" Elanil asked.

Duke nodded. "Skin and bones. Looks like you've been hung up to dry with the jerky."

"Well, we can't have that," Elanil said, gripping the pitcher of water. "Let me rehydrate you." She upended it on Duke's curly hair, sending water streaming down her face.

Duke spluttered. "You'll pay for that!" She launched over the table, broken arm and all, and tackled Elanil from her seat.

I chuckled as I watched them roll around the grassy lawn of the Pointed Ear. Who knew fighting would be the first sign the village was on a path to recovery? I was on my second slice of pizza before Duke declared it a draw while her face turned blue in Elanil's headlock.

"When is she coming?" Duke asked as she plonked herself down at the table and pulled free a slice, the mozzarella stretching like bungee cords.

I looked east along the highway. "Shouldn't be long." I turned to Elanil. "Nervous?"

Elanil scoffed and picked up a slice. "After what we've been through, you think I'm scared of your mom?" Her knee began bouncing.

I draped an arm around her shoulder and pulled her into me. "She'll love you, don't worry."

Elanil dropped the slice back to the board. "What if she doesn't? What if—what if she doesn't want you dating a girl? Or worse—an elf?"

I kissed her cheek. "She married an elf, remember? And I think she would prefer me dating a lass than a lad. We are far less trouble."

"Well," Duke said, picking up her second slice, "you're about to find out." She nodded down the highway.

A horse-drawn cart rounded the bend into Belbury, swaying side to side with two people on the bench—Mom on the right, the mayor on the left.

I chewed my lip, a mix of excitement and fear rioting in my

stomach. Arthur would have told her I killed someone. Would she think different of me? Think her daughter a murderer? My legs tensed. Would she blame me for Pop's death?

Elanil placed her arm around the small of my back. "We will handle this together," she said and rested her head on my shoulder.

Duke groaned and shoved a full slice of pizza into her mouth. "You two make me sick," she said, spraying food over the table as she picked up her third slice.

I watched the wagon. Maybe spray painting the mayor's horse black would help calm my nerves. My lips twitched upward at the absurdity. No. I wasn't in Barden anymore, and I wasn't the same lass I'd been. My stint in the country changed me, maybe even for the better.

I sighed and dropped my uneaten slice back to the board and walked to the road, squeezing Elanil's hand.

It wasn't until the cart reached the tavern's barn that Mom's eyes turned away from the mayor's and locked on mine. She stiffened, and my heart pounded. Should I wave? Hide? Laugh? Cry?

Mom leaped from the moving cart like a much younger lady and raced toward me. "Chalia!" she cried, hair streaming behind her.

My eyes prickled. "Mom!" I sprinted to her, caught her in front of the Pointed Ear's front door, and threw my arms around her neck. I glued myself to her, a weathered movie poster clinging desperately to the side of a building in the middle of a storm. She smelled of lavender shampoo, as she always did, and I grew lost in it. "I'm sorry for everything I've done—"

"Oh, Chalia," Mom said, stroking the back of my head, "I'm the one who's sorry. I should have explained everything to you from the moment you were born." She pulled away and looked at me through shimmering eyes. "You are my everything, and I thank God for you every day." She combed her fingers though my hair, eyes tracing every feature on my face. Then her gaze flicked over my head, and her eyebrows raised. "Oh, hello."

Elanil and Duke arrived.

"Hello," Elanil said, fidgeting with her shirt.

I grabbed Elanil's hand and pulled her forward like a shy puppy. "Mom, this is my friend, Elanil Zinvyre."

Mom smiled. "Nice to meet you, Elanil. I believe I know your parents."

"Yes, Mom said she remembers you fondly," Elanil said, looking at her twisting hands.

I wrapped an arm around Elanil's waist, and she went rigid. "Elanil is someone we will see a lot of."

Mom looked from Elanil to me, and then understanding sparkled in her eyes. Her smile widened, and she beamed. "I hope so!" She turned back to Elanil. "You can tell me how you make your hair shine like the sun. Barden's water has stolen the life from mine, I'm sad to say."

"Oh, y-yes, of course," Elanil stammered, glancing up. "It's more to do with—"

"I'm Bekka," Duke said, cutting Elanil off. "But everyone calls me Duke." Pizza sprayed from her mouth. "Happy to tell you the secrets for these golden locks, but it'll cost you a bucket of carrots." She shook her head, making her curly mane dance and dislodging a string of mozzarella.

Mom laughed. "Well, I best be getting my garden planted as soon as possible." Her eyes found mine again, and her smile faltered.

I dropped my arm from Elanil's back. "What's wrong?"

Mom shook her head. "Oh, it's nothing. Just . . . your smile, Chalia. I've forgotten how beautiful it is."

My heart swelled. I looked around, from Elanil to Duke, the Pointed Ear to the hill beneath the White Tree. I grinned and felt light enough for a breeze to blow me all the way to the brook. "All I needed was a bit of magic to help me remember where I'd left it."

"And carrots," Duke chimed in.

Mom laughed and pulled me in for another hug.

Everything was going to be all right.

My time in Belbury taught me many valuable lessons, the primary being certainty made fools of us all. Pop was right—it was not my place to live someone else's dream. As much as I loved Kingsley and would never forget him, Italy was his dot on the map, not mine. My dot was in a small village with a large and magical secret. A village of wonder and adventure and memories. A village with a tough-as-nails dwarf and an elf of impossible beauty.

A village to call home.

I hope you enjoyed reading The Fire I Called as much as I enjoyed writing it!

I will be immensely grateful if you leave a quick review on Amazon. These reviews are an essential resource, and it's sad but true that readers of e-books seldom bother to post their comments, good or bad! You can also make suggestions in the course of writing a review. Believe me, I read them all.

Thank you!

If you enjoyed The Fire I Called, be sure to check out my other fantasy novels:

The Traitor in the Trees
The Other Side of Blood
The Curse of the Spider-riders
When Magic Follows Midnight

And don't forget to leave a review on Amazon, I'd love to hear from you!

www.ingramcontent.com/pod-product-compliance
Lightning Source LLC
Chambersburg PA
CBHW030521120726
47904CB00005B/1572